Dangerous Conjectures

A Novel

Brian Finney

PRAISE FOR DANGEROUS CONJECTURES

Admirers of Brian Finney's earlier novel *Money Matters* know that there are few contemporary writers as adept at turning headlines into fictional fuel. In *Dangerous Conjectures*, a professional couple in the Bay Area struggle with multiple national crises—the start of the Covid pandemic and the growth of QAnon among them. As Adam and Julia navigate the rapids of their personal and professional lives, readers re-experience the last year, where a pandemic and a parallel "virus of massive misinformation" made that journey so difficult. Finney's characters are us, and their struggles our own.

— David Peck, author

Brian Finney weaves the early months of 2020 into an allegory of privilege as we witness the piercing of the Gosford family's Silicon Valley bubble. Confronted with the impending pandemic, QAnon beliefs, incel revenge, false accusations, addiction, and the danger that poor judgement can beget, this compelling tale makes us question our own actions and responsibilities as we move forward into an unsure normal.

— Sandra Ann Miller, author and founder
of The L.A.L.A. Society

In *Dangerous Conjectures*, Brian Finney's brilliantly conceived new novel, the social context is the internet's web-shadowed world (an ever-darkening web) of our present day. The politics are sexual as well as cultural, inevitably divisive and impossibly personal—this is a world where both our secrets and our intimacies are certain to be betrayed. Disturbing and prescient, this is the novel you need to read today.

— *David St. John, author*

SCIENCE IS HIS RELIGION.
A PANDEMIC IS HER UNDOING.

Dangerous Conjectures

Brian Finney

... she may strew
Dangerous conjectures in ill-breeding minds
—William Shakespeare, *Hamlet*, Act 4, scene v (14-15)

... do not spread the compost on the weeds
To make them ranker.
—William Shakespeare, *Hamlet*, Act 3, scene iv (153-154)

ACKNOWLEDGMENTS

Many of my friends and family helped make this book better with their creative suggestions. I want to thank James Acheson, David Peck, Melvin Scheer, Leo Braudy, my nephews Steven Kaplan and Angus Finney, and Jacky Lavin, my wife. I so appreciate the time and care you all took reading through earlier drafts.

I am truly indebted to Laurie Winer for a painstaking and inventive line edit that had a significant effect on the much-improved form the book finally took.

I am also grateful to Sandra Ann Miller for voluntarily copy-editing a late draft in great detail.

I owe thanks to Leila Aguilera for a beautifully designed jacket and textual layout. She responded to my numerous requests with professional patience and expertise.

In particular I would like to thank Nanda Dyssou and Coriolis Company for once again providing highly professional advice on every aspect of producing and marketing this book.

PREFACE

THE NEW YORK TIMES. Wednesday January 22, 2020

Bipartisan Confirmation of Director of CISA

At a Senate hearing before the Committee on Homeland Security David Crawford was unanimously recommended for confirmation as Director of the recently reconstituted Cybersecurity and Infrastructure Security Agency (CISA). Unlike many recent Senate hearings this one was marked by informality and bipartisan agreement. In his testimony David Crawford introduced his six children and paid special tribute to his wife, Clara, who he said always keeps him grounded. Most of the discussion focused on the need to provide security for the 2020 cycle of national elections.

THE NEW YORK TIMES. Thursday January 23, 2020

Exposed: CISA Chief's Emails to Mistress

Late yesterday, Politico reported that a hacker has captured the emails of David Crawford, the newly nominated Director of CISA and the likely person who will lead the country's cybersecurity efforts. Politico also received copies of sexually explicit emails purportedly sent by Crawford to a Lebanese woman living in Virginia, Isra Nasri. Ronald Dearborn, the

Chair of the Senate Committee on Homeland Security, declared that the hearings would be extended in the light of this development. The CISA, he added, was actively searching for the source of the hacking.

At a news conference David Crawford denied writing the emails, saying they were forgeries. The president tweeted "DISGRACEFUL. David's so great. Must be the Dems." However, later the same day, Isra Nasri announced through her lawyer that the emails were genuine and that she'd had a relationship with David Crawford for the past two and a half years.

A dam was no longer sure. Was this the first time he had become aware that Julia was getting more stressed? She was not the stressed-out kind. But recently, she'd changed. She worried. She worried a lot. About seemingly unimportant matters. Adam wished he'd taken more notice of this earlier.

Outside, the January night air was unusually cold and crisp for the Bay Area. He and Julia were propped up in bed watching Google News on his laptop. Julia kept pulling her long black hair back behind her shoulders, something she did when feeling anxious. Lucky, their much-indulged Maltipoo rescue dog, lay curled up at the end of the duvet staring at Adam with his irresistible brown eyes. Liz, their daughter, was fast asleep in the next room. They were fortunate. For all of her nine years she had been a great sleeper.

The news was focused, of course, on the alarming spread of the coronavirus in China, which had just expanded its lockdown to encircle thirty-five million of its citizens. Thirty-five million! Meanwhile, ten patients in Northern California were being held in isolation awaiting results of testing. Adam and Julia watched the president at a press conference insisting that everything was under control. That's when Julia's temper, inherited from her father, Arturo, erupted and she began ranting.

"Here we are in the epicenter of the outbreak in our country, and all the government can say is to stay calm, nothing to worry about?" She looked like she would burst into tears any moment.

Adam pointed out that the president's main justification for re-election was the economy, so he was naturally focused exclusively on that. She kept at it. "Great! So now we all have to pretend that there's nothing to worry about?" As a scientist Adam had to admit that, indeed, the virus was highly infectious and had no respect for national boundaries. That it was only a question of when, not if, it spread beyond China. "So, I'm right to be concerned," Julia said. Yes, sure she was.

Wanting to get off the subject, he asked her to guess who came to his office today, which of course she couldn't. Two agents from the CISA, he said. She asked what that was. He told her it was the Cyber-security and Infrastructure Security Agency, the Homeland Security division in charge of protecting the 2020 electoral process.

"You're suspected of being a hacker now?" she asked, recovering her characteristic sense of humor.

He told her that they wanted his help in tracing the identity of the person who had hacked the emails of the man slated to be CISA's director.

"I remember now. The sleaze ball who was having an affair that was exposed just as he was about to be nominated by the Senate as director."

"That's him. These days an affair is no big deal, especially in the president's eyes. It was lying to the Senate that tripped him up. The president and apparently everyone in the White House were furious at the way he was outed by a hacker. They're after blood. Not that it's that easy to trace a hacker."

She folded her arms across her chest. "I hope the hacker doesn't get caught."

"At any rate—and this is confidential—"

"Confidential!" Now she was almost out of the bed. "This government calls all its shady dealings confidential—"

"All right. All right. I'm just repeating what these two guys from the CISA were saying—that they were dealing with highly sensitive material, by which of course they meant politically sensitive material."

"Assholes! So what do they want from you?"

"They knew about me teaching that graduate seminar in hacking. They asked me to make it an exercise for my class. Have the students try to trace the hacker of the CISA director's emails."

"And why would you want to take on that can of worms?"

"They offered to make a seven-figure contribution to UC Berkeley in return."

"Whoa! A bribe to do their dirty work."

"That's one way of seeing it."

"How else can you see it?"

"University science departments depend heavily on federal funds to balance their budgets, as you know."

"Yes. A corrupt way for the government to keep universities in line."

"Academics, like businessmen, have to walk a fine line between financial and ethical demands."

"Where is the line between ethical and unethical? No, please don't tell me, because I won't agree with you. So. You're going to take this on?"

"How'd you guess?"

Adam had always envied Julia her clear-cut responses to issues, even though they often left him embarrassed at what he thought of as his more nuanced and considered stance. The more he argued with himself on the pros and cons of something the further he felt from resolution. Ever since his schooldays he'd simultaneously congratulated and criticized himself for this disposition. And while he admired Julia's hardline liberal stance on things, another part of him looked at their radically divided country and thought that the near paralysis of Washington was because almost everyone there adopted as hard a line as she did. Both of his reactions were sincere but mutually exclusive.

The result? An impossible search for compromise. So, he ricocheted between the two opposing views, depending on which was most compelling at any given moment. He wasn't proud of this attitude, but he couldn't see how to escape it. Truth was complex.

Julia took no prisoners. It was all or nothing for her. She came from a traditionally left-wing, working-class, Stockton family and, over time, she'd developed a more radical attitude than either her Mexican American father or mother born in the mid-west where she went to the University of Minnesota. After a period working as a journalist for *The Mercury News*, Julia had joined the ACLU of Northern California, the perfect employer for someone with her purist views. She worked her way up to become an investigator for the legal/policy team, where she could satisfy her single-minded pursuit of right-wing iniquities with Public Record Act requests calculated to embarrass the government.

Recently she had researched the case of a US citizen of Pakistani descent who'd been placed on the government's Suspicious Activity Report list for attempting to buy a large quantity of computers. In fact he was only doing his job as the purchasing agent for his Silicon Valley computer consulting company. Julia gleefully witnessed the government's discomfort at being outed for its blatant attempt to racially profile him. The government attorney was forced to issue a grudging apology. Julia was good at finding the hard evidence the ACLU legal team needed to win a fight.

After closing the laptop, Julia announced that she hadn't been sleeping well the previous few nights. "I wake up from a nightmare and have to get out of bed to make sure I don't continue with the same dream as soon as I get back to sleep. That means I stay awake for an hour or more before dropping off. That can happen two or three times a night."

When Adam looked into her face, he saw dark circles under her beautiful brown eyes.

"I'm sorry that's happening to you. Sounds like your anxiety's playing up again."

"That's pretty obvious." With that she reached into her nightstand drawer, took out a thermometer, and she held it in her mouth until it pinged.

"Well?" he asked.

She looked annoyed. "97.8. But these digital thermometers are known to be unreliable."

She replaced the thermometer and pulled out a bottle of Ambien. She swallowed two green pills. Funny, Adam thought. He could have sworn that Ambien came in white tablets.

He said nothing. It was Friday night and she didn't need to drive anywhere first thing.

Adam asked himself if he should have taken more notice of the way Julia's temper was growing shorter? He'd always believed in respecting other people's autonomy. He guessed that was a reaction to his dad who spent his life trying unsuccessfully to control what his mother said and did. He had always wondered why his father persisted when she never gave an inch. If his father had been a model that he had reacted against, his mother had helped shape much of what he had become. Still, he hoped that he had kept her at a sufficient distance to develop his own identity.

Q

Yes! A family outing, thought Julia. The two of them had decided to make it a cooking-free day. Well wrapped up for the cold, all three of them walked down College Avenue to Market Hall. The prepared foods there were so good you'd never want to cook your own meals again, were it not for the prices. They made straight for the entrées. Liz pointed through the curved glass covering to the macaroni and cheese. Julia stopped herself from saying that this was the least healthy choice available. Julia went for vegetable tajine and Adam settled on chicken lasagna. They added a side of grilled veggies and moved on to the desserts. Liz opted for ice cream, Adam for chocolate bread pudding and Julia abstained. They rounded off their purchases with a loaf of multigrain bread and a bottle of red Burgundy.

The bill came to over $100. Exiting the store with a large bag in each hand Adam nearly knocked over Roberto, a local homeless guy who looked in his eighties but was likely half that, stationed just outside. Of course that was Roberto's intention. But the disparity between what they had just bought and his request to spare a dollar hit home. The need for guys like Roberto to beg for food from people like them made Julia mad—and embarrassed. Adam put down the bags and reached into his shiny leather wallet for a five-dollar bill. She grasped his hand and pointed to a twenty. Adam gave the larger bill to Roberto. Roberto mumbled as he stared at the money. Then he broke into a grin. "Guess I will be living it up esta noche."

"Don't spend it all on spirits," Julia kidded him.

"Can we have some spirits, too?" Liz asked her.

"Smart girl you've got there, señora," Roberto said.

"Too smart," Julia replied as she urged a hypnotized Liz to move on.

"I didn't know you could buy spirits. In the story about Aladdin's Lamp they come out of a bottle." Liz said.

Adam and Julia laughed.

"The spirits we were talking about come out of a bottle, too, but they don't turn into genies. Swallowing them can leave you fuzzy."

"Fuzzy?" Liz asked.

"Unable to walk or think straight."

"Genies sound much more fun."

As they headed home Adam remarked, "This morning I was reading that there are around 28,000 homeless in the Bay Area."

"A house of your own was the American dream the Boomers all bought into," said Julia. "Now Gen Alphas like Liz face an impossible choice: join the five percent or give up on that dream. Not that I ever subscribed to it. To hell with the dream. It's a mirage that allows the rich to become even richer. Watching my father chase it through the bars of Stockton cured me of that illusion."

They turned the corner of Florio, walked halfway up the block and up the long drive leading to their house. Nine years ago they had taken out a hefty mortgage on this roomy 1930s house hidden from the street behind a mass of overgrown trees and bushes. It had a large interior yard between the garage and the house that offered Liz and Lucky an ideal play space. It also featured a large back patio where they had meals, and watched the birds and squirrels fight for food.

"I can't help feeling that, when she grows up, Liz and her generation will curse us for leaving them with such a mess," Adam observed.

Liz looked up at Adam with her shining gray eyes. "What mess, Daddy?"

"Nothing, sweetheart," he replied in the maddening way adults have of avoiding children's need to know what's happening in the world they are about to enter.

Q

Adam had always loved Sundays. Leisurely breakfast and maybe a third cup of Blue Nile blend with the bulky *New York Times* and the *San Francisco Chronicle* full of advertising supplements. Walk with Liz and Lucky to Chabot Park, giving Julia time to herself. Phone his mother.

His mother had been widowed for three years. His father, a certified financial planner, had succumbed to a stroke when he was only sixty, leaving her comfortable. She stayed on in the house that Adam had been brought up in. Although she was only a few miles away he rarely saw her. But they chatted on the phone most Sundays.

"Hello, Mom. How's life in wonderful Glen Highlands?"

"Now, Adam. Don't make fun of Glen Highlands. One day you'll inherit this house and the lifestyle that goes with it."

God forbid, he thought. He had no desire to live in that all-white neighborhood.

"What have you been up to?" he asked.

"Actually, I have some news for you. As you know, I have been spending a lot more time with the committee now that the primary is only five weeks away." His mother had always been politically active. Three years ago she was elected to the Alameda County Democratic Central Committee.

"Well," she continued, "at last week's meeting they elected me chair."

"Congratulations! You deserve it."

"I've spent most of my waking hours since then trying to familiarize myself with everything the committee is doing. Like reasons for endorsing Measure A to help finance Alameda Unified School District. And the bond measure to upgrade fire stations in the unincorporated areas of the County. The list goes on."

"I'm sure it does," he said, anxious to divert her from a topic she could expound on for hours.

"How's Liz doing?" she asked after a pause.

Adam experienced his usual sense of guilt at not having taken Liz to see her during the week.

"She has a cold," he said truthfully.

"Better that she stayed home," his mother said, letting him off the hook.

"By the way, I hope you two will be voting for both County measures this March," she half asked, half demanded.

"Come on. You know we will." Adam reflected that, once children have grown up, they speak to their parents more brusquely—or is it brutally?—than they do to anyone else. Except maybe their partners. And they—the parents—are usually unbelievably restrained in their response.

Adam did his best to make up for his last remark by returning to her favorite topic: "It's great news about your being chair. It shows how much trust the other members have in you."

"You're as much a flatterer as your father."

"He was more of a charmer for sure."

"You have your moments."

"Now who's doing the flattering?"

He continued, "Julia and I were wondering whether the coronavirus will impact the elections."

"No chance," she said. "The president's ratings are currently higher than usual. So he has no interest in seeing the primaries postponed. Besides, we only have a very small number of infected people here. It's not like we're in China."

"I know. But viruses are notoriously unpredictable." There was a pause.

"How's Barack?" he asked. Barack was her new kitten. Adam was still annoyed that she had named an animal after his favorite president.

"How do you think? An adorable bundle of mischief. Just this morning I caught him trying to chew through the cable connecting the power to the TV."

"That's scary. What did you do?"

"I shouted at him and he rushed under the sofa."

"And where is he now?"

"Purring on my lap."

"You treat him better than you did me."

"Now, dear, you know that's not true."

"Whatever you say," he said, while thinking how differently they remembered the past.

There was an awkward silence. "I have to make Liz's lunch," he said. "So I better go, Mom. Fight the good fight—for all of us."

"You bet I will. Say hello to Julia. And give Liz a kiss for me. Goodbye, dear."

The phone went dead. Apart from that brief allusion to his childhood, their conversation had steered clear of anything really personal. Why, he wondered, were they both so anxious to avoid talking about matters of the heart? Or just feelings? Had he acquired that habit from her? She was always so calm and controlled. Like him, she hated scenes. Excess of any kind. And her relative wealth had allowed her to maintain control over her circumstances most of the time. As a kid he'd thought she was really cool. Never worked up. Someone who planned ahead and was rarely caught by surprise.

Now he saw it more as a defense mechanism, a way of trying to fend off the unpleasantries of life—not possible of course. It required a selective take on things. And a refusal to acknowledge that any selection was involved.

So much for the myth that men marry their mothers. Julia couldn't have been more different. Volatile, quick tempered, emotionally charged, she was like kelp swept this way and that by the tides of her blood. Was that difference what made him fall for her? And her directness. And her passion. Not to mention how attractive he found her—long iridescent black hair, high cheekbones, piercing brown eyes and sensuous lips. He guessed theirs was a marriage of opposites. Or was it of complements? Jack Sprat and his wife. They sure had had no difficulty licking the platter clean. At least up to that time.

Q

The next morning Adam was shaving as the TV morning news anchor announced: "The coronavirus outbreak continues to spread, with the death toll now rising to at least 145 people in China where nearly 60 million people are on partial or full lockdown..."

"Listen to this Facebook post," Julia interrupted. She was still in bed, reading stuff on her cell. "It comes from a member of the Stanford Hospital medical board: 'Take a deep breath and hold it for more than 10 seconds. If you complete it successfully without coughing, without discomfort, stiffness or tightness, it proves there is no fibrosis in the lungs; it basically indicates no infection.' It goes on to say that, if you drink water every fifteen minutes, it will flush the virus from your throat into your stomach where acid will kill it."

"Sounds like another rumor to me," Adam replied.

Adam always was a skeptic. She admired him for it. But sometimes it made her mad.

"What makes you think that?" she asked.

Julia had found herself both fascinated and terrified by anything to do with the virus over the past few days. It was becoming an obsession, the idea that death was so close to all of them, silently stalking them out there on the street. It filled her with a kind of fear she'd never encountered before. She guessed it was the first time in her life that she'd even thought about the possibility of dying. *To sleep, perchance to dream.* More like a nightmare from which you couldn't wake up— because it turned out you weren't asleep.

But Adam, with his scientific training, immediately questioned this home cure.

"Let's have a look at it," Adam said. Wearing only his boxer shorts, razor in hand, he came to look over her shoulder. "See. Facebook has added a link to the CDC website. I bet if you click it that it will debunk the posting."

Julia duly followed the link and read a redirected message from Stanford Healthcare warning that this misinformation was not from Stanford University.

"Too bad," she said. "I guess we'll all have to take our temperatures every morning."

"You really think that's necessary?"

"We could be facing an epidemic here. And one of the first signs that you've been infected is having a fever."

"Epidemic?"

"That's what the media is calling what's happening in China."

"China is not the US."

"Then why has the mayor of San Francisco just activated an emergency operations center to centralize responses to outbreaks of the virus?"

"I guess you have a point."

"You bet I have a point."

Adam withdrew. She knew he thought she was being alarmist. But wasn't it better to find out if you had been infected, especially when you could be putting others in danger? Adam had always downplayed any possibility of getting ill. He carried around an aura of invulnerability, as if he were exempt from life's exigencies. That trait was part of what attracted her to him in the first place, having been brought up in a volatile and unstable family. But now she found herself getting irritated by him. He was just too damned collected. He was treating her growing alarm as a caprice. ¡Maldita sea! Why would he take risks with his own family?

It was strange. After Adam had convinced her that the cure was fake she felt less secure than she had before. She guessed this was because the online world of rumors offered her a refuge of sorts. A refuge from the material world where deadly viruses could attack her unseen.

Returning to the mirror Adam saw that he had nicked his neck with the razor, which brought their exchange to an end.

Q

Tuesday and Thursday mornings were always a frantic rush to get up, shower, have breakfast and drop Liz off at Chabot Elementary on his way to the university. At 10 a.m. he taught a large one-hour sophomore class, Internet and Network Security, followed at 12 p.m. by Advanced Topics in Computer Security, a three-hour graduate seminar. It was the students in that seminar whom the Homeland Security agents wanted to trace the hacker.

That Tuesday morning turned into a sequence of minor disasters.

As he was getting out of bed he saw a sizeable blood stain on the far end of the duvet where Lucky slept. He examined Lucky and saw that, sure enough, he had chewed a hot spot on his right back thigh. Admonishing Lucky as he cleaned him up—pointless apart from allowing him to vent his frustration—Adam searched without success for his cone, something Lucky hated having to wear.

"Julia, do you know what's happened to the dog's cone?" he asked.

"It's where you put it after the last time—in the bottom drawer in the closet where it always is," she replied. "Why is it men have such a hard time finding things?"

"But it's men who actually do stuff with the things."

"Oh, please. Don't get me started on that this early in the morning."

Adam fixed the cone on a resisting Lucky and gave him a rub on his tummy— "Sorry, buddy, but it's for your own sake" —before making for the shower. There, he managed to drop a large new bar of soap on his toes. By evening they'd probably turn dark purple.

He went down to the kitchen and sliced a banana onto Liz's Honey Nut Cheerios. He'd poured milk onto them before he realized that she was still upstairs.

"Time for breakfast," he yelled up from the bottom of the stairs. No response. He climbed up to her room and found her still in her pajamas.

"Why aren't you dressed, sweetheart?" he asked.

"I couldn't do it," she said.

"Couldn't do what?"

"Solve the algebra problems in my homework."

"Why didn't you ask me to help you last night?"

"Because you had your friends over and that lasted forever."

"I'm really sorry. You know, I would always make time for you if you asked me."

"What am I going to tell Ms. Fulsome?"

"Just explain that your parents weren't there to help you last night, but that your father has promised to go over the problems tonight. The most she will do is ask you to bring her the answers in your homework tomorrow."

"Are you sure, Daddy?"

"If you want me to, I can stop and talk to her when I drop you off."

"Please don't do that."

"Why?"

"I'll talk to her, Daddy. Just leave it to me."

"OK. But you need to hurry up. We're leaving in fifteen minutes."

"Don't worry. I'll be down real fast," she said, now smiling.

Liz had barely reached the breakfast table when Julia's cellphone sounded. As Julia reached for it her sleeve caught the handle of her mug of coffee and knocked it over. A flood of hot coffee raced over the tabletop and poured onto Adam's lap.

"So sorry, *cariño*," she said, barely suppressing the impulse to burst out laughing at his predicament.

"Ow! You sure drink your coffee hot," he called back as he rushed upstairs to change.

Of course he was late leaving with Liz, and rain was pouring down. When they reached the end of the drive, he realized that he had forgotten to take her packed lunch. He ran back to the house where a grinning Julia greeted him with the lunch box. "My absent-minded professor," she teased. He ran back to the car drenched, and willed himself to drive under thirty to her school.

When he reached the Berkeley campus the lot was almost full and he had to park on the highest level. Then, he realized that he'd left his office key at home and had to borrow a duplicate from the department office. By the time he got to class he was eight minutes late. After he'd started his presentation at least another six students crept in by the rear entrance and slid sheepishly into their seats. That made him feel a little less guilty. But he couldn't put his all into the class and the result was obvious in the distracted faces of many of the students. Each class was a new challenge, and he knew he had failed to meet this one.

That day's topic was the California Consumer Privacy Act that had just come into effect at the start of the year. This was a new digital privacy law that allowed consumers to opt out of the sale of their personal information. When one student expressed indignation at this encroachment on the workings of the free market, he uncharacteristically lost his cool and asked sarcastically, what made her think any market was totally free? Didn't the New York Stock Exchange have a trip mechanism? She looked flustered and didn't respond. After class he apologized to her, explaining that he was feeling frustrated by his own failure to connect with them. She silently accepted his apology and left. That class, he told himself, was definitely not a success.

What is that saying? "Setbacks are just learning experiences." He wasn't convinced. Sometimes setbacks are just setbacks.

He went directly to his car to keep an 11:30 appointment with the chief lending officer at the Bank of America on College Avenue. He and Julia were applying to refinance their mortgage. The rain never let up.

Q

They'd just finished their dinner. Adam had cooked a zucchini frittata and asparagus. The dirty plates were still on the table. Half of Julia's meal remained on her plate. Liz was in her room doing her homework.

"You didn't seem to have much of an appetite tonight," Adam observed.

"I told you, I spent the day at a regional conference at the Hotel Vulcan."

"Union Square? You're moving up in the world," he teased.

"If only! At any rate, we were given a buffet lunch and I ended up eating more than I intended."

"It must have been good."

"Yes, it was. Especially the cold salmon and asparagus." Adam raised his eyebrows.

"I know," she said. "I should have told you before you started cooking." She paused. "Then I ran into Dave, of all people."

"Dave?"

"Dave Ira. You know. My boyfriend when I met you."

"Oh, that Dave," he said dismissively.

Julia thought back to the night she met Adam. It was at a mutual friend's rowdy party in the Mission District. She and Dave had been arguing before they'd arrived. What was it about? Oh yes. Her new red dress. He thought it looked *sluttish*—that was his term. She told him she felt sexy in it. She thought it was a perfect outfit for drinks and a relaxed weekend evening. He was acting sulky and aggressive at the same time. She hated the way he could brood for days. Usually the sulking built up to a frightening outburst of temper. Still, his eruptions of anger would clear the air, like the downpour that often follows a clap of thunder. Strangely his near-violent outbursts actually turned her on in some inexplicable way. Yes, it was perverse. But that was what had kept her hooked on Dave—until Adam turned up. Reliable Adam, who seemed to offer reassurance to everything and everyone who entered his world.

Unlike Dave, who wore a Harley Davidson t-shirt and blue jeans bagging out at the knees, Adam looked elegant, wearing cream dress pants and a colorful patterned shirt. Dave's hair stuck out in all directions as if he'd just got out of bed, and with his stubbled ruddy complexion he wore a sullen expression. Adam had an elongated face, well-groomed fair hair, pale skin with bright blue eyes and a long thin nose—vaguely Scandinavian, she had thought (it turned out that his grandfather was an immigrant from Denmark). In the course of that evening Dave kept downing bottles of Corona Extra while she talked and flirted with Adam, who talked and flirted back.

The two men were so different. Dave was as volatile and quick-tempered as she, while Adam was everything she wasn't. Totally cool. Full of charm. Someone you knew you could rely on. In fact someone, she had told herself, with whom you could spend your life.

The two men met only twice. The second time was after she had dumped Dave for Adam, who was helping her move her things from her studio apartment into his place. Dave turned up to collect a few items of his that were still there. He looked defeated and resentful. Adam left Julia and Dave alone to say whatever they needed to say to one another. Of course, that soon degenerated into a nasty argument that ended when she told him not to forget to take his framed photo of them vacationing in Stinson Beach.

"You think I'm just an image that can be trashed?" Dave asked.

"You can put it where you like," she said provocatively.

"This is where I'm putting it," he said, smashing the glass over her head. She reached up and, saw that her fingers had blood on them. She rushed to the bathroom to grab a towel and pressed it on the gash. On her return to the living room Dave had already left and Adam was hurrying over to her to see how bad the wound was.

"That was thirteen years ago," Adam said.

"I know. So weird. He's a night clerk at the Vulcan."

"Then why was he there at lunch time?"

"That's exactly what I asked him. He said they were short of staff for the conference and were paying him overtime to help out."

"And—"

"He told me that I had ruined his life. Called me a Stacy."

"What's a Stacy?"

"I have no idea."

"Let's Google it," he said, pulling out his cell phone. "Wiktionary. Here you go: 'Slang, sometimes derogatory. An attractive woman who is sexually active.'" He searched further. "Oh, man! It's a derogatory term used by Incels."

"What are Incels?"

"Let's see what it says here. Incel stands for involuntary celibate."

"That sounds weird. Go on."

"'Some men build a grudge against popular alpha females because they seem sexually out of reach. They think Stacys only give out to what Incels call Chads, good-looking alpha males.' Pretty pathetic."

"A great excuse to blame women for a man's failing."

Adam continued his search. "Listen to this: 'On November 2, 2018 Scott Beierle, a 40-year-old vet, shot to death a 21-year-old Florida State University student who he barely knew. The police turned up numerous postings describing his hatred of women who he blamed for rejecting him.' It goes on to define the Incel as 'characterized by resentment, misanthropy, self-pity, self-loathing, misogyny, racism, a sense of entitlement to sex and the endorsement of violence against sexually active people.'"

"Well," she said, "that's all I needed—a woman-hater taking an interest in me."

"He took an interest in you?"

"He asked me to have a drink with him after the conference ended."

"And did you?"

"No, thank God. But my refusal must have convinced him that I'm a Stacy. Another rejection causing more resentment."

"Did he leave you alone after that?"

"Only after promising that he would get in touch soon."

"He'll just move on to his next object of resentment."

"*Mierda!* That's easy for you to say."

"What makes you think he won't move on?"

"He's not the type to give up on a grudge easily. He's not the forgiving kind."

Those were all white lies. The truth was that Dave had succeeded in coercing her into having a drink with him after the conference.

Coerced? She guessed part of her wanted to be coerced, wanted to be—what? Taken out of herself? Maybe she was hoping that Dave's obsessions would drive out her own.

She joined him at the Sports Bar a few doors down from the Vulcan. He'd already had several beers. Here we go, she thought. Her own stupid fault for giving in to his pressure. He was dressed in black pants and white shirt, as if ready to go on night duty. Even his shock of dark hair was plastered down. He was examining his appearance in a mirror next to the booth he was occupying. Was that what Incels did? Incels were fixated on their supposed unattractiveness. But he was good-looking enough, in an uncouth way.

He'd already got Julia a beer that sat glistening on the counter.

"So! You turned up, then."

"I said I would. And here I am."

"Looking as appetizing as ever," he said, his eyes fixed longingly on her breasts rather than her face.

"Well, thank you."

"Someone else's meal now, though."

"You could say that, although I wish you would stop talking about me as if I was an item on the menu."

"That was meant to be a compliment. You make me real hungry, is all I can say."

"Why don't you order some wings?"

"As long as you agree to be the entrée."

"Come on, Dave. You know I'm married."

"That's what's wrong with the world. All the desirable women are married."

He took hold of her left hand and held up her fourth finger with its wedding ring.

"What are you staring at?"

"A symbol of married slavery." He grinned.

"That's what you'd like to think, isn't it? That all of us married women are longing to be freed. Just so that we can satisfy your sexual fantasies."

"Not all married women. Just you. I guarantee you wouldn't regret it."

"You're forgetting that I already took that journey with you."

"Until your Chad arrived."

"Who's Chad? If you remember his name's Adam."

"Just another stuck up alpha male."

"I'm leaving if you're going to spend the time bad-mouthing my husband."

"I'd rather be focused on your mouth," he said touching her lips with his fingertips. "Or any part of you." He grinned at her suggestively.

She pushed his hand away. "You really haven't changed one bit, Dave."

"That's right. I'm the same guy who turned you on back then. Admit it. We had a wild time together. Why are you trying to hide the fact that you still want me?"

"What makes you think that?" she asked. Strange though, she still felt powerfully drawn to him physically even as she was repelled by his crude behavior.

"Why else would you meet me here?"

"Please don't fool yourself."

"Okay. Okay. Drink up, then. I need another beer."

But she wasn't about to have another beer with him. "Got to go," she said curtly, as she quickly stood up and made for the exit before he could stop her.

What was it that drew her to him? She asked herself that as she walked to the BART Metro station at Montgomery. So much about him was off-putting. No. Downright repugnant. Yet, she couldn't stop herself responding to his magnetic force. And the pattern his magnetism shaped her into was unlike any other in her life. The charge coming from him overpowered her own dislike and fear of him. Luckily she hadn't let him perceive that. At least she hoped not.

Q

That afternoon Adam and his graduate students reported the results of their investigation to the two CISA men who attended the seminar. With their crew cuts and dark suits they looked like stereotypical Secret Service agents in a police procedural. All that they lacked were dark glasses.

The hacker or hackers didn't appear to be that sophisticated, Adam reported. They hadn't written self-erasing code. But they had hidden behind a proxy server. His students had quickly identified the digital door through which the hackers had entered Crawford's email account. Next they had used a Domain Name Server to identify the hacker's IP address. Using tracerouting they located the hacker's Internet Service Provider in San Francisco. The metadata of the leaked emails led his students to conclude that they were dealing with a relative amateur.

What was most revealing was his students' exploration of the hacker's emails which repeatedly referred to Crawford, the nominee for director of CISA, as an agent of the deep state. This paranoid belief in the existence of a deep state suggested that the hacker was a white nationalist, as white nationalists had a paranoid conviction that government policy was secretly controlled by the deep state. His emails also had frequent references to QAnon.

Adam had come across this bizarre conspiracy theory before, but now he decided to look more deeply into it. Apparently, it originated with a posting in October 2017 on the anonymous online forum,4chan, by someone calling himself "Q". Q is the highest level of clearance in the US government. Claiming to be a senior official in the White House, Q used a tripcode to post allegations that a Democratic cabal of Satanic pedophiles constituted a deep state that controlled the media and the government.

Q's followers, who all posted using the hashtag "QAnon," believed that Robert Mueller's Russian investigation had been a ruse, and that, in fact, it was Hillary Clinton and Barack Obama who were in thrall to Putin, and who were also into raping and killing children. The president, the group believed, had figured all this out when he was a mere candidate and was devoting his presidency to busting up this evil group. Arrests were (always) imminent.

What most surprised Adam was the popularity of QAnon. One source reckoned that in 2019 there were over 22 million tweets using that and related hashtags. Over 60,000 a day! How could such an absurd idea have caught on so widely? he wondered. But then he lived in the protected world of academia, one in which rationality and reasoned argument supposedly prevailed.

Adam's graduate students were familiar with QAnon postings. So were the two agents. As soon as they heard that the hacker might be a QAnon follower the agents backed off as if they'd been bitten. Adam had expected them to serve a subpoena on the ISP to obtain the name and address of the hacker. But they insisted that doing so would open them to charges of political bias. Adam tried arguing that QAnon hardly qualified as a legitimate political party or ideology. They replied that he had no idea how different political calculations had become with the current administration. They instructed him and his students to drop the investigation and keep it secret. This seemed exceedingly strange to Adam, but his students didn't seem particularly bothered.

After the two agents left his students agreed that the case wasn't worth any further class time spent on it. The hacker was just another subscriber to a lunatic conspiracy theory who also had a rudimentary expertise in computer hacking. Adam accepted their vote to move on and thought that was the end of the matter.

But Adam couldn't move on. He was stunned. More than one thousand Facebook groups that collectively claimed millions of members believed that the Democratic party condoned Satanism. This immense online universe walled itself off from any factual questioning or doubts.

Adam lived in two worlds, he reflected. One was the external world, the other a digital fantasy world that appeared to be far more appealing than the actual world with all its disappointments and hazards. For the inhabitants of the digital world, theirs was the real world. If the material world failed to conform to their world, they altered reality to make it do so.

Listening to the news on the way home, Adam learned that Beijing had confirmed over 4500 coronavirus infections. The US had just recorded its fifth case. Nevertheless, the Health and Human Services Secretary assured everyone that, "at this point Americans should not worry for their own safety." Adam couldn't help questioning this bland reassurance. It didn't send him into a blind fury as the president's similar comments had done with Julia. But it made him ask: Is it really possible to contain a new infection of this sort within a country's borders? And what if people could be infected without showing symptoms, as with other diseases, which would allow the hidden virus to spread exponentially?

Come on, he told himself, you're being over-cautious. We know next to nothing about Covid-19 and how it behaves. Forget it. He switched the car radio to KDFC which was playing Beethoven's "Für Elise" for the thousandth time and continued his slow drive home down College Avenue.

Q

Adam's department held its meeting on the last Friday morning of the month. He took the opportunity to spend an hour in the gym before the start of the meeting.

Most of the faculty hated those meetings where the same few colleagues spent most of the time grandstanding and fighting with one another, mainly to obtain reductions of instruction time in return for undertaking administrative tasks on tedious, time-consuming committees. Still, these tiresome meetings were a small price to pay for the privilege of teaching only thirty weeks a year. Adam and some of the others spent their time quietly catching up on their emails and social media while holding their cell phones just below the conference table.

Adam sat next to Anna, a colleague who was one of the few close friends he'd made in the department. They sometimes played tennis together and had lunch or late afternoon drinks together when their schedules permitted. Their research interests overlapped in the areas of computer security—specifically network security monitoring and intrusion prevention—and electronic voting (both technology and its policy implications). Julia complained that she couldn't understand what these research areas referred to. The few times Adam had invited Anna home, they tended to drift into shop talk that excluded Julia, so he'd given that up.

Anna and Adam soon found more in common than their mutual research interests. She was one of only half a dozen female faculty in his large department. And she combined the disciplinary rigor of his male colleagues with a sensitivity to human foibles that they seemed to lack. He found most of the men a little too cold and factual. He may not be a vortex of strong emotions himself, he reflected, but he preferred the company of those who showed more emotional intelligence—as Anna and Julia did.

"You free for lunch after today's marathon?" he asked Anna as he settled down, put the agenda on the table in front of him, and pulled out his phone.

"You bet. Just what I need after this circus," she replied brightening.

"Can't wait," he grinned.

Anna had the additional advantage of not looking like the typical academic scientist. She didn't wear work-suits and pumps. Neither did she seek anonymity in formless shirts and trousers. She mainly dressed in jeans and form-fitting shirts, while often, like today, wearing high heels and lots of lipstick. She had close-cut jet-black hair and glittering gray eyes. She also had a floral tattoo on her upper left arm and a stud in her cheek. She had plenty of sex-appeal and she knew it.

The only interesting item on the agenda concerned a push to repeal Prop 209, initiated by some of the university's Black students. Prop 209 was an anti-affirmative action measure passed in 1996. A Black Republican colleague named Thomas Cain adamantly supported the measure, while another professor named James Trust supported the students and wanted to reintroduce affirmative action.

After Thomas offered a passionate defense of the status quo, James mounted a vicious personal attack on him, claiming, among other things, that Thomas vastly exaggerated his struggles as a child brought up by impoverished grandparents. How this related to Prop 209 Adam couldn't understand. But for about twenty minutes the meeting was in uproar as colleagues rushed to defend Thomas from this ad hominem attack. James eventually apologized for needlessly personalizing the debate and another colleague brought up a study showing that Berkeley now had one of the lowest percentages of Black students in the UC system. Finally a vote was taken with the majority supporting the effort to repeal Prop 209. After that, they returned to an agenda filled with trivia and banalities.

At 12:30 the meeting broke up after the chair tried to forge yet another reconciliation between the increasingly divided factions within the department. Poor guy, Adam thought. What a thankless job.

Anna and Adam walked in the warm sun over to Kimshi Garden, a Korean noodle place on Durant Avenue. After they'd ordered their lunch (he had pan fried seafood udong, and Anna chose tofu soup with shitake mushrooms), he asked her whether she had heard of QAnon.

"Of course," she replied. "Why do you ask?"

He recounted the entire business with the two agents and admitted that until very recently he had known hardly anything about Q's postings.

"Well, they spent a lot of their time posting on 8chan. When 8chan got shut down in August last year, users like QAnon migrated to 8kun where they have their own board."

"And how seriously do you think people take QAnon?" he asked.

"Well, there are the 35 current or former congressional candidates who've endorsed QAnon. And the president regularly retweets QAnon posts. Look at videos of his rallies and you'll see Q signs everywhere."

"Unbelievable. And they all believe that when the president mentions the deep state he's referring to a gang of Satanic pedophiles led by Hillary Clinton?"

"Not all of them. Some don't believe the pedophile and Satanic allegations. But they all are convinced that the deep state is real, that it has liberal leaning members embedded in the highest echelons of the government, and that the president is preparing to arrest them—not to mention Hillary Clinton, George Soros and Bill Gates—and send them to Guantanamo Bay. They call it the Great Awakening."

"Sounds like the Rapture."

"Exactly. QAnon is more like a religious cult than just another conspiracy theory."

"With Q as the Messiah."

Anna paused from eating and looked directly at Adam.

"I'm sure you know that conspiracy theories become popular when people's critical faculties are overwhelmed by a sense of helplessness. Their supposed access to secret truths restores their sense of control. They give them a feeling of self-empowerment."

"Interesting," he said. "I noticed how Q's followers are convinced that they are uncovering buried meanings. How dangerous is that?"

"If you look at Q's posts he—I am assuming it's a 'he'—is extremely adept at suggesting various scenarios without ever committing himself fully. That sets off his followers on wild goose chases. For instance, he'll remind them that Q is the seventeenth letter in the alphabet and hint that the president will mention the number seventeen in one of his speeches or tweets over the next few days. Sure enough, sooner or later, the number seventeen crops up in something he says."

"And no one has identified who Q is?"

"They all agree that he must be an important official in the government. Some even maintain that he is the president himself. But Q uses the Tor app to remain anonymous."

Adam told Anna about the strange way the two agents had suddenly backed out of the inquiry once QAnon was implicated. She also found it odd.

"But that's enough craziness for one day," Adam concluded. Their coffees arrived with the check. "What's happening with you?" he asked.

"Actually I'm thinking of researching a paper on new threats to the 2020 election, which overlaps with your interest in QAnon."

"Sorry. I meant your life outside academia."

"Oh, that," she laughed. "I just broke up with a man I've been seeing for the past three months. That's a long time for me."

"Still playing the field?"

"You could say that. I like to keep my lovers at arms' length."

"And why is that?"

"They're more exciting that way."

"Driven by the pleasure principle?"

"Freud had a point."

"And how are married guys like me governed by the pleasure principle?"

"I guess you exchange the thrill of intense desire for the guarantee of long-term satisfaction."

"Sounds like a very bourgeois exchange. Like investing in government bonds, say."

"In my experience a lot of married men want and get both forms of pleasure."

"I can certainly understand why you might have ample access to such information."

"Now you're coming on to me," she said smiling, leading Adam to think that she wouldn't be averse to a serious move on his part. But that was not his intention.

"I was just acknowledging the undisputed fact that you are attractive," he said steering the conversation back to safer ground.

"I don't mind a compliment, especially coming from a handsome guy like you."

He looked at his watch. "You make the time fly. I better be off. I have to pick up Liz from school in a half hour. Thank you, Anna, for helping to erase this morning's tedious meeting from my consciousness."

"You did the same for me." She gave him a light kiss on the cheek, and they parted.

Q

Saturday was Julia's favorite day of the week. It was not as leisurely as Sunday. But more fun things usually happened that day—like shopping for clothes or shoes (especially shoes). Or lunch out with friends. Even a movie if they could arrange a sitter for Liz.

Before she could indulge herself this particular Saturday she owed her mom a call. Pouring herself another cup of coffee that morning, she punched in the numbers.

"Hello?" a voice answered.

"It's me, Mom. How're things?"

"This morning my sciatica is bothering me a lot."

"I'm sorry to hear that. Are you doing all your exercises?"

"They're too damn painful to do today. I took Advil, but it doesn't seem to have made any difference. Walking is the worst. When I sit down I don't feel it so much."

"Have you talked to your physical therapist about it?"

"Some help she is. She's not around weekends. Some people have it easy, if you ask me."

She used that phrase frequently and it annoyed the hell out of Julia. It made her want to reply, "But I didn't ask you."

"Why don't you call to make an appointment for Monday," Julia asked.

"And be in pain all weekend?"

"An alternative is to go to urgent care and ask them to give you a stronger pain killer."

"I've got a better idea. I'll ask your father to go to Connected Cannabis and get me some THC."

"Where's he now?"

"Stuck in the bathroom with the paper."

"Is he still sober enough to drive there?" Her dad had a serious drinking problem. He often had his first beer of the day with breakfast. By lunchtime he'd upgraded to whiskey. By mid-afternoon he was usually snoring in his chair in the den or outside on the deck. As a child Julia had learned to avoid him altogether in the evenings when he grew unpleasant and sometimes violent.

"I doubt he would pass the breathalyzer any time day or night," Laura, Julia's mother, said.

"Didn't you say he joined AA a couple of weeks ago?"

"That's right. And lost interest in a week. You know your father. Without a drink in his belly he can't stand himself."

"And with a drink in his belly I can't stand him."

Julia recollected some of the worst scenes from her childhood. Like when he chased both her mother and her out of the house shouting "*Putas de mierda*" and waving a kitchen knife in the air. That time he left them shivering in the rain for an hour before unlocking the door. Or when she had to spend half the night locked in the bathroom after he'd tried to thrash her with his belt because she'd hidden his only bottle of scotch.

"Now, dear. Don't be talking about your father that way."

"Why not? You know how he behaves when he's smashed."

"When he's smashed he never knows what he's doing."

Julia found she was digging her fingernails into her palms until they hurt. "There is no excuse for what he tried to do to me as a teenager." She found it really hard to talk about this chapter of her life, which her mother always diminished or denied. But she wasn't about to collude with her denial.

"What are you talking about?" her mother asked.

"Come on. You know very well what I'm talking about. His drunken visits to my bedroom when I was a teenager."

"He did no such thing." Why did she keep trying to make her mother admit what she refused to face?

"Are you telling me that you don't remember the time I had to yell for help because I woke up to him pulling my pajamas down? You had to come and pull him off me."

"You're making it up. I did no such thing."

"You might kid yourself, Mom. But you can't kid me. Do you think I could forget something like that?"

"You're not remembering right, Julia. He never did that."

"You never stood up for me," she replied bitterly.

"I don't know what you're talking about."

"Bullshit, Mom," she shouted into the mouthpiece. Julia was close to tears, which only infuriated her more.

"Don't swear at me. I'll be upset all day if you go on like this."

"Forget it, Mom," she said.

There was an awkward pause. Julia was remembering the times she had had to wrestle and kick her father off her in bed. Luckily, drink robbed him of his strength. He would usually end up on the bedside floor cursing her with slurred swear words. Just *un viejo verde*, a dirty old man, her father.

"So, what do you think about this virus going around?" Julia asked her, trying to get the bitterness out of her voice.

"They're saying it's only affecting people in China. And who cares about them?"

Yes, she was also a racist, Julia reminded herself. Not that she was alone these days. Only that morning Julia had read a tweet: "Because of some folks in China who eat weird (foods) like bats, rats, and snakes, the entire world is about to suffer a plague."

"I heard," her mother went on, "that they deliberately spread the virus as a means of population control."

"You know that the virus is beginning to spread to this country."

"What do you mean?"

"They've just confirmed the eighth case here in the US. The Defense Department is preparing housing for thousands of travelers who'll need to be quarantined here when they arrive from abroad."

"Is that so?"

"It sure is. And yesterday the president issued an order restricting travel from China."

"But just this morning I heard the Secretary for Health and What-ever-it-is say that the risk of it spreading to Americans is low."

"Since when have you believed a government spokesperson?"

"You got a point there. Those bastards'll say anything to keep us all quiet."

"That sounds more like the mother I know."

"If only Bernie was in charge we wouldn't have to worry about catching some foreign virus plus we'd all have free healthcare."

"I totally agree." Julia didn't want to spoil their unusual moment of agreement by pointing out that there was no known cure for this virus.

"Nice talking to you, Mom. Got to go now. Bye."

"Goodbye, dear. Give Liz a hug from me."

"Will do. Bye again."

That afternoon at Julia's urging Adam and she went to the Rialto Cinemas in Elmwood to see Steven Soderbergh's *Contagion*, a 2011 movie enjoying a comeback because it was about a pandemic. It had been praised by scientists for its accuracy. Besides, it had a great cast including Matt Damon, Gwyneth Paltrow, and Jude Law, who played a conspiracy theorist selling a fake cure.

When the film shows the riots that broke out after food supplies and tincture of forsythia dried up, Julia realized she was truly frightened. There was a scene showing the streets of San Francisco littered with trash and discarded clothing. All the fears that were keeping Julia up at night closed in on her. As she watched the crowds of hungry Americans storm an empty truck that had been delivering food rations, knocking down one of the female leads in the rush, Julia felt lightheaded. And the looting of banks, pharmacies and grocery stores stoked new terrors she had not even considered.

Back home, she looked up at Adam across the table doing something on his cell phone.

"Adam. I want to ask you something."

"Yes?"

"I know you'll think I'm being paranoid. But I've been reading about the spread of the coronavirus. It's getting a lot worse."

"So?"

"Would you promise me to wash your hands whenever you come into the house from anywhere?"

"I usually do."

"I mean every time. Even if you've just taken the trash out."

"That seems a little excessive."

"Would you do it for me?"

"I'll tell you what. I'll do it whenever there's been a chance that I've come into contact with someone else or with a surface that someone else could have contaminated."

"But how do you know the trash can, for example, hasn't been handled by the guys with the trash truck?"

"I don't."

"Exactly my point. So why not just wash every time?"

"Because there is no reason to, after, say, I've taken Lucky for a walk."

"What about the gate handle that is used by the mail person, the gardener, Teresa, you name it?"

"What about them?"

"So you don't care enough for me or Liz to take such a simple safety measure?"

"Of course I do. I promise to wash my hands any time I've had contact with anyone or anything that could be infected."

"You just don't get it. It needs to be all or nothing. Half measures are not going to make me feel safe."

"And acting irrationally will make me feel ridiculous."

"Screw your rationality. I'm talking about life and death."

Adam looked taken aback. "Okay. Okay. I'll do it to make you feel better. But I still can't see the point of doing it every time."

"As long as you do it I don't care how you feel about doing it. All right?"

"All right!"

That night she dreamed that she was being pursued underwater by a giant octopus. She was a small silvery fish. She kept darting behind rocks on the dark ocean floor. But soon one of its tentacles would appear round the rock edge seeking to trap her with its suckers. Finally it cornered her in a cave, blocking the entrance with its amorphous bulk. Even though she was a fish she could hardly breathe. She tried to plead with it, but only bubbles emerged from her fish's lips. As it drew her with its tentacles into its gigantic mouth she screamed, which started her awake. Adam drowsily asked her what the matter was. Just a nightmare she said, shaking. It took her an hour to get back to sleep.

Q

It had been a typical Sunday, filled with routine chores, like gardening for Adam and like laundry and doing her nails for Julia. They had a large back yard running downhill to a stream that trickled most of the year, but that turned into a raging torrent after spring rainstorms. That Sunday morning it was unusually warm for the beginning of February. Adam was clearing a pile of debris in the stream that would likely flood their neighbor's yard further down the hill in the next storm. Liz was helping him, as she claimed, by raking the sodden leaves and branches he had retrieved into pretty patterns.

After lunch they decided to give themselves a break by going for a walk with Lucky, now happily free of his cone. Liz opted to stay home and make chalk drawings on the driveway.

On the way back a Rottweiler barked furiously at Lucky from behind a gate. Before they knew what was happening it jumped right over and charged at Lucky, who cowered behind Adam's legs. Adam shouted at the large dog to go away, but it tried grabbing Lucky in its jaws from around Adam's legs. Adam kicked the dog as hard as he could. As the Rottweiler backed off it set up a howl that brought its elderly owner, a red-faced, white-haired man, running out. Grabbing his dog by the collar, the old man yelled at Adam that he was going to report him.

"You know what the SPCA will tell you?" Adam replied. "Alameda County requires all dogs outside an owner's yard to be leashed. Your dog was attacking mine."

"My dog was just protecting his territory," he shouted back while his dog was growling ferociously and straining to get at Lucky who was still cowering and whining with fear.

"This is not his territory. This is a public sidewalk," Adam told him.

"You must be one of those wet liberals who needs to hide behind the law."

"And you must be one of those right-wing nuts that hates any law that restricts your right to be a jerk," Julia called back. "*Vete a la chingada!*" she yelled at him.

"Why don't you go back to where you came from?" he shouted.

"Because I'm there already, bigot," she spat out.

As a parting shot Adam called out, "If your dog gets out and attacks ours again I'll report you to Animal Services."

"Get lost, asshole!" he yelled back.

Julia felt her anger and despair welling up. So many Americans were allowing political differences to erase everyday civility. It seemed to her as if their society was approaching its own Big Bang, implosive rather than explosive.

Once they had turned the corner she remarked, "Goddammit. It's as if our Hater-in-Chief has infected everyone with his poisonous tweets."

"You're right," Adam agreed. "He's spread a virus of hatred just as deadly as the coronavirus."

"Speaking of which," she said, "I'm really worried about Amy. She hasn't been feeling well for a couple of days now. I need to call her when we get back."

As they opened the gate into the front yard of their house Adam let Lucky off the leash so that he could run over to lick Liz who was just finishing her chalk drawings. Among them she had marked out squares for hopscotch.

Julia picked up the shell Liz was using as a marker and threw it onto the first square, then hopped her way to 10 and back to 2, picked up the shell and hopped just short of clearing the first square.

"You lost, Mommy," Liz said with a giggle. "My turn." After throwing the shell onto the second square she completed the circuit flawlessly. Of course she'd been practicing while they were out walking.

"Did you know," Adam said, "that two thousand years ago Roman soldiers played hopscotch to improve their speed and strength? Some also carried heavy weights while they hopped."

"Who needs Google with you around?" Julia joshed.

"Daddy. Won't you play with us?"

"Sorry, sweetheart. My knee's playing up after this morning's work in the garden."

"Then I'm the winner," Liz announced, pleased at her victory.

"We'll have to find you a prize when we go in," Julia said.

Adam turned his attention to a chalk drawing Liz had made a little way off. It consisted of a woman sleeping on a couch, a young girl kneeling by her side watching her, and a man driving a car.

"What's this, Liz?" he asked.

Liz looked shyly at him. "Guess, Daddy."

"Are they the three of us?"

"Right, Daddy."

"And why is Mommy asleep and you watching her?"

"Sometimes Mommy doesn't wake up when I talk to her."

"Maybe I was feeling very tired," Julia suggested, hoping they'd drop the subject.

"No matter how loud I call her she doesn't answer," Liz insisted.

"I'm sure she would answer if she really heard you," Adam said.

"That's a fact," Julia said, taking a deep breath.

"What's my prize going to be?" Liz asked Julia.

Relieved at the diversion, she replied, "The prize is a surprise. So I can't tell you."

"Let's go in then," Liz said making for the house with Lucky barking happily at her heels.

Julia gave Amy a call. The two had been roommates at college. They'd grown so close that even their periods had synchronized.

"How're you feeling?" Julia asked.

"Terrible," she rasped. "I've got a sore throat."

"Have you taken your temperature?"

"Yes. It's 99.0."

"That doesn't sound like the dreaded virus."

"I guess not. Talking about the virus, have you heard the charge going around on Twitter and Facebook that the new 5G networks are responsible for its spread?"

"No," Julia said. "How can they do that?"

"They say that radio waves, emitted by 5G technology, are causing changes in our bodies that make them succumb to the virus."

"Really?"

"Yes. And we have two 5G cell towers close to the Bay Bridge toll."

"That's spooky."

"It's frightening, if you ask me."

"Listen, Amy, I have to go. I hope you get over that nasty throat of yours soon."

"Thanks, Julia. Stay safe."

After she'd ended the call Adam, who had been listening to her end of the conversation, said, "I'm coming across that rumor about 5G circulating on YouTube and Facebook. You do know it has no scientific validity."

"How can you be so certain?" Julia asked provocatively.

"For a start WHO's said that no one's ever been made sick by radio frequency fields."

"And does everyone accept that opinion?"

"There are a few academics who have become critics of it. But no expert has found any connection between 5G technology and the coronavirus."

"Whatever you say, wise one. I've got to put these cupcakes in the oven."

And there it ended for the moment. But later that afternoon Julia searched Google and found that the issue was less clear than Adam made out. One article reported that 180 scientists and doctors from 36 countries had warned the EU that 5G technology would lead to massively increased exposure to electromagnetic radiation. At the same time another scientific paper pointed out that because 5G requires more towers each one runs at a lower power level than 4G resulting in lower exposure to radiation. Adam could be right. But Adam's attempt to reassure her only added to Julia's mounting stress.

Q

That Monday Adam had to be on campus for an afternoon meeting of the Graduate Admissions Committee, one of the admin duties he signed up for, under duress. So, he dedicated the morning in his office to grading student papers, a task he disliked only less than attending committee meetings. Not a day he looked forward to, especially with heavy rain.

Part way through the morning there was a knock on his office door. It was one of the undergraduates from his Internet and Network Security class. Students from this class rarely came to see him. He guessed computer students naturally tend to do everything possible through technology rather than personal contact. This student looked young for a freshman. He had blond hair and his face and arms were tanned light gold. He was wearing blue jeans and a Bernie t-shirt emblazoned with, "NOT ME. US."

"Good morning," Adam greeted him. "Please sit down."

The student sat down gingerly on the edge of the chair opposite.

"I'm sorry, but I don't remember your name," Adam said apologetically.

"Roman Prior," he replied.

Adam looked up his grade on his computer. He was a B- student.

"And what can I do for you?"

He handed Adam a mid-term paper on election cybersecurity. Adam skimmed through it. As is often the case with freshmen he was getting sidetracked from his topic with a number of associated issues, such as the threat of ransomware and the likelihood of legislative intervention (zero currently). Towards the end Adam noticed a diatribe against congressional Republicans' obstruction to several House attempts to safeguard electronic voting.

"What's the thesis of your paper?" Adam asked.

"The need for voter-verified paper backups."

"Exactly. So you need to throw away pages 3-5 and 8-11, which have nothing to do with your thesis."

"But pages 3-5 recall the Bern Report, the Stanford study of the 2016 Democratic primaries showing that, in states with a voter paper trail, Bernie won 51% while in those without a paper trail he only won 35%."

"You are aware, I take it, that this so-called report was not a peer-reviewed article in a scholarly journal, but a paper published by two undergraduates on social media, and that it failed to account for other variables?"

The student sat up straight and fired back, "I bet you're a Biden supporter."

"Who I support is irrelevant to your paper."

"Who you support has to influence your response to pro-Bernie arguments."

"First, you're assuming that I am a Democrat. Next, that I oppose Bernie. But what matters here is that you're relying on evidence that lacks scholarly credibility."

"So what you're saying is that I need to rehash the mainstream centrist views about the need for paper ballot backups if I'm to get a good grade?"

"I don't recall saying anything of the sort. But I suggest you stick to your main thesis and avoid introducing ideas that smack of conspiracy theories."

"Great," the student muttered rising and bolted out of the room without a goodbye.

Badly handled, Adam told himself. He should have taken the Bern Report apart piece by piece, instead of getting diverted by the political issues. Damn. He felt as if he were waging a one-man fight against an army of rumors. Hamlet surrounded by lying courtiers.

After grading another eight papers—he counted how many as an incentive to get through them—another knock on his door was immediately followed by the appearance of Anna.

"Got a moment?" she asked.

"Sure. Anything for a break from reading poorly argued papers."

"I wondered whether I might interest you in co-writing a paper possibly for *Scientific American* on hacking computer voting systems, focusing on states' election-management systems."

"That certainly interests me. As you know, it's an area I've been looking into for a chapter in my next book. Infiltrate the systems with malicious code and you can spread it to all the individual voting machines."

"I thought that particular aspect might interest you."

"Funny the Russians didn't exploit that vulnerability in 2016."

"Afraid perhaps of retaliation? At any rate how about my sending you an outline of my ideas and you responding with yours?"

"Sounds good."

She paused to sneeze in the crook of her elbow. "By the way," she added, "after you asked me the other day about QAnon I looked up their recent posts. Do you know what their current obsessions are?"

"No. I've been preoccupied with other stuff."

"Have you read any Q or QAnon posts on 8kun?"

"No. I never took the time to sign up for 8kun."

"I was just looking at some on my cell before coming here."

Anna moved round to his side of the desk to share her phone with him. "Oh, before we go to their posts, this is an email a Montana judge sent a *Washington Post* reporter who had poked fun at Q."

Whether Q is real or otherwise, there is a movement started by the hypothesis of a Q and somebody behind the scenes standing up for the average American citizen. Patriots are uniting against people just like you. Your world of fake news and liberal agendas that give away our country to foreigners and protect the Clintons and Obamas is coming to an end. Wait for it ... you pathetic, snobbish asshole.

"That serves by way of introduction," she said. "Next are a couple of recent posts on 8kun by Q in person.":

What is the primary benefit to keep public in mass-hysteria re COVID-19? Think voting. Are you awake yet? TRUST THE PLAN. Q

"And .."

What happens when people learn the TRUTH? What happens when people WAKE UP? They will not be able to walk down the street. Nothing can stop what is happening. THE GREAT AWAKENING. Q

"Q knows how to keep his followers hooked," Anna said. "He always remains elusive by using open-ended questions and inviting his readers to fill the blanks." She scrolled up to read another post.

Follow the White Rabbit into The Great Awakening where our QAnon QArmy must Question The Narrative to bring Dark To Light. QAnon #WWG1WGA

"That stands for 'Where We Go One We Go All,' a signature rallying call for QAnon," she explained. "Here's a good one..."

WAKE UP PEOPLE!!! Satanists have always Ruled our World. Thank #GOD for @realPresident & #Q team. Fighting the Good Fight for humanity. QAnon

"Even God gets his own hashtag," she remarked laughing.

She glanced at the time.

"Got to get to class," she said and promptly left.

"Bye," Adam called after her.

He and Anna seemed to be entering into a closer relationship than before. Or was he mistaken? Probably.

In this self-contained cyber-world facts were irrelevant. Or maybe, everything that happened in the real world was converted by QAnon followers into evidence that the deep state was the enemy of right-thinking—and Right-thinking—Americans. In their minds behind the scenes a real battle was taking place and the outcome was in no doubt. That absolute certainty made them feel better about themselves. While their jobs grew more precarious and their rents grew exponentially, online they belonged to a conquering army whose victory lay tantalizingly close.

After the committee meeting he called Julia at work to discuss what they would eat that evening. Before they had reached a decision a beep indicated she had a call waiting. After a short wait she came back on the line sounding disturbed.

"Got to hang up," she said. "Business call."

"Okay. Bye, honey."

Adam didn't know why, but she didn't sound like her usual self.

Q

It was Iowa's primary. The first in the election cycle. The president was running unopposed, while the Democrats were divided amongst a half-dozen candidates, ranging from former Vice-President Joe Biden in the center, to Bernie Sanders on the left, a self-described Democratic Socialist. The president tweeted that he hoped Sanders would win. Of course he would say that. Much easier to beat.

That evening Adam and Julia had tickets to see *Hamlet* at the Berkeley Rep. It had been raining solidly all day. They left Liz in the care of Julene, a young Black teaching assistant they had gotten to know at Liz's school. On their way to the theater in the car they heard on the radio that the Secretary of Health and Human Services had declared a public health emergency.

"About time," Julia exclaimed. "Did they really think the president's ban on travelers from China was going to isolate us from the virus?"

"Only last Thursday he was saying at a Michigan rally that we had it under control."

"All he can think about," Julia said, "is whether it'll affect the stock market and his re-election in November."

"He sure is no calculating King Claudius. It's as if Polonius was king." Their arrival at the parking lot ended their conversation.

The play was well produced. Although the actor playing Claudius outshone the star playing Hamlet, Adam found himself strongly identifying with Hamlet. Was it his insistence on proof before turning to revenge? Or, more likely, did Adam share his sense of impotence as he ricocheted between right and wrong? As Hamlet put it, "There is nothing either good or bad, but thinking makes it so." Yes, that was it. Too much thinking always left Adam paralyzed. Like him, Hamlet put his trust in what he called "god-like reason" in a world where "reason panders to will." That last phrase summed up for Adam the current state of America, a country where millions rejected science to deny global climate change, just as the president denied the possible arrival of a major pandemic. And offered arguments to reinforce these prejudices.

On the drive home Julia said, "Poor Ophelia! How those men controlled her. Even Hamlet dumped her without telling her why."

"That's not true," Adam said. "He only turned on her after realizing that she had agreed to be planted on him by the King."

"So Hamlet takes out his anger on her instead of the King. What was she to do? Endanger her father's position by refusing to do what the King demanded?"

"Okay, she was as conflicted as Hamlet. They were both victims."

"And that justifies Hamlet's abusive treatment of both Ophelia and his mother?"

"He was torn by competing loyalties."

"He was a pathetic prevaricator, that's what he was. And his failure to make up his mind caused the death of both the women in his life."

"You'd rather he'd been like Laertes?"

"At least Laertes was decisive. Unlike Hamlet, when he felt injured he went straight for revenge. Hamlet's endless delays caused the deaths of so many innocent characters. Laertes only killed one person. And good riddance."

When they got home Liz was asleep. Driving Julene home in the rain, Adam asked her how the teaching was going.

"I love teaching elementary kids. They're still so direct," she replied.

"That's great."

"Unfortunately school is more an exception than the rule."

"What do you mean?" he asked.

"In school they have created an atmosphere of fairness. But, where I live, in Oakland, there's no fairness."

"How's it unfair to you?"

"We're all scared of the cops."

"Even Black cops?"

"You bet. They suck up to the white cops."

"That must mess with their heads, if you ask me."

"Knowing that doesn't make our life any easier. My brothers are terrified that if they're stopped by a cop they'll end up getting shot. Martin, my oldest brother, will turn around and return home if he spots a cop coming towards him. As for me, I'm scared I'll meet one of those cops that target women when I'm alone."

Adam didn't know what to say.

"It not fair. What's so special about my skin they treat me different?"

"Honestly, I don't get it either," he said.

"Thank you. But you're like part of the teaching community. That's different. The world outside your campus is filled with menace and danger for me. I have to watch out what I do and where we go every time I leave home. You've simply no idea what it's like. You can't have. It's now starting to make me angry as hell. And the anger's driving me crazy. It's not what I want to be feeling. But it's everywhere. It's like my fate. Who wants that?"

They had reached her house. As she thanked him for the lift, Adam saw that her eyes had filled with tears.

On the drive home he felt angry, apologetic and confused. He recollected Hamlet's reflection that, like Gertrude, we—what is it? — "skin and film the ulcerous place, Whiles rank corruption, mining all within, Infects unseen." That's why the play haunted him—because Danish society was similar to his, one that was infected deep within while maintaining a surface appearance of health and sanity. Like the poison in Hamlet, Adam thought, the invisible coronavirus might be considered an analogy for a similar sickness running unchecked within the body of America.

Q

The day after Julia had had a drink with Dave he began to bombard her with daily emails sent to her work account. He must see her again.

He knew she needed him because he wanted her. She was acting superior. It wasn't fair to him. It was all the fault of the feminists. Feminists wanted men to behave as if they had no sex drive. Sex was what made men men. Women needed to stop turning them into lapdogs. That's what Julia had done to Adam. Unlike Adam, Dave was a real man. That was why women were afraid of him.

One email in particular exposed his delusion that we are all still living in the Stone Age. "In the natural order of things women should be afraid. But the modern digital world has fucked up relations between the two sexes. Back in primitive times men like me could just grab what we wanted. Now everything is reversed and women have the upper hand. But secretly you still want your men to be like me. You want to be seized and made an instrument of my pleasure. That's your destiny. That's what gives you the most pleasure."

This deluge of bizarre beliefs showed no sign of stopping. Julia reluctantly agreed to meet him in the hopes of once and for all ending his siege by getting him out of her life. Who was she deluding? At least a part of her wanted it. At any rate she agreed to meet him in the bar of the Hotel Vulcan at six and told Adam she would be working late.

When she arrived Dave was sitting in a circular booth in a remote corner of the bar dressed in the same outfit as the week before. He had almost finished his beer. He gestured for her to join him and signaled with two fingers for the waitress to bring another round of beers.

"So," he said, "you came."

"I said I would."

"You never know with a Stacy whether they'll stand you up."

"I wish you'd stop calling me a Stacy."

"You know what a Stacy is?"

"Yes. I googled it. Maybe you've forgotten that I come from a working-class home. Hardly your typical Stacy."

"But you're sexually irresistible and you dumped me for a Chad. That's what Stacys are like."

Their beers arrived with condensation misting the sides of the glasses. Conflicted, she delayed her response while she took a big gulp.

"If that's your definition of a Stacy I plead guilty. Because the reason I agreed to see you was to ask you to stop emailing me. Can't you just leave me alone and move on?"

"I wish I could. But you've gotten into my system. You know how much I want you. I think about you all day—and night when I'm on duty at reception."

"There's really nothing I can do about that."

"Oh, yes, there is."

"And that is?" Despite herself, Julia found herself flirting with him.

"You know the answer to that."

"Look, we were a couple all those years ago, and it came to a natural end."

"No it didn't. I already told you that you ruined my life when you ditched me."

"Come on. Let's not exaggerate."

"You don't believe me? I couldn't work for months after. I was depressed and they put me on meds. Which reminds me."

He reached into his pants pocket and brought out a small bottle. Opening it he popped a tablet into his mouth and swilled it down with a gulp of beer.

"Like one?" he asked her.

"No."

"It's Oxy. Sure you wouldn't like one?"

She hesitated. Since agreeing to meet him she'd been wound up. Was she making a huge mistake? She needed something to calm her down. She'd been taking OxyContin for a while. It might not eliminate her anxiety, but it relaxed her and filled her with feelings of pleasure.

"Why not?" She took one from him.

"I'm sorry if our breakup had that effect on you. But it was clear we weren't meant to spend our lives together."

"I couldn't have sex for over a year. And when I did, no woman could make me as excited as you could."

"Thanks for the compliment," she said, laughing at him to lighten the mood.

"Drink up." He signaled for more drinks. "So that's why you owe me."

"You think life should work like a double entry ledger account."

"Don't get clever with me. I'm talking real basic stuff. Desire. Satisfaction."

"And what would change if I gave you what you're asking for?"

"Everything. My need would go. My obsession with you. I'd respect myself again. Get on with my life."

Two more beers arrived.

She really wanted to believe him. She had no wish to ruin anyone's life.

She took a long sip of beer and looked him in the eyes, eyes that signaled overpowering desire. He was sending out waves of it. And it was infectious. Like a virus. She felt a strong urge to plunge into those waves and be carried wherever they took her. Would surrender to him free her from him and him from her? Or would he renege on his promise and expect her to relieve him again and again?

"How do I know that you would stick to your side of the deal?"

He could feel that he was going to get his way. "I've already told you. One time would make us even. God's truth."

"Since when have you started believing in Him?"

"Now you're stringing me along. You know what? I'll give you a bag of Oxys for free if you agree."

"Trying to bribe me now?"

"Say you'll come with me."

"Come where?"

"There's a whole empty section in the hotel. I have a pass key. We can take our choice."

Julia looked around her as if seeking to escape. She realized it was herself she couldn't escape from. "Just this once only. You understand?"

"I've already told you. Let's go now. I can't wait any longer."

His desperate need was catching. She disliked and wanted him in equal amounts.

"Very well," she said getting up. "Lead on."

They left their half-finished beers on the table with some cash and took the elevator to the tenth floor. At the end of the corridor Dave unlocked a corner room and closed it behind them.

With his back to the door he pulled her against him and she could feel the hardness of his erection pressed into her stomach.

"I can't wait any longer, bitch. Start by giving me a hand job."

Adam would never speak to her like that. She hated to admit to herself that it turned her on. She didn't want to feel shame at this moment; she knew that would come later.

He forced her hand down so that she could feel his throbbing through his pants.

Undoing his fly and seizing hold of his erection made blood start coursing powerfully through her body.

"What are you waiting for?" he croaked into her ear.

His eyes were shut tight and the expression on his face was closer to pain than pleasure. She started pumping him real slow. He groaned and said, "Stop playing around with me." She ignored him. So he grasped her hand in his and began to speed up her movements.

"That's good," he groaned taking his hand off hers.

"Don't stop now," he said as she came to a stop to show him that he needed her.

She grinned up at him. He responded by slapping her face.

"I'll get really rough if you try messing with me. Move your hand. Now."

To her surprise the slap made her feel more excited. Was she that perverse? She had no time to consider. Renewing her hand movement she could feel the blood pulsing faster through the veins of his rock-hard penis. She knew he was about to explode. Shouting a prolonged "YE-E-ES!" he ejaculated all over the floor as she moved swiftly to the side.

She found herself shaking with unfulfilled desire.

"Get undressed," he demanded peremptorily.

"Yes, sir," she found herself saying.

They both stripped in record time.

"Now lie face down on the bed," he commanded.

She did as he said.

"Not like that, you silly bitch."

She felt a powerful smack on her butt.

"Ouch! *Hijo de tu chingada madre!* What do you think you're doing?" she protested.

"Shut your mouth. Should I use a condom?"

"I'm on the pill."

He grabbed both her legs and tugged her backwards until he could fold them at the edge of the bed, leaving her upper torso face down on the bed cover. Before she knew it he had pulled her legs as wide apart as they could go and forcefully thrust himself inside her producing an equal mixture of sharp pain and intense excitement.

"Now I'm going to fuck you like the whore you are."

He grasped her hips tightly with his hands and used his body like a battering ram so that each push into her felt like it was going to split her open. Once more she realized that for her pain mixed with pleasure was far more exciting than pleasure alone. How strange. She lay there waiting for each violent thrust to take her closer to the climax she now had to reach. Faster and harder he pushed as she abandoned all control and let out scream after scream that seemed to turn him on more.

Suddenly he came inside her. She knew he didn't care whether she was satisfied or not. But he couldn't just stop and before he could slow to a stop with a wild shout she came too.

They lay there for a minute or more before he withdrew from her.

"See? I knew you needed me. Don't tell me that was like married sex. That's real sex. With the man in control. Sex as it was originally intended, before feminists messed it all up with their 'no means no.' A real man knows when 'no' means 'yes.'"

Already she was flooded with a sense of shame.

"Seeing what a success that was, we should arrange for a repeat sometime soon," he said, grinning. He was now sitting naked on the bed.

"Wait a moment. That wasn't what we agreed, you lying bastard," she said, getting really angry now as she started dressing.

"I only agreed to get you up here. I knew once I'd banged you hard enough you would come to see that that was what you really wanted. A man who wants you bad enough to make you do whatever he wants. That's what turned you on."

"Listen carefully, *imbécil*. I only agreed to come here with you because you promised to leave me alone after this one time."

"Don't try to tell me what I can do. Face it. You loved every minute of it. So of course we're going to do this again."

"No. We're not, you jerk. Ever."

She was fully dressed by that time. She made for the door. Still only in his underpants Dave started up and grabbed her by the arm. Reaching into his discarded pants he pulled out a bag of Oxys and thrust it into her hand.

"You'll come when I need you, or I'll ruin your life as you did mine."

"Let me go, damn you. This is the end. Got it, you dumb shit?"

"Wait and see."

He let her go and she stormed out of the room as fast as she could, bumping into a porter in the lobby as she rushed out.

As she walked to the BART station at Montgomery grasping the small bag he'd thrust at her she cursed herself for being so gullible. *Mierda!* She didn't even like Dave. She knew getting tangled up with him would be a disaster. She hated herself. She despised herself. What a fool she was.

They'd split up all those years ago when she finally made herself face how impossible he was. Why had it taken almost two years to realize that? There was no avoiding it—because sex with him was more exciting than anything she had experienced before or after him.

After him! Sex with Adam belonged to another universe. Adam was always considerate about her needs. He would never omit fore-play as Dave had. He was always concerned that she had come as well as he. He would never force himself on her. If she didn't want it, he would never try to persuade her to change her mind, let alone insist. He was what should be the perfect lover for any woman who really respected herself. They had had some marvelous moments in bed to-gether. But he had never taken her to the level of wild excitement that Dave had just done.

Realizing that made her feel even more wretched. Adam was her true love. Dave was a crazy temptation that she should have resisted. It was his sheer need that had broken through her defenses. Come on. What a poor excuse. Admit it. She had given in to her own desire, a desire to be sexually overwhelmed by a man who was driven by his own urgent physical need.

She was filled with dark and confusing thoughts. Was she really a masochist? Was she most aroused when pain accompanied pleasure? Out of the past arose a phantom she had buried deep down. Her dad. Those late-night visits to her bed when she was a teenager. His grop-ing hands. His making her grip and pump his erection. His attempts to get his fingers between her thighs. He never succeeded in that. Her fights to push his hand out from under her bedclothes often left Julia hurt. But when he would leave, she would find herself aroused by that residual pain. Sometimes she would even use her hands to bring her-self to a climax. That's pretty sick. That's truly messed up. Thanks a lot, Dad. She could hear him saying, "Just playing, *chica*. Relax, can't you." And her hissing, "Stop it, *papá*. Get out of here." She needn't have hissed, because Mom knew very well what he was up to and chose to pretend it wasn't happening. Or that she couldn't hear. Some parents they were. But you didn't get to choose your parents. You just had to learn to cope with the ones you had.

When she got home Adam was already in bed. After letting Lucky out in the back yard she had a quick shower and slid quietly into bed. In a short while she felt Adam fit his body into the shape of her back. Slowly, his hand moved up from her hip to her breast. She gently moved his hand back down and drifted off to a disturbed sleep.

Q

On Tuesdays and Thursdays when the University was in session Adam and Julia were in a rush as they had to get Liz to school and themselves to work. This Thursday morning Julia seemed unusually distracted and left almost all the preparations to Adam. She was more concerned with taking her temperature than helping with the morning exodus. As Julia's commute to San Francisco took longer than his to Berkeley, he usually drove Liz to her school on his way to campus. At breakfast, he read in the newspaper that the president was furious with the media and the health community for blaming him for the country's slow response to the outbreak of the virus. What really bothered the president was that as a result the polls showed that he would lose to any of the Democratic front runners. Still, he was an expert at the blame game. When in trouble, always point the finger at someone or something else. It had worked for him up to then. Adam had no time to wonder at the gullibility—or was it fidelity? —of his core supporters as he rushed to clear the breakfast table, remembered to feed Lucky, wheeled the trash bins out onto the street, and shepherded Liz into the car.

On the short trip to Chabot Elementary Liz said to him, "Daddy, why does Mommy need to take pills all the time?"

"What do you mean 'all the time'?"

"She took one this morning." He hadn't noticed. "She nearly always takes one when she gets home from work. And last weekend, I saw her take another one after lunch."

She also, he reflected, takes one when going to bed.

"Your mother tends to get worked up about things more easily than I do. So she takes anti-anxiety pills to calm herself down."

Although he felt he had reassured Liz, he made a mental note to take more notice of Julia's use of meds.

Because Liz's school started early Adam was usually in his office well before nine. That morning the department chair phoned him to thank him for the check the university had received from Homeland Security. Adam told him that he hoped it would help them put more resources into their research on cyber security for the November election. Of course the chair said he would. But no doubt he would channel most of the money to artificial intelligence, as that was his research specialty.

Isn't that the kind of power that induced individuals like him to undertake such a thankless job? Fortunately for his sanity Adam was not into power. Unfortunately that left Adam powerless when competing for limited funding. And Adam had to live with that, just as he'd had to live with the stream of lies that had poured out of the White House for the past three years. Live with a society that preferred a fictional world to the real one. Live in a world infected by a virus of massive misinformation. Repeated often enough, lies assumed their own material presence.

And contemporary absurdities like QAnon infuriated him. He may not have much power, but he was deeply invested in fighting for the truth. He agreed with Hamlet—we were not given reason to let it "fust in us unused." *Fust* was a great word. What words did we use instead? Stagnate. Fossilize. They had none of the charge of *fust*—that was something Adam felt compelled to fight.

If truth really mattered to him, Adam thought, shouldn't he get off his butt and investigate first-hand the cesspool of lies, including those of QAnon? Where to start? He'd heard that the president was due to hold one of his rallies in San Jose that coming Saturday. Attending one of the president's rallies ought to help Adam better understand why the president's followers swallowed all his blatant lies. Not something he relished spending most of a day doing. But too bad. It was time he stopped railing against the president's base and learned first-hand what was going on. Then, he could publish something.

During his office hour Anna joined Adam in his office to discuss their proposed research paper. Something between them had changed. Why was he now responding to her as not just a colleague but an attractive woman? A door had opened at their last meeting. This could be just a current mood or phase. Or was his marriage in trouble? If so, why? Maybe there was something he had done to alienate Julia.

Yet, apart from the physical aspect, he and Julia seemed to be just as close as they had ever been. The only difference was that she seemed more anxious and short-tempered lately. And she was uncharacteristically repeating falsehoods about the virus without first looking up the facts. The outbreak really seemed to have shaken her. And yet there were only 11 confirmed cases of infection in the country.

What Adam couldn't deny was that sitting side-by-side with Anna looking at his computer he felt an electric current running between them that he had never felt before.

That evening the ten o'clock news was full of the fiasco the Democratic caucuses in Iowa had turned into. No certified results, although informal exit polls predicted a win for either Bernie Sanders or Pete Buttigieg, with Biden trailing fourth. Julia, who felt the Bern powerfully, was much cheered by this result. Of course the president added fuel to the fire by tweeting that the Democrats who wanted to run the country couldn't even run a simple caucus. He also pointed out that he had won the Republican vote in Iowa by 97 percent. Here we go, Adam thought. The first of a series of election primaries. The start of months of campaigning. What a time-wasting ritual.

The same broadcast showed the president making claims about the virus that went against all common sense: "Once the weather starts to warm up the virus will weaken and disappear."

"Very likely," he remarked sarcastically.

"I wish I could believe him," Julia said, and she sounded as if she really did want it to go away. "Yesterday I talked to Amy who claimed that the virus was caused by big pharma wanting to increase its profits."

"That's not even remotely plausible," he replied. "How would the CEOs of big pharma expect to avoid being infected? Or are they so greedy that they are willing to risk dying from it to inflate their share price?"

"All right. All right. Take it easy, can't you?"

He was so tired of hearing so many unfounded conspiracy theories that it was hard to contain his anger. Which wasn't fair.

"Sorry," he said. "I'm feeling over-tired tonight. Forgive me, please, and forget what I said."

Of course, you can't forget something once it's said. But this was the best he could do. Julia was evidently feeling overwhelmed with a sense of helplessness at the relentless spread of the infection. There was nothing like a good conspiracy theory to alleviate the sense of confusion that the virus produced. He told himself that he should have shown more sympathy for the fears that were running wild in her, while at the same time offering her better information. He went to sleep promising himself to be more supportive of her tomorrow.

Q

The first thing Julia noticed when she got home from work was the large Band-Aid on Liz's forehead.

"What happened to you, sweetheart?" she asked her.

"I fell off my bike in the driveway."

"Daddy was teaching you to ride your bike?"

"Yes. It wasn't his fault. He told me to watch out for Lucky, who was chasing round me like crazy. But he got in front of me. To avoid hitting him, I swerved into the hedge and a branch scraped my forehead."

Julia turned to Adam. "I thought we agreed that we'd wait until the summer break before we gave Liz riding lessons."

"Yes, we did. But, as usual, Liz twisted me round her little finger, asking me why we bought her a bike if she wasn't allowed to learn how to ride it."

"You could have waited for me to get back before reversing a decision we made together."

"I'm sorry, You're right. I'm just putty in her hands."

"That's an easy excuse."

"I know. I know. I should have waited."

Liz intervened. "Please, Mommy, don't take it out on Daddy. I pestered him like crazy until he gave in. Blame me."

"You've already had your just reward," Julia told her. "I hope that's not a nasty gash hiding behind that Band-Aid."

"Daddy says I won't even need to cover it up by tomorrow."

"Okay." She turned to Adam. "Time for a real drink. It's the end of the workweek."

"Margarita?"

Adam knew that she preferred liquor, especially when she didn't have to go to work the next morning. He made her favorite margarita on the rocks with Herradura Silver tequila, Mr Stacks triple sec, orange liqueur and lime juice, poured watermelon and strawberry lemonade into a glass for Liz, and opened a can of Corona Extra for himself.

Julia judged this might be the right time to tell Adam about the nonstop emails she'd been getting from Dave since she'd stupidly agreed to meet him two days ago. Of course, she had to censor the sexual part. She'd deleted quite a few emails that alluded to their disastrous meeting. One she'd received that morning read something like: "You'd better reply to me or you'll regret it. Your silence makes me wish I'd punched you in the face right after I came. That way you'd never forget me." Another read: "Modern women like you are degenerates. You're attention whores in your tight dresses. You only want to fuck Chads because they have money. Last Wednesday you learned what was missing from your life."

Even after her deletions there were more than a dozen emails from him sent over the last two days. Most of them said something to the effect that she had ruined his life when she dumped him, that he'd entered a depression that he had never fully recovered from, that his life since then had been abysmal, that he'd never been able to have a stable relationship with another woman, that he hated her for doing all this to him.

Julia showed Adam a sample of these emails.

"How did he get hold of your work email address?" Adam asked.

"That would be easy. Like UC Berkeley, the ACLU lists all its personnel and their email addresses on its website."

"Yes, it's a problem. We're all so accessible now."

"So what do you think?"

"Dave may be mentally twisted, but he's very careful not to leave himself open to charges of harassment. I suppose you could tag it as abusive email, but it's hard to act on such vague threats as 'You'll be sorry.'"

"Then what can I do?"

"You could start by blocking him access to your work email account."

"Why didn't I think of that sooner?"

"I'm sorry this has happened at a time when you're already feeling stressed."

"What do you mean?" she asked defensively.

"Just that recently you seem anxious a lot of the time."

"Come on. You're exaggerating."

"Even Liz has commented on how regularly you're taking pills," he said, noting that Liz was absorbed in her cellphone in the adjacent den.

"The last thing I want is for Liz to start worrying about me."

"We both worry about you, honey. Would it help to consult somebody?"

"You mean a shrink?"

"Or a counselor."

"Give me a break. How about refilling my margarita? And please add more lime this time."

While Adam was at the counter refreshing the drinks, she called out to him, "I forgot to tell you that I also looked up Dave's posts on Twitter. Apart from the prevalence of #realPresident, the hashtag that came up most frequently was #QAnon."

"Really?" Adam was all attention.

"Yes. You know what that is, right? Did you know that they think JFK Jr. is still alive and helping our president to out the secret state?"

"Right. Some of them believe Kennedy is Q, the anonymous poster of what they call 'breadcrumbs,' or snippets of secret information."

After returning with the drinks, Adam gave Julia a detailed account of what he knew about QAnon, how the two government agents wouldn't investigate anything associated with it, and how that aroused his suspicions. He finished by saying that, because many Q supporters regularly showed up at the president's rallies, he was planning to attend a rally in San Jose the next day. When she asked him why, he said he needed to see what was persuading so many people to subscribe to QAnon's ideas.

"You mean you're willing to spend over an hour driving each way to have to sit through one of those lying, hate-filled speeches?" Julia asked.

"I believe that the truth will always win out against the kind of misinformation that QAnon trades in. But, as I don't really understand why it—or this president—attracts vast crowds, I need to experience it. How this poison spreads."

"Well, whatever you do, don't let your true loyalties show while you're surrounded by those fanatics."

"Don't worry. I won't be wearing a REAL MEN DON'T GRAB t-shirt. I'll look the model of neutrality."

"I won't feel okay till you get home, *cariño*."

"I should be back between four and five."

"Just be careful."

They left it at that. But that night, Julia had a dream in which Adam was dressed in a few torn rags and being chased by an angry mob of Bacchantes led by Dave. So much for a smattering of classical education. Maybe it was the margaritas' fault. Lying awake after this nightmare, she laughed at her dream for substituting Dave in place of a god. But then she remembered that, after all, Dionysus was the god not just of wine but ritual madness, and that Dionysian rage was at war with the rational world. Dave fit that set of attributes well enough. Then had she substituted Adam for herself? Was she the prey for not believing in the crazed cult Dave embraced? She remembered the fate of the king who denied the cult of Dionysus—torn to pieces by the Bacchantes. That kept her awake for over an hour.

Q

Adam set off for San Jose at nine that Saturday morning to leave plenty of time for the president's 2 pm rally. He had already obtained a ticket for the rally online. It was a perfect day, cool and sunny.

As he had anticipated there was a long line of cars stretching for at least five blocks waiting to enter the car park. Crawling slowly forward, he passed groups holding signs HONK FOR THE PRESIDENT, and pop-up roadside stalls selling every kind of paraphernalia including drink and snack cartons with the MAGA logo on them, all sorts of jewelry showcasing the letter Q, and even Great Awakening coffee. There were also some protestors who stood at the entrance manipulating a giant balloon float depicting the resident as a screaming orange baby. After parking Adam joined another long line on foot, waiting to pass through a fairly serious security checkpoint. Banners couldn't be larger than a specified size. No selfie sticks. T-shirts with acceptable slogans were allowed. He had chosen a plain blue baseball hat and white t-shirt with no graphics or text.

While in line, he spoke to a white couple in their sixties standing behind him. They said they were recently retired and had driven from Las Vegas to be there. They called themselves Front Row Joes and had attended over a dozen of the president's rallies. The man —Call me Ron —turned out to be a vet on disability. He had been an Army engineer who had taken part in Operation Desert Storm in 1990, and had served in Afghanistan and Iraq. He suffered from bronchitis and had difficulty breathing, symptoms of what he called burn pit exposure. He told Adam that he and his wife of forty years loaded up the SUV with a deep cycle battery that powered their camping stove and electronics, and drove it to any of the president's rallies that were within a few hundred miles. It had been a way of life for them for more than two years. The rallies never failed to give them a lift, no matter how repetitive the president's speeches were.

When they were admitted Adam was immediately reminded of one of those tent revival meetings he had seen in old black-and-white movies. At the same time it felt like a rock concert. The speakers blasted music by Frank Sinatra, Elton John, The Rolling Stones, and other pop favorites. Some supporters were dancing. The energy emanating from the crowd was powerful and infectious.

Adam took a seat and looked round for Q signs even though they were banned by security. Fortuitously a man in his thirties right in front of him stripped off his MAGA t-shirt to reveal another beneath it emblazoned with "WE ARE Q" and, on the back, "The Great Awakening."

"Hi," Adam said, as friendly as he could. "So, you're a follower of Q, I see."

"Q's the real ticket," he replied seriously as he turned around in his seat. "He's got top clearance and lets us know what's actually going on in the White House."

"I always find him hard to decipher," Adam said.

"He has to be careful what he reveals because he knows the deep state also reads his postings."

"And the president?"

"He's in the know. Is this your first rally?"

"Yes, it is."

"You'll see. He never fails us. He'll emphasize a point he's making by joining the tips of his thumb and third finger to make a Q sign." He showed Adam how it was done.

"Is that so?" Adam asked, friendly.

The man's companion twisted round in her seat and said excitedly, "Yes. And there was the time that Straka, I think it was, warmed up the crowd in Cincinnati and ended with our motto— Where We Go One, We Go All. If that's not proof the president is one of us, I don't know what is."

She was wearing a MAGA cap backwards on which a gold Q glimmered above her face.

"And," she went on, "there was also that rally when the president picked out a baby and said it was beautiful. It had a Q on the back of its onesie."

"The president's just waiting for the right moment," the guy added. "It won't be long now, Q thinks. Then, all those disgusting perverts will be arrested and sent to Gitmo. They have sex with children!"

Adam was surprised to find that, outwardly, this couple didn't seem to be mentally unbalanced. He tried to look neutral but interested.

"Bill Gates is one of them," the man continued. "He is one sick billionaire. Did you know he helped spread the coronavirus to boost pharmaceutical companies? And they're making the viruses. He and the Clintons believe in population reduction and they want to implant all of us with microchips to control us."

"That's news to me," Adam said. "Where did you learn that?"

"It's all over Facebook, YouTube and Twitter. Gates knew the virus was coming in 2015. His wife admitted that their basement was stockpiled with food back then."

"Wasn't that because he thought that a pandemic posed a greater threat to everyone than nuclear war?" Adam asked.

"It's all part of his plan to use the outbreak for his personal gain," he responded.

"Is there any evidence to support that?" Adam asked.

"Is there any evidence not to?" he replied.

"They're all in it to serve their own dirty interests," she added. "As the president said yesterday, his enemies are only inflaming people's fear of the virus to hurt his election chances."

"Fat chance of that," the man said. "Look at the enthusiasm here. Nobody here cares what those crazy liberals say. They're crazier than loons. We've got our man in the White House and he's staying there for four more years."

On hearing these words, a nearby contingent began to shout, "FOUR MORE YEARS!" Soon the entire auditorium was reverberating with the chant, which eventually segued into a long loud cheer and much waving of hats and banners.

Adam surveyed the banners. GOD, GUNS AND THE PRESIDENT. FINISH THE WALL. WOMEN FOR THE PRESIDENT. VETERANS, BLACKS, and PATRIOTS – FOR THE PRESIDENT. MAKE LIBERALS CRY AGAIN. And: LIBERALS FOR THE PRESIDENT.

Later a video played on a large screen with cheering soldiers and a somber voice telling them that only the president could be trusted to make the right decisions for Americans. Workers wearing "Voter Registration Strike Force" logos methodically moved along each row clipboards in hand. Merchants selling flags, stickers and hats worked the crowd with equal purposefulness. Everyone was excited and happy to be sharing their excitement with everyone else.

A woman in her thirties next to Adam said quietly to him, "Not everyone believes that QAnon stuff. I don't. I don't even always believe the president. I wish he didn't say some of the things he says. But he's taking the country in the right direction. So, he has my back. He understands what it's like for people like me to live from one paycheck to the next."

"But how can he," Adam replied equally quietly, "when he's so wealthy?"

"He speaks my language," she said adamantly. "He's not like all the other politicians who spew out whatever they think their voters want to hear and then act in their own interests."

"Could I ask you what kind of work you do?"

"I have a franchise on a Burger King restaurant in Fremont. It just about pays my bills. But I never have enough to put any money aside."

"So, what did you think of the large tax cut the president got passed in 2017? Did it help you?"

"I can't say it made a big difference to my income. But look at what an amazing effect it's had on our economy. So I did get to benefit from it indirectly."

At that moment her attention was caught by a small group of GOP officials standing at the bottom of the steps leading up to the stage.

"You see that guy wearing a red t-shirt and cowboy hat over there?" she asked Adam.

"Yes. Why?"

"Because he's the leader of my QAnon group."

"I didn't know that QAnon was an organization. I thought it was just an online thing," Adam said.

"That's what most people assume. We started getting organized last year."

Adam focused on him and realized to his surprise that the man with whom he was having an intense conversation was the vice president. That cast QAnon in a very different light for him. It had become far more than just a digital phenomenon. Evidently, there was a direct physical link between it and the White House. No wonder the president refused to denounce QAnon. It had to be a secret arm of the president's re-election campaign.

Just then the crowd let out a collective shout as the vice president climbed onto the platform. Adam had always wondered what made him tick. He seemed content to live in the outsized shadow of the president. But before that he'd been an unpopular state governor. Was he just another hold-over from the patrician class of Republicans? How far did he go in supporting the president? All Adam knew for sure was that he was religious and thought abortion should be outlawed.

His speech stuck to familiar talking points and Adam could not detect any true feelings. But he knew how to work the crowd. "I'm here for one reason, and one reason only, and that's that we need four more years of this president in the White House."

Up went the chant of FOUR MORE YEARS that seemed to go on for minutes while the vice president smiled and clapped in time. That whole crowd seemed like one sensibility now, with a renewed sense of their power and self-confidence. It was like a bonding ritual from which they all emerged unified and strengthened.

The vice president went on to list what he said the president stood for—jobs, workers, faith, family and the American flag—and after each of these he added, "When the president stands up for jobs —or workers, or faith —I stand with him!" He ended with the inevitable "KEEP AMERICA GREAT," and finally, "GOD BLESS YOU ALL," and exited waving. The energy of the crowd grew as they knew they were about to see the man they loved.

The president entered with the lights low, his silhouette projected onto the giant screen while the song "Macho Man" blared from the speakers. This triggered ecstatic cheering, whistling and waving of placards. This demonstration of mass adoration in turn energized the president. He clapped and did a little jig to the music. After the cheering finally subsided he began by telling the crowd how proud he was to be in the great state of California with thousands of hard-working patriots who believed in God, family and the country. The crowd erupted with shouts of "USA, USA!" He quickly moved on to attacking the Democrats "The lying Dems. They have no idea what they're doing. They can't even count their own votes in Iowa."

He went on to praise his own achievements: the best prosperity anyone's ever had; no one thought it could be done; seven million new jobs; the most powerful military anywhere in the world (hardly his achievement); an all-time historical high for the stock market; a hundred miles of wall on the Mexican border. Up went the shout, "COMPLETE THE WALL!". He warned the crowd that the "new democrat hoax" was this virus that China had sent here, but he reassured everyone that, with the warmer weather, it would just go away. They cheered more.

Adam looked round at the faces as the president became semi-incoherent: "That's a dirty swamp. You have some really evil, dirty, horrible people. Like to say nice, everyone's nice. They're not good. They're not good people." What the hell was the president talking about? He never identified who the horrible people were. Apparently he didn't need to. The crowd knew. They lapped it up. Trashing an unseen enemy made them feel better. Just like dismissing the unseen virus reassured them. It made them feel united. It made them feel like winners.

The president ended with just such an appeal for unity to the already united crowd: "Together we will make America wealthy again. Together we will make America strong again. Together we will make America proud again." He pumped his arms to each section of the crowd and exited to the tune of "You Can't Always Get What You Want." An ironic choice, thought Adam.

As he made his way to his car, Adam imagined what the fact checkers at the *New York Times* and the *Washington Post* would have to say about his latest bullshit. The president had promised a vaccine within months, when it was over a year away. He claimed he had won the popular vote in 2016, if you deducted the millions of illegal voters. The list was seemingly endless. Windmills caused cancer. Redemption money from illegal aliens was paying for the wall. He grossly exaggerated everything—"crowd sizes at his rallies, his ratings in the polls. He had lost touch with reality.

But none of that mattered to those attending the rally. The infection of untruths had already passed through them, leaving them immune to fact checkers, scientists, and those for whom reality still mattered. The crowd was made up of deprived and disappointed working-class Americans who, above all, needed to feel good, and to hell with anything threatening that need. And the president, in turn, fed off the crowd's vibes. Each needed the other to generate that feeling of well-being, of mutual admiration. What were facts compared to that euphoria? Everyone wanted that high.

Adam thought back to the 2016 election. Those earlier crowds had been filled with anger. They had really wanted to lock Hillary up. They were convinced that every immigrant was after their jobs. Now, there was none of that anger. This year the mood was more one of celebration, a conviction that their candidate was bound to win a second term, that they were on the right side. Let the good times roll.

As Adam was driving slowly from the car park, he passed a group of protestors waving banners with NOT MY PRESIDENT, NOPE and LOCK HIM UP. As he passed them he recognized a few of them as students of his. They both stared at him, amazed. He never allowed his own political opinions to show at school, and now he could hardly blame them if they concluded that he was a closeted Republican.

Q

After Julia had left for a lunch date with Amy, Adam sat down with a cup of coffee to make his Sunday call to his mother. He could see Liz through the window throwing a stick for Lucky to retrieve in the backyard.

"Hi, Mother. How's it going?"

That put the onus of what to talk about on her.

"Hello, Adam. Everything's fine on this end."

That didn't work. There was a pause.

"How's Liz been this week?" his mother eventually asked.

"She's been learning to ride her bike and managed to fall into the hedge and cut herself."

"Oh dear. Did she have to have stitches?"

"No. It was just a scratch."

"But what about tetanus?"

"Don't worry. She's had five shots since she was born."

"Thank goodness for that. Before you got married, I used to worry myself sick that Julia would turn out to be an anti-vaxxer."

"No chance when she's married to a scientist."

"But she does tend to buy into rumors spread on the internet."

"Really? I hadn't noticed," he lied.

"Only last month she was talking to me about the threat of fluoridation. She seemed to think it was possibly a Chinese plot to undermine Americans' health."

"That's strange. I've never heard her say that."

"She knows better. As you say, you're a scientist."

"I know her best friend, Amy, is prone to believe that kind of stuff. But she's a lot more gullible than Julia."

"Just because Julia's down-to-earth doesn't mean that, in some matters, she's not irrational."

"True. But I'm still surprised by her thinking that. I'll ask her to explain it to me this evening."

"Please don't do that. She'll only blame me for telling you. Being a mother-in-law is tortuous enough as it is."

"As you wish."

"Just remember, in any marriage, it's healthy to retain a degree of skepticism."

"What are you getting at?"

"All I'll say is that you trust anything Julia tells you. Nobody is above a little deceit at times."

"Whatever you say, Mother."

She sighed heavily. Another awkward pause.

"So, what do you make of the Iowa Democratic caucus?" he asked.

"We could have done without that mix-up in the vote count. The results leave me uncertain who to back."

"Who are your top picks?"

"Either Buttigieg or Biden. I thought it would be Biden.

"So you're not a fan of Bernie's?" he asked.

"No one calling himself a socialist stands a chance in this country. Most voters don't know the difference between a socialist and a communist."

Adam decided not to tell his mother about his visit to the president's rally. She would only see it as some sort of betrayal. So instead he warned her to be extra careful of this new virus. The global death toll had now exceeded 900. Everyone agreed that people over sixty were especially vulnerable. It didn't help that she had undergone chemo for breast cancer the previous year. She thanked him, but he could sense from the tone of her voice that she wasn't about to change anything she already planned on doing, like attending her committee meetings for Alameda County Democrats. When even his ultra-careful mother was willing to dismiss medical warnings, what chance was there that the rest of the country would listen if things got out of hand here?

Julia returned mid-afternoon from her lunch with Amy in a good mood, something that had become rare recently. Adam was in the living room with Lucky curled up at his feet reading *The Hacker and the State*, a fascinating book about the battle for dominance in cyberspace.

"Welcome back," he said. "How was lunch?"

"We went to La Note. You know, the French restaurant on Shattuck."

"And you had?"

"Croque Madame."

"And how is that different from Croque Monsieur?"

"It adds a poached egg to the ham and cheese filling in the sandwich."

"Sounds like an improvement."

"It was delicious. And it came with a perfectly dressed green salad with fresh herbs."

"And to drink?"

"A double cream latte."

"I'm envious."

"You seem to prefer political rallies to indulging your palate," she said teasingly.

"That's one experience I don't have to repeat, I'm happy to say."

"I thought you said you were surprised at how everyone enjoyed themselves. Didn't that include you at all?"

"I was too conscious of the misinformation that was being doled out."

"What is it they call him? A serial liar."

"One woman I talked to told me she knew he lied, but it didn't matter to her. He spoke to her in her language. That was what counted."

They let the topic lapse.

"So," he said, "how's Amy?"

"She's over her throat thing. For a few days she thought she might have gotten the virus. But her temperature never rose above 99 degrees. She did have some interesting news about the origin of it."

"Oh. And what was that?"

"She'd read an article in the *Washington Times* that cited some former Israeli military defense officer who said that the Wuhan Institute of Virology was the only lab in China capable of working with deadly viruses. A part of it does research on biological weapons. He says it's possible the virus was accidentally leaked from the lab. The lab was about twenty miles from the Hunan seafood market where it may have first infected people."

"You know what a right-wing rag the *Washington Times* is?"

"Of course I do. I'm not a baby," Julia shot back.

"But you think this story's credible?"

"I see no reason to doubt it."

"Okay. Let's look it up on the internet."

Adam pulled out his laptop and located the original article back in early January.

"Look at this," he said. "Immediately after he alleges that a leak may have occurred he says, 'So far there isn't evidence or indication for such an incident.'"

"Lack of evidence doesn't mean that something didn't happen. Think how many criminals have escaped punishment for lack of evidence."

"But there is evidence that it *didn't* happen," Adam said, Googling an article in *Nature*. "Look at this. Researchers have sequenced the genome of the new virus and concluded it couldn't have originated in a lab." Adam continued to search in his computer. "And look—here's this open letter in the *Lancet* from twenty-seven public health scientists insisting that the coronavirus originated in wildlife."

"All right. All right," Julia replied crossly. "You always swallow anything asserted by scientists. Seeing what's going on all around us, I've every right to suspect the worst."

"You might have a right. But I've got a right to put my trust in hard evidence, in facts, not rumors."

"Now you're acting superior, as if I were a child who knew no better."

"I'm disagreeing with you. That doesn't mean I feel superior."

"Oh, damn! I can feel a headache coming on. I'm going to get an aspirin."

With that, Julia, no longer in a good mood, flounced out of the room.

Hell. These days, Adam reflected, just defending the facts comes off as offensive to Julia. Just what was going on? She now habitually turned a difference of opinion into some kind of aggression on his part. He wished he knew how to reverse what was happening. Okay. You could never go back. But how could they go forward in a different direction?

Q

For Julia, Monday was always the hardest day to get herself to work. Although she was employed by the ACLU as an investigator, the position sounded a lot more glamorous than it was. That morning she was charged with updating the table of authorities, that is the dozens of previous cases that acted as precedents to the case they were working on. Not exactly stimulating investigative work. The case accused ICE of failing to release immigrants with serious health conditions from civil detention. One of the precedents involved a case pursued by the Southern California ACLU in conjunction with an LA immigrants' rights organization. Julia remembered spending a week in LA compiling evidence for it with the organization's researcher, Jenny, a delightful woman who was the director's girlfriend. They had her over to dinner and Eduardo turned out to be a talented cook of Mexican food. The remaining precedents were just tiresome statistics.

Around midday, Adam called her to ask her where they kept the mustard that he needed for a sandwich he was making.

"It's in the fridge, of course. Bottom shelf of the door. Why do you always have such a hard time finding things?"

"Centuries of conditioning, I guess. Even my father wasn't allowed to do anything in the kitchen."

"I'm so happy I belong to Generation Y."

"You know what? I feel likewise."

"Well, bully for you."

"It's true. Sexual equality means that neither is dependent on the other for anything."

"Except for knowing where the mustard's kept." She was not letting him off the hook that easily.

"Touché! I'd better let you get on."

"Arrivederci."

"Ciao!"

Julia joined her two assistants for lunch at the Oasis Grill just down the street from the office. It was sunny and seventy degrees, and all the patio tables had been taken, so they took a table inside next to a window. Julia ordered their house Greek salad. Jill, twenty-three, was blond, and fun. She chose a tabbouleh salad, and Tina, a year older, shy, and inhibited, had falafel sliders.

"So how were your weekends?" Julia asked them.

"Too many drinks. Too much to eat. Too many men," Jill replied with a laugh.

"And yours, Tina?"

"Too few drinks. Too little to eat. Too few men."

They all laughed.

"Or women?" Jill asked.

That came as a surprise to Julia. Was Tina gay? Bisexual?

"Just parents," she replied.

"That sounds like a pain," Jill said.

"Actually I get on with my parents pretty well," Tina reflected. "Does that sound weird?"

"Sounds like arrested development to me," Jill said.

"Why does everybody think that you have to rebel against your parents to be independent?" Tina asked.

"I don't see how you can drink or have parties let alone one-night stands if you still live with your parents," Jill replied.

"You can always go out for that," Tina said.

"Sounds very restrictive to me," Jill said. "What do you think, Julia?"

"Me? I'm a wife and mother. I'm lucky to go to a couple of parties a year. Drinking too much is still an option. But the rest of it's no longer possible," she lied.

Tina intervened. "You come across as so negative about married life. But Adam sounds marvelous and Liz obviously gives you so much pleasure."

"Thank you, Tina. Sometimes I need to be reminded of that. Being unattached can be lonely, but it can also be so intensely exciting that married life can seem to be tedious by comparison."

"I'd love to have a permanent partner and child like you," Tina said.

That remark stayed with Julia as they walked back to the office. To the outsiders she looked happy and content. Why then was she so stressed? What was wrong with her life? Or was it her? Why couldn't she just enjoy what she had?

She thought back again to her time with Jenny and Eduardo. They even worked for the same organization. Yet they appeared so satisfied with their life together. They even had a short argument one evening that only seemed to leave them more united. Recently, her disagreements with Adam seemed to be pushing them further apart. Or maybe they only seemed that way to her.

The commute home was a nightmare. Her Embarcadero BART station was closed for some emergency—the rumor among those thronging the blocked entrance was that a passenger was under a train). So, she had to walk to Montgomery Street, which was overflowing with diverted passengers. It took her at least half an hour to get onto a train that then stopped between stations for random periods of time all the way to Rockridge.

When she entered the house Adam and Liz were both worried.

"Where've you been, Mommy?" Liz asked.

"Trying to get home. My station was closed, and everything went downhill from there." After giving Liz a hug and a kiss, Julia threw her coat and briefcase on the sofa. "Haven't you eaten yet, sweetheart?" she asked looking at the laid dinner table.

"No. We were waiting for you," she said.

"Adam. What's going on? Liz must be starving."

"Since you didn't call us, we expected you back any moment."

"But I could have been held up for hours."

"I assumed that, if that were the case, you'd have called us."

"For some unknown reason my cell wouldn't connect the call."

"You still could have texted me."

Adam was always so damned logical. It made her feel exasperated.

"Why does everything have to stop until I get home?"

"We always wait until you get home." Adam was stirring something on the stove. "Dinner's ready."

"Serve yourselves. I need a drink before I do anything."

Adam went to the drink cabinet. "What can I get you?"

"Please, please give Liz her dinner now. I'll fix my own drink."

Julia poured herself a generous glass of red wine and swallowed a large mouthful.

After serving Liz Adam turned to her. "What's got into you tonight?"

She flopped down on the sofa with her wine, pulling her discarded coat from under her. "I did all this research on a case I was given, and late this afternoon the lead lawyer announced that he wasn't going to pursue it, owing to some legal technicality. All that work wasted."

"I'm sorry. But there's no need to take it out on me," Adam said, returning after placing Liz's dinner in front of her at the table.

"It's all very well for you waiting in comfort back here at home." Julia realized that she was envious of Adam's relaxed work schedule. And a little pissed off. "I was stuck in a tightly packed mass of people waiting to get on the train, and an equally packed train being breathed on by strangers who might be infected with the virus."

"Come on, Julia," Adam said with some exasperation. "There's a minute number of confirmed cases in California."

"Six, one of which is person-to-person."

Adam was taken aback by her up-to-date knowledge. She'd been conscientiously keeping track of the spread of the virus for at least a week. It seemed almost obsessive.

"What's six out of the state's forty million?"

"Who cares about the odds if you happen to be the one that gets infected?" she asked as she poured herself another generous glass of wine.

"The chances of your getting infected are infinitely smaller than are those of your winning the lottery."

"I don't care," she shouted. "I don't want to die." To her surprise she found she was crying.

Liz rushed over to her from the table. "Please don't die, Mommy."

Julia pulled her close to her and managed to say between sobs, "I promise I'll do my best not to."

As Liz looked into her mother's eyes Liz's too filled with tears.

"It's OK, sweetheart." Julia tried to regain control of herself.

Adam came over and put an arm round her. "Don't you worry. We're not going to let anything happen to Mommy. We both need her too much."

Julia chimed in, "Liz, the best way you can make me feel better is by eating your dinner."

"But I'm not hungry anymore. Please, please don't ever leave us, Mommy."

"Now, now, Liz," she said. "It's just your mother being silly. Take no notice of her."

Julia turned to Adam. "I just need to do something upstairs." With that she left the room, hoping things would return to normal by the time she returned.

That evening in bed they were both looking through the headlines on their cellphones. It occurred to Julia that they were both watching more news than they used to do.

"Listen to this," Adam said. "In India, the *Wall Street Journal* reports, Swami Chakrapani Maharaj, president of the Hindu Mahasabha—a century-old organization that advocates Hindutva, or 'Hinduness'—declared that 'consuming cow urine and cow dung will stop the effect of infectious coronavirus'. There's a conspiracy theory that's not going to get a lot of traction on social media."

"On the other hand," she replied, "here's one that will spread like wildfire. In his inimitable way of expressing himself the president announced from the White House lawn: 'Now, the virus that we're talking about having to do—you know, a lot of people think that goes away in April with the heat—as the heat comes in. Typically, that will go away in April.' He can't even construct a coherent sentence."

"You don't have to be an epidemiologist to know that is not how viruses behave."

Eagerly she said to him, "So, you do believe it's going to get worse?"

"Yes, I do. Viruses spread as fast as the president's misinformation does."

"That's what I was afraid of," she said. "Speaking of misinformation, did you hear that the idiot-in-chief said that his New Hampshire rally today was attended by forty to fifty thousand people when the venue had a maximum capacity of twelve thousand tops?"

Adam chortled.

She turned off her phone and switched off her bedside light.

Q

On Tuesdays and Thursdays Adam had a one-hour gap between classes. He settled down at his desk and, without even thinking, found himself searching for the latest QAnon mentions.

The first page he came across was a piece in the *Daily Beast* dated two weeks before. Headlined "Toxic Mythology," it described a miracle cure called "MMS" — Miracle Mineral Solution —that was being promoted by QAnon followers. With thirty-six million Chinese locked down, QAnon followers were advocating drinking or spraying the mouth with this mixture of bleach and citric acid to kill the coronavirus. It was being offered for sale by a Mexico-based church, Genesis II Church of Health and Healing, for $45. Despite warnings from the FDA that "Ingesting these products is the same as drinking bleach," and despite a woman dying from drinking it in 2009, it was being widely endorsed by prominent followers of QAnon. "MMS the whole shit out of everything," said one QAnon promoter on YouTube.

As he wondered what would make so many Americans believe such insane and dangerous advice, he became aware of someone standing at his open office door.

"I've brought you my outline for our paper," Anna said, waving a folder in the air.

"Come on in," he said, happy to see her.

She came around to his side of the desk in order to lay the folder in front of him, rested her hand lightly on his shoulder, and asked, "What are you looking at?"

Instantly a shock shot through him. He thought she felt it, too. Recovering, he told her about MMS.

"I'm having a hard time understanding how crazy cures like this catch on," he said.

"All it takes is magical thinking," she joked.

"It's easy to dismiss this stuff as internet derangement," he said, "and feel superior. But, even after attending that rally, I still can't account for the way the QAnon people construct a whole alternate reality, and they all agree to it. It's so strange. It feels like a dystopian novel."

"Really! You really went to the president's rally?"

"I really did."

He clicked on a page of images and motioned for her to pull up a chair next to him. He scrolled through photos he'd taken during the rally—Q signs on banners and clothes, excited faces in the crowd, a sea of arms and placards, the president basking in the adoration.

"QAnon has gotten under my skin," he said. "How can I rebut these theories when I'm unable to comprehend what makes their fictions so popular?"

He went on to describe his day at the rally.

"Fascinating," she remarked. "Haven't you partially answered your own question? The answer lies in that feel-good euphoria you witnessed. Just think of how tough their everyday lives are. Living paycheck to paycheck. They really believe immigrants are going to take their jobs from them. And they vote for the people who want to remove the pathetically few safeguards left between them and homelessness and hunger. And now an added source of fear—the coronavirus."

"But they deny the virus," he said.

"Still, their lives kind of suck, and QAnon not only makes them feel like they are smarter than the people they think look down on them, it also promises a magical solution to their problems. It simultaneously works on their paranoia and offers them hope. When the president defeats the bad guys, their lives will finally be what they're supposed to be. It puts them on the winning side. Besides, how could QAnon be wrong when so many other people accept its assertions?"

"But surely a part of them knows that the part about pedophiles, satanic cults, and the deep state, is made up, right?"

"Probably some of them do. It's just like you or me going to the movies. Part of us remains judgmental, apart from what we're watching. But that doesn't stop the other part of us suspending our disbelief and enjoying the story. If that makes you feel on top of the world, and reality never does, why choose reality?"

Anna leaned over him and searched for a page on his computer. She smelled of jasmine blossom.

"Look at this," she said.

It was a *New York Times* piece titled: "What Happens When QAnon Seeps from the Web to the Offline World."

"'Offline World' caught my attention," she said. "As if the online world was the real one."

He scanned the piece. It said that, since its inception over two years earlier, QAnon followers had surfaced in political campaigns, criminal cases and campus scandals across the nation. It cited a June 2018 incident, in which an armed man from Nevada drove his armored truck onto a bridge near the Hoover Dam and engaged in a 90-minute standoff with police, demanding the release of the Inspector General's report on Hillary Clinton's email practices. The next month another guy from Tucson was arrested for occupying a cement plant he accused of sheltering a child sex-trafficking ring. Two months later another man took a crowbar to the altar of a chapel in Sedona, yelling about the Catholic church's sex trafficking. All of them declared their adherence to QAnon.

What surprised Adam the most was the number of politicians who endorsed QAnon, including six current Republican congressional candidates and a city council member who quoted one of Q's drops as if it were a verse from the Bible: "To quote Q No. 2436. . ." Yes, by December 2018 Q had uploaded 2,436 posts, most of them bewilderingly short and enigmatic. Of course, trying to decipher the meaning of these breadcrumbs or drops was what hooked them. It made them feel autonomous, in charge of their own research.

"If you try to trace the origin of any of these conspiracy theories," Anna said, "you find they start off as relatively innocuous speculations. You know, 'What if...?' or, 'It's likely that...' Then, with every repetition, they mutate—fill in some blanks, acquire more certainty, become more powerful."

"Sounds just like the coronavirus. The parts of the coronavirus genome that accumulate many mutations are more flexible and more likely to survive and replicate. The same is true of lies. Which makes them preferable to the truth."

"Right. We are threatened with not only a possible pandemic, but an infodemic of misinformation."

"Both kinds of virus work largely out of sight—"

At that moment they both reached out to the keyboard to find something on the computer. He found his hand was on top of hers. They looked at one another and burst out laughing. But Anna didn't try to remove her hand from under his for what seemed a long time. When she finally retrieved it, she smiled at him and shrugged her shoulders. It was as if she were saying that the next move had been his, and she was sorry he hadn't made it. Or, alternatively, that she knew he was married, and understood how torn he felt.

"I was about to show you," Anna said, "a place on Facebook where QAnon amplified a false narrative, that Asians are more susceptible to the coronavirus than white people, who are said to be immune to it."

"So white people think they have nothing to worry about."

"It also increases the prejudice shown to Asian Americans like me."

"Because of the virus's origin?" he asked.

"Yes. But that kind of rumor has very real racist implications for anyone with Asian features. For instance, on the subway, I've noticed recently that some white passengers would rather stand than sit next to me."

"That wouldn't be me," he said jokingly.

"So you say," she said getting up and making for the door. "But it reveals an unpleasant truth about these conspiracy theories. They always target somebody. There's nothing like a common enemy to bring everyone together."

"Remember, you also have friends," he called out to her as she left.

Just what's happening here? he asked himself. Sure, they both felt a strong attraction for one another. But this was madness. Wasn't Julia enough? Maybe that was the source of his conflict. She had been enough for him. But, recently, he didn't feel as if he was enough for her. It was hard to pin down. But some undercurrent was sweeping her in a different direction from his. It wasn't anything tangible. But he felt it in her fear of catching the virus, her conviction that she'd die from it, as she blurted out last night. Was the virus now secretly attacking their marriage? For sure, it was undermining their sex life.

Easy enough to blame Julia for his desiring Anna. The truth was that didn't require any excuse. What left him uncomfortable was the feeling of being caught in a flash flood that was too powerful to resist. The feeling of losing control. Or resignation. Like Hamlet's, "If it be not now, yet it will come."

Q

Wednesdays was the day Teresa, their housekeeper, came. She was in her fifties, Mexican American, immigrated here as a child, had a green card, and spoke English well with a very slight accent. She was great with Liz and Lucky. Well, why not? She had raised two daughters, now in their late twenties, and currently had a small poodle. Roberto, her husband, did garden work and sometimes helped Adam out with large projects in their yard.

That morning Liz was complaining of an earache. When Teresa learned this, she said that both her daughters had suffered from earache as children. The first time, she'd assumed it would cure itself—with the help of raw garlic—but she ended up having to take her daughter to urgent care to have her ear drained. The next time she took her daughters right away and was given antibiotics that resolved it within a couple of days.

Adam rang their doctor's office and was given an appointment for five that afternoon.

"Do I have to go to school today?" Liz asked.

"You know the answer to that. Of course you do," Julia said quickly. She knew Liz could always get around Adam more easily.

Adam said he and Liz would pick up a pizza on their way back from the doctor's office. Julia voted for pepperoni, told Teresa she might see her if she got back before six, and left for work.

Julia got home at sunset. Rain clouds obscured the sun making it look like nighttime. As soon as she closed the front door behind her, an agitated Teresa rushed up to her.

"What's the matter, Teresa?" Julia asked. Teresa's eyes were darting from Julia to the windows.

"You didn't see anyone as you came in?"

"No. Why?"

"Oh, dear. Give me a moment. My heart is beating so fast, I can't catch my breath."

"Let's both sit down at the kitchen table and you can tell me what's wrong there."

"You bolted the front door?" Teresa asked.

"I'll do it right now," Julia said.

After locking the door she poured a glass of water for Teresa who took a large gulp. Finally, she started, "I was just finishing up in the kitchen when I looked up from the sink and saw this angry man glaring in at me through the window. He raised his hands like this"—she made two tight fists, narrowed her eyes and squinched her face. "I screamed and rushed to lock the front door. Lucky was barking furiously."

"What did he look like?"

"I'm not sure."

"Was he black, white or what?"

"White."

"Was he tall or short?"

"I would say medium height."

"Was his hair dark or light?"

"Dark. And he was wearing a dark hoody. That's all I remember."

"So, what happened next?"

"I heard him yelling and swearing."

"What exactly was he yelling?"

"He said…" Teresa shot her a look to prepare Julia for the language. "He said, 'Tell that whore to stop f—,'" she hesitated, "'fucking with me. She's a stuck-up fraud. Tell her…' I couldn't catch any more of what he was saying."

"How long ago was this?"

"A minute before you came in. I'm amazed you didn't run into him."

That really spooked Julia, the thought of encountering Dave—who else could it be?—in the dusk out there.

All this time Lucky had been pawing her to tell her he had to go out urgently. Julia summoned up her courage and, telling Teresa to stay where she was, took Lucky out into the yard. It was still gently raining, and all the wet vegetation glistened with reflections from the yard lights. She comforted herself with the thought that, if anyone was lurking out there, Lucky would start barking at them—though he was hardly a natural guard dog. All Lucky did was rush over to the grass and pee for the longest time.

On her way back into the house, Julia took in the mail.

"There's no one out there now?" Teresa asked fearfully.

"It's all quiet on the western front," Julia replied.

"*Gracias a Dios*," she said.

Julia sorted through the bills and solicitations for money, and came across an unstamped envelope addressed: JULIA, obviously hand delivered. On opening it, she saw it was written all in caps:

YOU THOUGHT YOU COULD JUST CHUCK ME AWAY LIKE A PIECE OF GARBAGE? NO SUCH FUCKING LUCK. ANSWER MY EMAILS OR YOU'LL BE SORRY. I'M GIVING YOU 24 HOURS. AFTER THAT WATCH OUT.

"Christ!" she exclaimed. She realized she was trembling.

"What's the matter?" Teresa asked.

Julia took a deep breath.

"It's all right. Listen, you're not walking back to the bus stop alone. I'm calling a taxi to take you home."

"There's really no need," Teresa protested.

"Believe me, there is."

Julia called a cab, then fed Lucky. Anything to stop herself from thinking.

But after Teresa had left she gave in to her true feelings, sobbing and wailing. How had Dave discovered where she lived? Did he intend to hurt her... or Adam... or Liz? Or even Lucky?

This was all too much. She went up to her bedside cabinet and took out the Oxys that Dave had given her. For a moment she hesitated.

But her need won out. Soon her mind would stop whirring round, torturing her with all the nightmare scenarios.

As she came downstairs she heard the front door open. Adam was back with Liz and a pizza.

"So what's the verdict?" Julia asked.

"Antibiotics for seven days," Adam said. Extracting one tablet and giving it to Liz with water, he said to her, "Don't you worry, sweetheart. By tomorrow morning the earache will start feeling better."

"Can we have our pizza now, while it's hot?" Julia asked..

"Why not?" Adam said and opened the box on the kitchen table.

"Anyone want a plate?" Julia asked. Both of them were already biting into their first slice.

She tried to sound calm as she told them what happened, trying to keep the fear out of her voice for Liz's sake. But recounting the experience started her off shaking again. She passed Dave's note to Adam to avoid reading it out loud in front of Liz.

Liz of course was alarmed.

"How long ago was he your boyfriend?" she asked.

"A long time ago, sweetheart, before I met your dad."

Adam finished reading. "We could file a police report," he said without conviction.

"What action can they take without a positive ID?"

"Of course, you're right." He looked frustrated.

"I could buy pepper spray, I suppose."

"That's not a bad idea."

"I have to admit that I was in such a state before you got back that I took an OxyContin."

Both Adam and Liz stopped eating and stared at her.

"I didn't know we even had OxyContin in the house," Adam said.

"I got it online," she lied.

"Mommy, isn't OxyContin an opioid?" Liz asked.

They both look at her surprised.

"It is," Julia told her. "But how do you know about it?"

"Last week our teacher invited a specialist to talk to us about opioid addiction."

"And what did she say?"

"She said that, in our county, one opioid prescription is written for every two people."

"Anything else?" Julia asked.

"Yes. We were all taught what to do if someone at home showed signs of an overdose."

"And what were you taught to do?"

"If someone falls asleep and stops breathing we were given a spray called Narcan to use. We were taught to, 'Open, insert, and spray.'"

Adam and Julia exchanged glances.

Liz continued, "We were given two sprays to carry in our backpacks. So, you don't have to worry, Mommy."

"That's good to know," Julia told her smiling. "Not that I think an occasional OxyContin can lead to an overdose." Julia was squirming with embarrassment. "Want any more pizza?"

"No thank you, Mommy."

"Then it's time for you to go and do your homework."

In bed later that evening Julia and Adam watched the news on his laptop. Bernie Sanders had won the Democratic primary in New Hampshire. Biden came in fifth. A Republican senator remarked,

"A socialist is now the front runner for the Democratic nomination for president. What's his top priority? A complete government takeover of healthcare in America."

"QAnon," Julia observed, "seems to be evenly split between those seeing Sanders as another Satanic Jew bent on strengthening the deep state, and those who think he's the president's best hope for getting re-elected."

Adam looked over at her surprised. "I didn't know you were following QAnon."

"Since we talked about it, I've checked out their Twitter stuff. Most of the posts read like the ravings of nutcases, but some of them are interesting. Not that I spend much time on it." She wondered if that was true.

"I'm glad to know that. The more I find out about them the more I despair of our future."

"Come on, Adam. We've always had crazies in America, from the moment it was founded."

"Of course you're right," said Adam, turning out the light.

He moved over to put his arms round her waist. He landed on her skin exposed between her pajama bottom and top. Aroused, he began to stroke her waist, her stomach and was moving up beneath her top to reach her breasts when she grabbed his hand to stop him.

"What's the matter?" he asked in a hurt voice.

"I'm too freaked out by Dave to respond tonight," she said. But the truth was that Adam's foreplay failed to arouse her, at least not tonight. She thought back to her encounter with Dave that had overwhelmed and so excited her. Sick. Sick! What could she say? She couldn't control how her body responded.

"I was hoping to take your mind off him."

"That was a nice thought. Let me take a rain check?"

They both moved to the edge of their own side of the bed and waited to be overtaken by sleep.

Q

Adam had barely gotten back to his office after his morning class when a student knocked on the open door. He recognized her as the young woman he had unfairly criticized in class a couple of weeks ago. She wore the obligatory torn blue jeans and t-shirt inscribed with #METOO. She had long blond hair with brown roots, hazel eyes, and bright red lipstick.

"Good morning, Ms. ...?" he hesitated.

"Natalie French," she informed him.

"Oh, yes. Natalie. And what can I do for you?"

"You just gave us back our first paper of the semester."

"Yes?"

"You gave me a C+."

"I see."

"Well, I'm not happy with the grade. I think you're being over critical in your remarks."

"Can I refresh my memory by looking at your paper?"

She handed it to him. It was a shabby piece of work that lacked proper research and did nothing but reproduce the findings of the principal textbook for the class.

"I'm sorry," he said gently, "but this paper needs much more work on it to get a better grade. You offer only one argument that comes straight out of your textbook and no counterarguments. Also you've failed to structure your paper. It meanders all over the place. You only cite three sources total. And even your citations fail to conform to the formatting guidelines I've made available to you online."

She looked nervous.

"Look," he said to her, "I'm willing to accept a complete re-write and give that a fresh grade."

"I could lodge a complaint that you discriminated against me in front of the class."

"How do you mean 'discriminated'?"

"That you attacked me in class because previously I hadn't agreed to offer you sexual favors."

"Sexual favors! What are you talking about?"

"I would be happy to offer them to you if you revise my grade to an A." She reached for the door to close it.

"Leave the door open please," he instructed her firmly. "I do not give grades in return for sexual favors. What made you think I might?"

"Some of the faculty do. We all know which ones."

"I sincerely hope you are misinformed."

"I'm not. But you are too square to know what's really going on."

She had recovered herself completely. Or had he simply misread the earlier signs?

"So, are you willing to revise my grade, or...?"

"Or what?"

"Or are you prepared to deal with a complaint of sexual harassment?"

"You are not helping the MeToo movement concocting false charges against faculty," he said gesturing at her t-shirt.

"Don't tell me you support MeToo."

"I do. And it upsets me to see a woman undermining it the way you are."

"And it upsets me to be the victim of your prejudiced grading. I'm serious. I will contact the Department for the Prevention of Harassment and Discrimination if you refuse to change my grade."

"Go ahead. See if lying gets you anywhere. It certainly won't earn you a better grade from me."

"We'll see about that. You've no idea what's going to hit you next."

"My offer stands—a complete re-write will be given a new grade. Now please leave my office."

She flounced out of the room muttering to herself.

Adam immediately questioned his response. Was he being too legalistic? Should he have offered her some kind of compromise? Say, a minor revision of her paper in return for a higher grade? That would be rewarding her blackmail out of self-interest. He wished he was more of a pragmatist. But he just couldn't live with himself if he'd caved in to her.

He realized that, if she took this further, it could have serious repercussions for him. Even temporary suspension while the investigation took place. So he phoned the department office and asked to see the chair. The assistant told Adam he happened to be free at that moment.

After sitting and exchanging a few pleasantries, Adam revealed everything that had transpired. Instantly the chair looked alarmed, as if the charge were an infected object that would need to be treated with wipes.

"Of course I believe you, Adam. But you know the way these things work now. She is the victim and you, the presumed aggressor, have to prove your innocence. The burden of proof rests on you, not her.

It may not be fair, but women making charges against men have for so long been treated unfairly. Now they are given the benefit of the doubt. At least at universities."

Adam didn't waste his time arguing the rights and wrongs of the procedure. He simply reiterated that he was telling him exactly what had happened, thinking that, if it came to a hearing, he could call him as a witness to his testimony at the time when the charge was first levelled against him.

The chair only offered, "We will have to wait to see if Ms. French files charges. If she does, we will have to follow the university procedures for complaints of sexual harassment, which will mean referring the case to the Title IX Officer."

"I understand," Adam said as he made for the door. "I just hope she has second thoughts before proceeding with this fiction."

On returning to his office Adam was visited by two undergraduates from the morning class. Both looked like outdoor enthusiasts with tanned skin, and muscular arms and legs. They both wore long, baggy colorful shorts and identical t-shirts with the logo RAISED RIGHT.

"Good afternoon, gentlemen," he greeted them. "Grab a seat."

"Thank you, professor," replied one of them, who would turn out to be their spokesperson.

"Please introduce yourselves."

"I'm Brad," the spokesman said, "and he's Michael." He nodded at his companion.

"And what can I do for you?"

"We were at the president's rally last Saturday. You didn't see us, but we spotted you."

"Yes," Adam said guardedly, "I was there."

"We didn't realize that we had a professor who felt as we do."

"Which is?"

"That the president is just what the country needs to shake up the establishment."

"The establishment?"

"You know, the deep state." Brad turned to Michael. "What does Q call them?"

Now they had Adam's attention.

"A cabal of high-level bureaucrats and military commanders left over from the Obama administration intent on overthrowing the president," Michael trotted out.

"So you follow Q's posts?" Adam asked.

"You bet," Brad said.

"And you believe all that stuff about satanic pedophile cults led by Democrats?"

"Of course we don't go along with some of the most extreme theories. But we do think there is a power struggle going on in the highest reaches of government, and that the president is aware of the actions and leaks of the deep state."

"Yes," Michael interjected eagerly. "The president is waiting for the right time to expose its members and expel them from the government and the military."

"I thought he was going to imprison them in Gitmo," Adam said to probe where they stood.

"I doubt that would be necessary," Brad said.

"It might be," Michael corrected him.

"Nah. That's just a fantasy favored by the extreme fringe of QAnon," Brad replied.

"And what is it I can do for you?" Adam asked.

Brad looked at Michael who nodded. Finally, Brad said, "We both belong to a local branch."

"Branch!" Adam exclaimed with surprise. "I had no idea QAnon had local branches."

"Civilians aren't supposed to know. Our group has about ten members, including a group leader," Brad told him.

"And who is he?" he asked.

"We all call each other by our Twitter handles. I can't really tell you more until I know whether you are interested in joining us."

"Joining you. Well, let's see. What does that involve?"

"You could come to one of our meetings and judge for yourself if you are interested. They haven't been very frequent. Mainly, they allow us to exchange news and information."

By this time Adam was having a furious silent debate with himself. Had he learnt enough about Q's adherents from the rally? Well, no. He still didn't fully understand what motivated them. He could go along with these two and get a lot more information.

"I wouldn't mind attending one meeting to see if it interested me," Adam said.

They both broke into smiles.

"That's great," Brad said. "Our next meeting happens to be this Sunday morning. Are you free to come then?"

Adam thought for a moment. "Sure. Where is it?"

"We'd be happy to pick you up."

"That sounds like a good idea. Where from?"

"We both live in a dorm off Bancroft Way. So, how about the corner of Bancroft and Barrow Lane?"

"Fine. At what time?"

"Can you be there at 9:30?"

"I'll be there."

"See you then," Brad said as he and Michael got up looking very pleased with themselves.

Once they'd left, Adam immediately wondered whether he was taking his inquiry too far. A year ago he would never have willingly spent a precious Sunday morning away from Julia and Liz. But things were different now. Maybe it was also because Liz was becoming more independent. What was done was done. He couldn't easily contact Brad and Michael to back out. So, that was that.

Q

Valentine's Day. Falsely associated with the ancient Roman festival of Lupercalia that celebrated Juno's chastity—according to Wikipedia. By the Middle Ages it became a celebration of love when ladies would adjudicate lovers' disputes. Thoroughly commercialized in modern times. Julia continued reading on her cell that, according to the National Retail Association, it has been estimated that US consumers will spend $27.4 billion for the holiday.

Sure enough, when she came downstairs in the morning, Adam had arranged a dozen red roses in a vase on the table and placed a Valentine's card on her plate. He never forgot all the special occasions—Mother's Day, their wedding anniversary, Christmas, her birthday. She should have been grateful. Yet, today, it all felt too predictable.

Not his fault. But she couldn't make her feeling go away.

"Oh, Adam. What beautiful roses."

She sat down and opened her card. It was inscribed: *There's nobody else I'd rather lie in bed and look at my phone next to.* Did she detect a hint there?

"What a declaration of love," she remarked.

"I thought you'd appreciate it," Adam replied grinning.

On the radio the announcer was summarizing the state of infections in China. "Yesterday, as China expands its diagnosis of the coronavirus, 14,000 more cases were reported, while deaths from it topped 1,300." Wow! she thought. This was huge and totally scary. "The CDC reported its 15th case of the virus, with 600 people returned from Wuhan held in quarantine."

Here it comes, she thought. So much for the president boasting he'd saved millions by banning flights from China. How could anyone be that simple-minded to think that someone wanting to get here from China wouldn't fly via an intermediate stop? How long would it be before they were experiencing thousands of confirmed cases here? The fear gnawed away inside of her. Only an OxyContin could temporarily dull her panic and relax her. In fact, she thought, she might just take one before leaving for work.

After lunch Julia was trying to get some figures together for a 3 p.m. meeting when her office phone rang.

"Yes?" she said. Silence. She felt a chill. "Can I help you?"

"You know you can help me. And how."

How the hell had Dave obtained her work number? From the directory of course.

"Dave. You've got to stop."

"No way. You owe me big by now."

"I owe you nothing. You lied to me. That won't work a second time."

"I'm not lying when I tell you I need you badly."

"It's no good. You don't get another chance. Forget it and leave me alone."

"Don't you understand? I can't leave you alone. I've got a hard-on just talking to you."

"I don't care what state you're in. You're not part of my life any longer. Please stop calling me."

"Just hearing your voice is making me come. Say something sexy."

She slammed the phone down. Returning to her report she found that the words made no sense to her. She was shaking with anger. First he invades her property, and now he was invading her workspace.

Dave called her four more times that afternoon, uttering obscenities, and she was beside herself. She called the Personnel Officer and told her she was being harassed on her office phone by an ex. The Personnel Officer said she'd get back to her. When the phone rang half an hour later she assumed it was her. But it was Dave.

"Get lost!" she yelled loudly into the phone. She slammed the receiver.

Jill looked at her over the glass partition. "You all right?"

"I'm being harassed by an ex," Julia explained.

"I know what that's like. I had one who pestered me for three months."

"Thanks a lot. That makes me feel a lot better."

The phone rang again.

What could she do? She picked up.

"Julia?"

"Yes."

"This is Susan from Personnel."

"Yes."

"About those annoying calls. I spoke to our service provider. They all came from a payphone on Market Street. So, there's nothing they can do."

"Damn. He rang me four more times since I talked to you."

"The only thing I can suggest is contacting the Federal Trade Commission. I can give you their number."

"Thanks for your advice. I'll see if cutting him off without saying anything will work."

"Good luck, then."

"Thank you, Susan."

There were no more calls from Dave that day. Either he gave up or he had to go to work. She was quite shaken. Her whole life could be so easily disrupted and made miserable. She took an OxyContin and left under-prepared for her 3 o'clock meeting.

By the time Julia got back home she'd partially recovered, especially once she'd been given a margarita. But as soon as she started to tell Adam about Dave's calls that day (leaving out the sexual parts) she got so upset she could barely finish her account. She asked Adam for a second margarita. Although he raised his eyebrows to express surprise at how quickly she'd downed the first, he knew better than to say anything. Julia felt as if she were on the edge of a meltdown.

"I think you did the best thing you could have done," said Adam returning with her drink. "Cutting him off without saying anything; that ought to take the oxygen out of it."

"It's easy for you to say that. But I'm really scared. And it's making me feel paranoid—more paranoid than usual."

"I'm sorry, honey. Sit back and enjoy your drink while I get a mushroom omelet together."

"I thought you were planning to cook a zucchini frittata." She couldn't stop herself being disagreeable.

"Yes, but I discovered that we didn't have enough zucchini left for that."

"Liz isn't crazy about mushrooms."

"I asked whether she'd prefer a cheese omelet and she opted for mushrooms."

"Fine. Personally, I'd have chosen cheese."

"I can do you a separate one."

"No. Don't bother. The way I feel it makes little difference."

Liz came in from the next room and asked Adam for help with some homework. Even Lucky followed them out, preferring their company. She felt abandoned. But then hadn't she, in effect, asked to be left alone? Yet, in reality, she longed for the comfort of family small talk.

When they had eaten their mushroom omelet—very tasty with fontina and garlic, even if she couldn't get herself to say it—Adam surprised her with a totally unexpected bit of news. He'd been accused of sexual harassment by one of his female students. He recounted her visit to him and his exchange with the department chair.

"Then, today," he continued, "the chair—that pompous ass—called me to say the student's filed a formal complaint with our Title IX office."

"That's horrible, Adam," she said sympathetically. Adam was the last man she knew who was capable of sexual harassment. This was really absurd.

Adam passed her a document headed "Notice of Charges of Sexual Harassment." After identifying the complainant and defendant, it summarized the charge against Adam: "That on Tuesday, January 28, 2020, Ms. French visited Professor Gosford in his office to discuss her grade. Ms. French alleges that Professor Gosford offered to give her a term grade of A in return for oral sex, an offer that she declined."

"What happens next?" she asked.

"Apparently, the Title IX officer decided that the university didn't need to place me on interim involuntary leave."

"That's a promising sign."

"I guess the chair's account of what I told him introduced enough uncertainty to avoid that step."

"And now?"

"I wait for the Title IX office to summon me to a hearing."

"And, presumably, your student gets a separate hearing?"

"For sure."

"So, it could boil down to he said, she said."

"Very likely."

"Which in turn will lead to some form of compromise?"

"I guess so. Like my having to attend additional sexual harassment prevention training. Or a deduction from my salary."

"How unfair to you, *cariño*" she said, reaching out her hand to grasp his.

"It's always possible the truth will prevail." He didn't sound convinced.

"In the current climate, people just assume all women tell the truth."

"I know. Besides, I believe that any compromise between the truth and fabrication is doing the truth a disservice."

"Is doing you a disservice."

"Welcome to our new 21st century world."

"You sound so calm about it. I'd be fucking mad."

"I am fucking mad. But I can only pursue my fight through these tortuous university procedures."

Julia got up and poured herself some straight tequila.

"Want some?" she asked.

"Thanks, but no." He was so maddeningly abstemious. "I'm going to wash up now."

"I'll dry," she volunteered.

"Better not," Adam replied, smiling. "Less breakage."

"Maybe you're right. But how dare you."

Later that evening in bed Adam wanted to celebrate Valentine's Day, starting with some foreplay. Julia simply couldn't get herself to even do that. She pretended to be asleep, which she nearly was, drugged with so much tequila. Her last feeling before drifting off was one of guilt.

Q

At breakfast Adam sprang his delayed surprise on Julia. He had reserved places for the two of them on a Chocolate and Wine Cruise in San Francisco Bay that Saturday afternoon. It may have been a bit schmaltzy, but they both loved chocolate and wine. So how could they go wrong? Easily, it turned out. He had arranged for Julene to come and be with Liz while they were gone.

The two-hour cruise left from Pier 40 at 1 p.m. It was an unusually sunny and warm day for San Francisco. They were ushered onto the three-tiered luxury yacht together with 108 other passengers by attractive female attendants. The higher up the income ladder you went, he reflected, the more you regressed into the earlier era of male privilege. Handsome male attendants? What was the point! They targeted the men because they were presumed to have paid for the excursion. As Bill Clinton said, always follow the money.

Once on board, they found themselves surrounded by tables and booths decorated with chocolate selections of every variety, as well as local winemakers offering tastings and a sprinkling of other wine merchants offering high-end vintages. The ticket for the excursion didn't include any of the products for sale, although there was a plethora of free samples.

The engine rumbled beneath them as they left the pier to start their tour of the bay. Adam suggested they pay the $40 each for a wine tasting at Chateau Montelena's booth and take their final sample to the upper deck. They were treated to the usual pretentious descriptions of the various vintages they tried: angular, complex, elegant, lively. As for the aromas, wines were said to smell like melon, passion fruit, fig, grapefruit, jackfruit, kumquat, not to mention beeswax, piecrust, and crème brulée.

They escaped with a 2016 Ramey Ritchie Chardonnay from the Russian River Valley, "featuring rich toasty notes of baked apple and dried pear flavors, with buttery accents emerging on the finish." On the upper deck they found a space on the rail among the crowd of passengers—mainly tourists, he guessed—and gazed at the receding shoreline of high rises as they headed for the Golden Gate Bridge.

"San Francisco always looks so beautiful from afar," Julia said. "But try working in it and the glamor soon wears thin."

"Maybe it should be called Santa Francisco," Adam said teasingly.

"That sounds mildly sexist to me," she replied.

"Excuse me," they heard, "but I couldn't help overhearing you. It always troubles me when I hear someone using that term."

A youngish white man with a "fashy" haircut, khakis and a white polo shirt with the number 88 on the back was leaning against the rail next to Julia. He had a Southern accent.

"And why is that?" Julia asked curtly.

"Because 'sexism' smacks of political correctness. And political correctness is just one way the liberal elites put men down."

"Put men down or treat them as equals?" Julia asked.

"Excuse me," a much younger woman the other side of the guy cut in. "Are you from around here?"

"We are," Adam answered. "Why do you ask?"

"It's just that we heard San Franciscans are about as far left as you get in this country."

"Maybe," he said. "But I distrust generalizations."

"But isn't it called the gay capital of the world?"

"It certainly has one of the largest LGBTQ communities in the world." he answered.

"There you go again," the guy said. "LGBTQ. What does that stand for?"

"Lesbian, gay, bisexual, transgender and queer," Adam replied.

"What's wrong with just 'homo'?"

Julia jumped in. "Because, for example, a bisexual is not simply homosexual."

"Where do you two come from?" Adam asked trying to de-escalate the underlying friction.

"We're both born and raised in Kentucky," he said.

"The Bluegrass State, home of Kentucky bourbon," she added.

"We have more barrels of bourbon being aged than the state's population," he said. "But I'm in tobacco."

"Where in Kentucky do you live?" Julia asked.

"Louisville," he replied.

"Didn't Louisville have one of the largest slave markets before the Civil War?" Julia asked. She frequently surprised Adam with obscure facts, the result of working for the ACLU, he guessed.

"We sure did. Those were the days when you could make a fortune in tobacco," he said.

"But at what a price," Julia retorted.

"After the Civil War a majority of the blacks left for the North. That means that over 90 percent of today's Kentuckians are descended from northern Europeans," he boasted.

"It's great to be white and live in a white state," she added.

"It's just the opposite here," said Julia. "Well under half of San Franciscans are white."

"That must be tough for you," he said.

"Why would you think that?" Julia asked. Adam could tell that she was now inching toward a fight.

"Because, as we European descendants say, 'We must secure the existence of our people and a future for white children.'"

"What about other people's children?" Julia asked, not giving an inch.

"Ask yourself: who have been the great leaders, the great thinkers, the great writers even—not that I'm a big reader—of civilization?" he said.

"Are you thinking of Confucius? Or Genghis Kahn? Or Muhammad? Or Martin Luther King?" Julia asked.

"Of course there might be a few exceptions," he said, annoyed. "But take King. He was a leader of the Civil Rights Movement, something that did enormous damage to this country."

"Really. How?" Julia asked icily.

"It broke God's Law. God never intended for America to become the melting pot it became after the Civil Rights Movement. Martin Luther King was no true interpreter of God's Word."

"But everyone interprets God's Word differently."

"The Bible is the family history of the white race, whose origins are listed in the Old Testament as the twelve tribes of Israel."

"What makes you think the twelve tribes were white? Jewish, yes. Olive-skinned like the Arabs, yes."

"Like the Arabs!" Both of them looked offended.

"What's wrong with looking like an Arab?" Julia asked, wanting to provoke them.

"You don't get it," he said. "We whites, including you, are facing an invasion by Islamicists, as well as Central Americans, and perverts from all over the world. They are a cancer invading the body of this great country. They want to extinguish us. I've heard it was them who intentionally spread the coronavirus here."

"Whoever told you that needs a lesson in geography," said Julia. "There have been over 200 deaths in Wuhan and none in the States."

Julia's ability to confidently summon facts was clearly annoying the guy in particular.

"You can quote as many fake facts as you please. But God's troops know who the followers of Satan are."

"I'd rather be on the side of Satan if being part of God's troops means hating the majority of the world's population, which you appear to do."

"You wet liberals don't realize that we are fighting the good fight to save this country for our children and our grandchildren. It's us or them."

"No. It's us *and* them," Julia said.

The guy turned to the woman. "Let's go before I lose my temper. Some people spend their lives with their heads stuck in the sand."

"And some people spend their lives hating everyone who's not exactly like them," Julia shouted at their retreating backs.

Those near them who had overheard the heated conversation did their best not to catch their eyes or get involved.

"How about sampling some chocolates?" Adam suggested.

"You weren't much help in that argument," Julia said as they slowly made their way to the lower deck where all the chocolates were laid out.

"I don't see the point of engaging with bigots like them. You're never going to change their minds."

"That doesn't mean that you have to stand silently by while they spout their hate."

"This was meant to be an escape from all that."

"It wasn't my fault that guy chose to butt into our conversation."

They now found themselves surrounded by displays of every variety of chocolate, each a winner of some competition somewhere. The first curated selection that caught Adam's eye was a #1 winner from Kentucky—bittersweet ganache with a bit of caramel and Jefferson County bourbon. Anything from Kentucky was out of the question now.

The wrappings were as fancy as the chocolates—pink cardboard boxes with gold ties, glass storage jars, see-through cellophane packets with red bows, even original paintings done in coconut butter.

They stopped in front of an Oakland chocolatier that he'd never heard of. He was offering samples of "elegant and complex micro-batch bonbons."

"Fancy trying one of these?" he asked Julia.

"I'm not crazy about bonbons of any kind."

They drifted on. The smell of chocolate in the confined cabin was becoming overwhelming. Another display featured three kinds of chocolate samples—dark, red wine, and Belize. Adam asked for a Belize. When he looked at Julia she indicated she was uninterested.

"The smell is making me feel nauseous," she said.

"Okay we'll get out of here. But, before we do, can I buy you a box of anything?"

"The last thing I want right now are chocolates. Let's go, please."

They ended up with no chocolates to take home. Just Julia in a bad mood.

Adam had hoped for a fun day and he had no idea the yacht trip would be so precious—in the wrong sense. It clearly offended Julia's working-class instincts. It had put him off too, with its appeal to the entitled few and tourists who could momentarily persuade themselves that they were savoring a privileged lifestyle. Sure, Adam liked wine a lot, but he found himself annoyed by the specialized vocabulary that made people think they were initiates of an elite secret society of connoisseurs. Those flowery descriptions were meant to persuade you that the outrageous prices were justified. The entire expedition had left him depressed. And Julia clearly blamed him for involving them in a scene that was so alien to their outlook and taste. On the drive home they both remained silent and annoyed with one another, although he had little reason to be angry at her.

He recalled that the original Valentine of Rome was martyred and had little connection to romantic love. Too bad.

Q

Brad and Michael picked up Adam, as arranged, in a beat-up red Honda CR-V. The car radio played rock songs Adam didn't know and the young men happily moved their bodies in time to the music. When Adam asked what address they were making for, they both avoided providing details.

"It's in the Tenderloin District," Brad volunteered.

"And what's the name of the guy running this thing?" Adam asked.

"We all go by our Twitter names. His is QChamp88."

"That's quite a mouthful."

"What's your handle?" Brad asked.

"AdamGosford13. Surely everyone is not going to address me by that?"

"We usually just use the first bit. Like Adam in your case."

"And what do you call QChamp78?"

"88. We call him Champ."

"I see. And you two?

"Our handles begin with our first name. So, no sweat."

"Got it."

"History of Violence" blasted on the radio and cut short the conversation as both students started singing along: "No one is safe. No one is safe from you."

Turning onto Eddy Street from Leavenworth they found a parking space without difficulty. A rough, young, long-haired, white guy who looked as if he lived on the streets rapidly approached and said, "Spare a five?"

Aggressively he stuck out a dirty, open hand.

"Forget it," Brad said. "We're students. No cash."

The panhandler zeroed in on Adam.

"You're no student. What about it? What's five bucks to you?" This wasn't a question.

"You have a strange way of asking," Adam said.

"Who the fuck do you think you are?" he shouted. "I told you I needed five bucks. What more do you want? Want me to lick your ass?"

Brad and Michael were looking at Adam as if to say, Let's get this over. He pulled out his wallet and found he only had twenties and four ones.

"That's all the change I've got," he told the guy.

"I saw those twenties."

"It's four or nothing."

"What a stingy motherfucker," he spat out as he grabbed the bills and stormed off down the street shouting, "Asshole! Prick! Tight ass! Jerkoff!"

"Welcome to the Tenderloin District," Brad grinned.

Brad rang the bell of an intercom next to a door with no name or number on it.

"Hello?"

"Champ! It's Brad and Michael. And we've brought Adam with us."

"Come on up."

After climbing two flights of cement steps, they were greeted at the front door by Champ. He was in his thirties, short-cropped hair, hard faced with tight lips and an aggressive stare. And dark glasses, though the apartment received no direct sunlight. He was wearing an open-necked blue shirt, dark pants, and white sneakers.

"So, you're Adam? I'm Champ," he said as he gripped Adams' hand with a vicelike hold.

"Nice to meet you," Adam replied, trying not to show the pain.

"Come and meet the others."

There were about eight others of various ages sitting in a variety of uncomfortable looking chairs, six of them men. He introduced each by name, but Adam felt unnerved and forgot each name as soon as Champ moved on. The three of them helped themselves to coffee on a plastic tabletop and sat down on an unoccupied sofa from which the stuffing obtruded out of an unraveled length of seam. The room was characterless—just a lot of second-hand, ill-matching furniture, an odd mat, a bare bulb hanging from the flaking ceiling, and dingy cream walls with a dirty single latch window.

"We're all here now," Champ announced. "So let me start by saying that this hasn't been a bad week for us. We've got what looks like a Socialist running for the Democrats against our guy this November. The day before yesterday the president retweeted one of our accounts that also tagged two hashtags, '#IslamisSatanism' and "#HitlerDidNothingWrong.' Yeah! And our new enemy, China, just reported 66,492 coronavirus cases and 1,523 deaths. As Q posted, 'A week to remember. Dark to light.'"

Wonderfully enigmatic as usual. Each QAnon follower could make it mean what he or she needed it to mean.

One of the older men, dressed in fatigues, who could have been a veteran, spoke up. "And did you read that post that white folks, unlike Asians, are immune to the coronavirus?"

A large red-faced woman added, "I read that everyone already has the virus from previous vaccinations. So, wearing a mask, as they're doing in Wuhan, activates it."

"Right. All those scientists pushing the president to take action against the virus are only in it for the huge profits to be made from coming up with a treatment," the first guy said.

"Everything about the spread of this virus smells fishy to me," Champ said. "This whole outbreak is just the latest hoax by the Democrats. It's something they dreamed up to hurt our president. But he's too smart for them."

The conversation continued along these lines for almost an hour, during which time most of those present aired a bewildering variety of grudges and suspicions, ranging from the supposed voter fraud in California during the 2016 election to criminal conspiracies being pursued by members of the deep state, including Bill Gates, Barack Obama, Hillary Clinton, Warren Buffet, and Joe Biden.

The group seemed particularly taken with the president's latest charges against Biden—about how he, Obama and other members of the deep state concocted all the allegations about the president conspiring with Russia. They were trying to take down their president. How could they call themselves Democrats when they were doing their damnedest to unseat a democratically elected president?

Adam held his tongue for fear of alienating the group. At the same time, Champ seemed to address his remarks directly to Adam and smiled in his direction when silently agreeing with something being said by one of the others. Towards the end Champ directed the discussion to current international politics.

"Did you see that breadcrumb from Q today? 'Iran plotting something big?' You wait. My information is that the president will announce that Iran plans to launch a massive cyberattack against our country with the aim of disrupting the primaries and undermining the president's chances of getting re-elected."

"We can do more cyber-damage to the Iranians than they can ever do to us," Brad asserted. "But won't the fake news ask the president for proof?"

"You're right, Brad," Champ said. "But I can foresee the response. The president or his National Security Advisor will claim that the evidence is crystal clear but cannot be made public because it is highly classified."

"Q-level security?" Brad asked.

"You got it," Champ answered. "I understand that the president will proclaim a threat of war, which will enable him to invoke Section 706 of the 1996 Communications Act."

Champ stopped there, knowing that no one else would have any idea what the Act or Section said.

"What's Section 706 say?" Brad asked on cue.

"I thought you might ask, so I looked it up on Google," Champ replied. "Section 706 gives the FCC authority to promulgate rules governing an open internet. To prevent the spread of Iranian disinformation, the FCC can take control of all internet traffic inside the United States."

"Oh, man," the vet-like guy said. "Finally, our man in the White House will get to veto the fake news."

"I wouldn't go that far," Champ said. "But the president, through the FCC, could target particular left-leaning websites."

"On what grounds?" Adam asked.

"That these websites were unduly influenced by Iran."

"And how would the government justify picking on these sites?"

"By claiming that their determinations were classified. You see? Foolproof."

"Great," Brad said.

"There are also other laws," Champ said, "that would allow the president additional powers to punish the deep state."

"About time," the large red-faced woman said.

Everyone seemed excited by this information, speculative as it was.

Shortly after this the meeting broke up. Champ's parting shot was a hope that he would see Adam back.

In the car Brad switched to an R & B station. Adam hardly knew any of the songs, but Post Malone's "Goodbyes" with its refrain, "I want you out of my hea-ead," struck a chord in him. Yet who or what he wanted out of his head he couldn't decide.

On the drive back he thought over the meeting. What a huge pile of manure they had all talked. Yet, just like the president's rally, the meeting had ended on a note of mutual congratulations and a universal feeling of euphoria. Everyone felt reassured by the prejudices they shared. Their private hang-ups gave way to a feeling that they were on the winning side of an all-important battle between right and wrong, good and evil, God and the Devil. They all saw things in black and white. Just trust your gut and to hell with any inconvenient facts getting in the way of your collective beliefs. They left the meeting no longer feeling like losers. Instead, they were conquering members of the army of the Lord. It beat even a church service. How appropriate that it was held on a Sunday morning.

Back home, Adam found Julia broken up by a tweet Dave posted that morning. It had already been retweeted more than a hundred times, she said. He asked to look at it.

"I don't want to show it to you," she wailed.

"Don't be silly. Let me see it. Please."

She handed him her cell phone. It began with a naked photo of Julia thirteen years younger looking shy and vulnerable. Underneath, the caption read, "This is Julia, the bitch that ditched me for a Chad called Adam. They live at 4739 Florio Street, Oakland. This Stacy thinks she's too good for me. WTF. She's so stuck up. Why don't you go kill yourself, ho?"

"What a total asshole," Adam said.

"That picture of me!" Julia wailed.

"Have you asked Twitter to take this post down?"

"No," Julia said tearfully. "I felt too humiliated."

"Why's that?"

"Everyone will blame me for letting him take a nude photo of me. It's awful." Julia was angry, but her eyes were filled with tears.

"Here, let me do it," he said, taking her phone. He punched in a request to Twitter to take down the post.

Looking at her nude figure on the phone, he said, "You look so beautiful. It's not as if you're offering yourself as a sex object."

"You don't understand," she shouted. "There I am, exposed to the whole world," she said, near tears.

"Think of it as a generous free offering to the world," he joked, trying to lighten the mood.

"It's all very well for you to laugh at it. But it makes me feel dirty.

I can just see some of my girlfriends showing it to their partners and asking them whether I turn them on."

"The part of it that worries me is his doxxing us."

"Doxxing?"

"You know. 'Docs.' 'Documenting.' Making public our address for everyone on Twitter and beyond."

"It makes me feel incredibly vulnerable. I hate him, the evil fuck."

"Let's at least mute Dave from your Twitter."

"What does muting do?"

"Muting and not following him means you won't see any more of his tweets and he won't know that you've silenced him. Blocking can infuriate a cyber stalker and send them to the next level."

"I'm feeling extra tired," Julia said. "Would you mind doing it for me, please?"

"If you want. There."

"Thank you, cariño. That's why I married a computer expert." Julia did her best to give the impression that she'd recovered her cool. But she still looked haunted. She quickly excused herself to go take a tranquillizer and Adam went upstairs to see what Liz was up to in her room.

Q

President's Day. Washington's birthday. Well, not quite. But today was the culmination of the three-day sales event that had become its real meaning for Americans. At a cabinet meeting last October the president claimed that he was following the example of George Washington in trying to profit from his presidency. The so-called fake media promptly identified this as his 13,500[th] false claim as president. For the past few months he'd been making an average of 22 false claims a day.

No one had to go to work. In bed checking out Google News on his phone, Adam read the principal headline: "President Alleges Iran Plans Massive Cyberattack." Wow! Champ apparently had good information. From Q? Was Q truly an important government official with the highest security clearance? Yesterday Adam had been convinced that Champ's inside dope was just more bullshit, in line with all the other groundless theories aired that day. He read on.

This morning the president spoke from the Oval Office. "I have been informed by my intelligence services that the Iranian state is planning a massive cyberattack on the United States in the very near future. They want to disrupt our primary elections. They also want to undermine my chances of being re-elected. As your president I am convening my National Security Council to advise me on an appropriate response. They will live to bitterly regret their plan to attack the most powerful country in the world."

Excited, he turned to Julia who was rubbing Lucky's upturned belly. He told her that Champ's prediction the day before was confirmed in this morning's feed.

"You see what this means?" he said to her. "I'm penetrating a network that receives advance classified information from top government intelligence services. QAnon is more than just a crazy set of postings. It has secret links with the White House."

"Do you think a visit to Fairyland today would still appeal to Liz?" Julia asked. It was clear that she couldn't arouse any interest in his investigation of the QAnon network.

"Fairyland primarily appeals to kids under nine," he responded. "But don't you think it is revealing that Champ knew what the president would announce the day before?"

"I guess so. Okay, then what about taking her to the Steinhart Aquarium?"

"Why don't we ask her?"

He gave up trying to get a response from Julia.

When they asked Liz what she wanted to do that day, she told them she'd arranged to spend the afternoon with a friend her own age who lived up the street. She was growing up fast.

Adam was really knocked back by the uncanny way that Champ had anticipated the president's announcement that morning. Attending the rally and the QAnon group meeting had turned out to be worth the trouble after all.

After breakfast Adam settled down at his computer to review all his tweets from the past and weed out the left-leaning ones. He didn't want Champ or anyone in the group to find him airing his liberal outlook, however indirectly.

For instance here was one he posted in January 2018: "POTUS terminates Commission on Voter Fraud rather than turn over its working docs to Democratic members of the Commission. So much for the president's claim that 3-5m people voted illegally in 2016."

He was surprised at how many tweets he needed to remove.

Adam even found a response he posted to a December 2017 tweet with a QAnon hashtag asking, "Why did so many DEMS, including Hillary and DC, have unsecured servers? They wanted to be 'hacked.' It's how they SOLD our secrets to our enemies." His response briefly described how those in the computer world knew there was no such thing as a totally secure server.

While he was searching Twitter he came across a retweet of a post suggesting that Michele Obama was really a man. A skeptic had questioned this, to which the re-tweeter replied, "Research it." Followers of QAnon are impervious to facts, he thought. They exist within a bubble that protects them from the everyday atmosphere in which everyone else lives.

Deleting his give-away posts was a compromise he was willing to make. But there was no way he was going to add right-leaning posts as cover. Besides, that might arouse more suspicion than sticking to a politically neutral history of tweets.

Once he'd finished his deletions, he emailed QChamp88 to say he would be interested in attending another meeting, while indicating that he had not abandoned his reservations about some of QAnon's more outlandish beliefs—he mentioned, as an example, the whole pedophile ring conspiracy. Champ responded promptly, inviting Adam to their next meeting the following Sunday, and providing him with the address and time. At the same time he added that, with a community the size of QAnon, there was bound to be a range of opinions some of which were mutually exclusive. Like Q, he believed it was up to every follower to research the material for himself and make his mind up accordingly.

Champ's handle led him to look up whether "88" had a special significance. It did. It turned out that "88" stood for "Heil Hitler," as "H" is the eighth letter in the alphabet. Apparently, it was commonly used by white nationalists across the globe. Of course, it could mean other things, such as the double directions of the infinity of the universe, which provided its users with a convenient cover. Champ, who was no dummy, if questioned, would no doubt fall back on that safer definition.

Later that afternoon Julia returned from a shopping trip with Amy.

"Did you find anything to tempt you?" Adam asked her.

"Have you even looked at me since I got back?"

"What are you talking about?"

"Do you see nothing different about my appearance?" she asked.

He looked her over carefully. He couldn't detect anything new.

"Is it your shoes?" he took a stab in the dark.

"Bravo. I left wearing navy blue wedges and return with new black ankle boots. What could be more different?"

"I'm sorry. I'm so focused on this QAnon thing that I'm becoming blind to the world around me."

"You always were blind to what I was wearing. I guess all men are like that. Except the few gay guys I know who have as good an eye for fashion as my women friends do."

"Sorry I'm not gay," he replied.

"There's no need to get sarcastic."

"Sorry again," he said.

Adam seemed to be spending a lot of time these days apologizing to Julia. Their entire relationship had acquired an edge to it. What was happening? And, come to think of it, why was Julia avoiding any sexual contact with him? Was that in itself causing the tension? Somehow he doubted it. More like a symptom. But he couldn't determine what was causing them to become competitive, even adversarial in their exchanges.

"By the way," Julia said, "did you hear that today a second person died of the coronavirus in Santa Clara County? Now people are dying in the US."

"No, I didn't."

"Too close for comfort. Amy told me she read online that people in countries such as India and Africa, who eat a lot of spicy foods, are not dropping like flies because spicy food is constantly flushing their lungs."

"But all food passes by the lungs. It doesn't enter them, as you well know."

"Too bad. I was thinking of cooking turkey chili for dinner tonight."

"Sounds like a great idea. Just don't expect it to flush your lungs or protect you from the virus."

"Then what does?' she asked.

"Your natural immune system is, so far, the only known factor that can fight it."

"That reminds me, I forgot to take my vitamins this morning." Julia got up. "I'm off to the kitchen to catch up on them," she called out as she exited the living room.

Her phobia about the virus was getting more pronounced, he reflected. What with taking her temperature every morning, obsessively washing her hands, and believing in quack prophylactics, she worried him. But what could he do? Any suggestion that she was overreacting only made her more defensive and less likely to listen to him.

He felt as if he was being swept out to sea by an undercurrent of fear more powerful than he was. All he could hope to do was swim at right angles to it. There was no way of swimming against it.

Q

While commuting to work on BART Julia looked up Google News on her phone. The war of words between Iran and the president was heating up. The Ayatollah denounced the Great Satan and said the president was concocting another fiction by alleging that Iran planned a massive cyber-attack on the US. Asked by reporters for evidence of a predicted attack, the president replied that the evidence was incontrovertible but highly classified. Instead, he threatened all-out war. Words, words, words, she remembered Hamlet replying when Polonius asked him what he was reading. Men waving their dicks at one another. Tiresome.

Was she becoming anti-male? Hardly. She was confused by the way she was turned on by the macho type she otherwise despised and turned off by the considerate type she otherwise admired. How messed up was that? It made her feel schizophrenic. But in the case of the macho president she had no such conflict. Why was he so complacent about the spread of the virus across the world? It was bound to spread here. It was already doing so. Before she could work herself up further, she reached Embarcadero.

At work she felt as if she'd eaten glass. She was getting cramps at regular intervals. She also was as nauseous as she remembered feeling during the early months of her pregnancy. The thought of drinking even a glass of water made her want to throw up. In fact, within an hour, she did throw up her breakfast. It put her in an even worse mood.

That day she was researching a case concerning police officers who were members of Facebook groups tied to Confederate, anti-Islam, and anti-government causes. They denied the authority of the federal government while claiming that local sheriffs and police chiefs were the only legitimate forms of law enforcement in the country.

Julia had asked Tina to gather any available evidence about one of these groups, the Oath Keepers, a far-right militia movement. The ACLU was considering suing it over its excessive use of force at a Richmond gun rights rally the previous month. Comparing Tina's material with her own research, Julia found some obvious gaps that left her wondering what other key elements Tina had failed to find or omitted. Julia called her over.

"Tina, this is a shoddy piece of work," she began curtly.

"What do you mean?" Tina asked nervously.

"Well, why is there no mention of the rally by Second Amendment supporters outside the Virginia Senate on January 13? Why is there nothing about the Oath Keepers providing armed security at the president's two rallies in Dallas and Tupelo in fall 2019? I could go on if you like."

"You only gave me this project yesterday morning. What I gave you is a preliminary set of incidents."

"Then why didn't you label this as incomplete?"

"Because I was planning on telling you myself that it was still a work in progress."

"But you didn't tell me before I read it. What am I supposed to think?"

"Why are you being so horrid to me?" Tina was close to tears. She always had been overly sensitive. She'd never acquired the necessary thick skin that women needed in a competitive workplace.

"What exactly is horrid about asking for a fully researched response?"

"But I just told you—" At his point Tina burst out crying and fled to the bathroom.

Jill looked daggers at Julia but said nothing.

What exactly was happening to her? It was obvious that she was taking out on Tina her own pain and consequent irritability. When Julia had sworn off OxyContin since Sunday, she hadn't expected to experience what she assumed were withdrawal symptoms. But that must be what was driving her crazy. It wasn't just her stomach cramps and nausea. She hadn't slept much at all last night, and she was feeling incredibly tired and depressed this morning.

No good reason to make poor Tina break into tears. That was not like her. So what did she need to do to stop acting like this? There was only one action she could think of. She reached into her purse and extracted two tablets of OxyContin and swallowed them without liquid. Two hours later she was joking with Tina and Jill over lunch.

When Julia got home that evening Adam was waiting to give her an update on the charge of sexual harassment. He had been interviewed by the Title IX officer on campus that morning. Her name was Elaine Krenshaw and she conducted the interview with great formality.

"She was very prickly. She started off," Adam said, "assuring me that anything I said would be treated confidentially. She asked me whether I wanted an advisor present to assist me, to which I said no. Next, she asked me to describe chronologically my actions on Tuesday, January the 28th, the day I supposedly harassed Natalie French. So I retraced my actions over that day. You know: Arrived on campus at 8:30. In office—with no visitors—until 9:55. Taught my sophomore class, Internet and Network Security, from 10 until 10:50. Five minutes before the end of the class, had verbal exchange with Natalie French about how free any market can be, followed by an apology after class for being too harsh in what I said. Elaine, as she asked me to call her, despite her barely concealed distaste for me, asked whether any other students had heard my apology. I told her it was essentially a private conversation, though other students were standing around talking to one another. 'You're sure none of them heard what you and Natalie were saying?' she asked. I couldn't say definitively whether we had been overheard or not. The entire conversation lasted probably no more than a minute."

"Hardly enough time to sexually harass anyone," Julia commented.

"Who knows? At any rate, Elaine seemed particularly interested in my movements between the end of the class and the time my graduate seminar started. I told her I went straight from the classroom to the parking garage and drove to Bank of America where you and I had an 11:30 appointment with the chief lending officer. Of course, you remember that. At any rate, Elaine wanted contact information for the lending officer and asked if it was OK if she got in touch with him. She also wanted to know how much time I spent at the bank and when I got back to campus."

"So what happens next?"

"Elaine has to interview any witnesses, such as students still in the room after the class and the lending officer. Natalie may also have come up with witnesses. Once Elaine's initial assessment is complete, she can choose to close the case, begin a mediation, or move on to a formal investigation. Every bit of this is cast in iron. It could be a nightmare. I actually began to feel as if I were being harassed by the harassment officer. But, as I never did anything, all I can do is repeat that and hope for the best."

"I really am so sorry," she said.

"Yep. It's a bummer." Unlike his normal confident self, Adam looked completely baffled and uncertain. He was used to being in control of his life, and he didn't know how to respond to a situation in which he could only react rather than act. Julia went over to where he was sitting and gripped both his upper arms from behind.

"It's a lousy place to find yourself in, *cariño*. But these things pass. We'll just move on and forget it once it's over."

"I know you're right," he said, putting his hands over hers. "But it's hard to see it in a longer perspective right now."

The news that evening reported that more than 2,000 people had died of the coronavirus across the globe. This confirmed Julia's fear that the virus would soon be attacking them with the same ferocity it did the inhabitants of Wuhan. She went to the bathroom and took an OxyContin. That would assure her of a good night's sleep. Why, she asked, did she ever think she could do without the pills? This was an anxious time, and she was doing what she had to do to get through it.

Adam was in bed waiting for her. She slipped under the duvet and turned off her bedside light in one movement, signaling her desire to go straight to sleep. As Adam settled resignedly into the curve of her back she could feel his erection. What was wrong with her? Why couldn't she surrender her body to his desire? No. His love. She had no answer.

That night she dreamed that she was checking her Facebook feed when an image of an octopus appeared. The octopus began to slither out of the phone and become engorged. Soon it was large enough to swallow Lucky who disappeared down its throat howling with fear. As it continued to grow in size, it turned its attention to her. But it didn't want to eat her. Its tentacles began reaching out for her thighs. She crossed her legs, then tried to roll out of the bed to escape it. She woke up on the floor shaking with fright. Adam slept through it all.

Q

That Wednesday the president declared a national emergency under the International Emergency Economic Powers Act of 1977. This seemed ominous. After taking Liz to school, Adam searched Google and found: "The International Emergency Economic Powers Act is a powerful authority that allows the president to declare a national emergency with respect to any unusual and extraordinary threat to the national security foreign policy or economy of the United States that has its source, in substantial part, from overseas." The president could apparently block and freeze any financial transactions with Iran, including any US citizens providing support to Iran. It sounded extraordinarily broad. Sure enough, he found confirmation that the president had also invoked Section 706 of the 1996 Communications Act and had already shut down two left-leaning national organizations and their websites that were concerned with getting out the vote.

Prodded by a breadcrumb from Q, QAnon went wild on Twitter.

Q: "Why has POTUS gone around the three-letter agencies?"

Q's posts were provocations demanding explanations that Q's followers enjoyed providing. His— or her) —followers quickly jumped in with their own interpretations of the emergency declaration.

"National Emergency? Bring it ON. POTUS is not messing around. Wait for arrests."

"We are the next generation minutemen! Ready for the GREAT STORM Sir!"

"Biblical prophecy is being fulfilled. Thy Kingdom Come."

"Trust the PLAN. The Cabal and the three-letter agencies are doomed."

"ENJOY THE SHOW! WWG1WGA" This post featured a sponsored ad for an emergency flashlight.

Its thread included one tweet protesting the presence of the ad— "STOP exploiting QAnon for YOUR financial gain." Adam couldn't believe it. He recognized the username, DaveIra43. This was the Dave who was making Julia's life hell. Adam took a look at his recent tweets:

"QAnon and Incels – what's the difference?"

He followed the retweet with: "I'll clarify. QAnon members are also frequently incels. The crossover is high."

Adam had never linked the two together, but it made a kind of crazy sense. Wouldn't incels seek reassurance from the self-confidence of the QAnon community? Here Dave was posting a piece of its craziness:

"Irregular warfare. Insurgency. STAY STRONG FOR GOD AND COUNTRY."

Scrolling down, Adam found a post by Dave that may have been about Julia: "Stacy, you have always been the best lay. You're hotter than any other bitch I've had. Forget Chad. Return to your destiny."

This was scarier than Adam had allowed himself to notice. Just how did you shake off the attention of someone as obsessive as Dave? Adam racked his brain for some tangible action he could take to make Dave back off. But he couldn't imagine confronting Dave with a weapon. With Julia counting on him to come up with some sort of solution, he ended up angry at himself. Was he a physical coward or did he truly believe that violence only begets violence? What a nightmare this was.

After dinner that evening Julia and Adam were sitting on the sofa, watching an episode of their current favorite video series, *Spiral*, a French police procedural. Liz was doing homework—supposedly—in her room.

"Is that your phone?" Julia asked.

Adam dug it out of his pocket. The call was from an unknown number.

"Looks like spam," he said. He turned it off and threw it down on the sofa.

A minute later Liz entered hurriedly and said, "Why are there a lot of police cars outside?"

Adam went to the front door while Julia pressed pause on the remote. As he opened it he was blinded by several spotlights focused on him. A voice from a megaphone thundered: "Put your hands on top of your head. NOW!" As his sight began to return he could see the barrel of a gun pointed at his head.

Shaken and scared of being shot, he did as he was told.

"Turn around and face the door." He obeyed again.

"Slowly walk backwards toward us with your hands on your head. SLOWLY, I said. STOP! Now, kneel down."

Terrified, he carefully followed every direction.

"Slowly move your arms down along your back. Good. You will now be handcuffed. Do not try and resist."

He wanted to scream NO but knew better.

Once he was handcuffed the police rushed into the house. Julia told him afterwards that Lucky started to run at the first officer to enter the room, but Liz grabbed him before he could get to him. Adam could hear the cops shouting commands to Julia and Liz and began to protest when an officer told him, "Shut up and this will go easier for everyone."

Next, he led Adam into the living room where a white-faced Julia and a sobbing Liz were sitting handcuffed on two chairs. Two other officers left the room presumably to search the house.

One officer was talking into a phone: "We have a man and woman in their thirties and a female child around nine in custody."

"What the hell is going on?" Adam managed to ask with fear-tinged indignance.

"We ask the questions," he said. "Name?"

Each of them gave him their name and confirmed that they were husband, wife and daughter.

"Why didn't you answer your phone when I called you?" the officer asked Adam.

"I thought it was a spam call."

"Do you have a gun in the house?"

"No we don't."

"Is there anyone else living here?"

"No."

"I need IDs for both of you."

Adam nodded toward his front trousers pocket from which the officer carefully extracted his wallet with driving license. Julia gestured to her purse. The cop examined their licenses and compared them to some document he had brought with him.

"Okay. You need to know that you are not under arrest. We have detained you for your own safety."

"Who or what is threatening us?" asked Adam.

"We received a call from your phone claiming that you had shot your wife and were holding your daughter hostage. You promised to shoot any police officer who tried to enter your house."

"That makes no sense. As you can see, my wife and daughter are fine."

"Please tell me where your cell phone is, so I can check your recent calls."

Adam gestured with his head to the sofa where he'd left it. The officer picked it up and asked Adam if he used facial recognition. When he said he did, the officer turned it on and held it up to Adam's face to get entry. After a minute looking through his recent calls and emails he turned it off.

"You can take the handcuffs off them," he told a fellow officer.

Once they were all free the officer said, "I'm afraid you are all victims of a hoax."

"A hoax?" Julia exclaimed.

"Yes, ma'am. Swatting— when someone who knows your name, address and phone number uses caller-ID spoofing and, in your case, a voiceover IP number to conceal their identity and location. The caller pretended to be Mr. Gosford."

"And you believed them?" Adam asked.

"If you had answered your phone, sir, we would not have had to go through this."

"Will you be able to trace the caller?"

"We will try. But scammers these days have figured out how to leave no trace."

Adam looked at Julia. They clearly both thought the likely hoaxer was Dave.

"We have a pretty good idea who the scammer is," Adam volunteered.

"I'm afraid we can only proceed on hard evidence," he replied.

"As I thought," Adam replied.

After the officer had taken down details of Dave as prime suspect, he said, "If that is all, sir, we'll leave you to spend the rest of your evening in peace."

Julia and Adam sat down on the sofa with their arms round Liz. She was still crying. Julia was visibly shaking. Adam tried to conceal his own shock.

Why is it men think they need to repress shows of emotion? Adam asked himself. Was he doing it for the sake of the other two? If he'd broken down with them, would that have been so awful?

Liz asked to sleep in their bed that night. None of them got much sleep.

Q

On her way to work Julia read that the president had warned Iran that, if any of its gunboats came within half a mile of an American ship, they would be blasted out of the water. The Ayatollah responded that any provocative act from the US would lead to Iran's closing the Strait of Hormuz. A CNN poll found that 63 percent of Americans considered Iran a threat to American interests. Another news item reported that the government had shut down a number of websites accused of funding or trading with Iran. In the process, it had also shut down several sites that the president had perceived as opposed to his ideas or his re-election. But when asked what the precise grounds were for their closure, the White House responded without blinking that this was classified information.

One of the websites taken down by the president's emergency powers was a voter registration organization in San Francisco. Why the president should feel threatened by an increase in registered voters was quite apparent, seeing how the majority of Americans were opposed to his latest abuse of power. Julia knew one of the interns at The Voting Foundation and called her after she had reached her office. She asked Julia if the ACLU would file an appeal on their behalf, as without a website they could hardly function.

Julia called her boss to ask whether they could intervene. Her boss said they were already reviewing the case but added that it was extraordinarily difficult to argue a case where the government pleaded national security and withheld what they claimed was classified evidence.

Early that afternoon Julia received a call from the principal of Chabot Elementary. Could she and Adam come in today? She wanted to discuss an incident involving Liz but wouldn't go into details. Julia called Adam, who said he could be there by 4:30. After asking for permission to leave work early, she confirmed the appointment with the principal, Ms. Johnson, and spent the rest of her time at work wondering what this could be all about.

On arriving at Chabot, Adam and Julia were told that Liz was in with the school counselor. They were ushered into the principal's office promptly at 4:30 and offered chairs, and water or tea. Ms. Johnson was Black, about fifty, gray hair and glasses. She gave off an air of competence and empathy.

"Liz has always been an exemplary student," she began. "We all find her eager to learn and cooperative in group situations. So, we were taken completely by surprise this morning at lunch break when she got into a physical altercation with Sandra, another girl in her class."

"That doesn't sound like Liz," Julia commented.

"I agree. This is a little delicate. Apparently, Sandra was sharing a tweet with some other children in the class that showed you, Mrs. Gosford, naked and was accompanied by some very nasty remarks about you. Obviously, this was an attack by someone who wanted to hurt you."

She was looking directly at Julia.

"I know the tweet you are referring to. The man posting it was someone from my past who has been harassing me for a while now," Julia explained.

"I see. I'm sorry." The principal hesitated. "And I'm sorry I have to fill you in on the details. It seems that when Liz approached the group, Sandra said to her something like, 'This says your mom's a slut.' More words were exchanged. Liz demanded an apology. Sandra refused, and it ended with Liz pushing Sandra backwards while screaming that she was a liar. Sandra lost her footing and hit her head. By this time some teachers had been alerted and Sandra was taken to the school nurse who bandaged a small cut but said she thought it possible that the girl might be suffering a mild concussion."

"How awful," Julia said.

Adam recounted the story of yesterday's terrifying raid by the swat team, after which none of them could sleep. "We all know that violence breeds violence," he finished.

The principal thought that could well be a mitigating factor. Strange how everyone resorts to pseudo-legalistic vocabulary on occasions like this.

"Do you know how Sandra is now?" Julia asked.

"I saw her with her mother when school ended. Sandra appeared to be fine. Naturally, her mother was furious and wanted to know if I was suspending Liz I told her that I couldn't share any information about Liz without your consent."

"So?" Julia asked.

"We never act on one incident alone. These are obviously quite dramatic extenuating circumstances. And, as I said, Liz has been an exemplary student. If you two don't object, let's talk to Liz and the school counsellor. We might be able to work something out."

"Of course," Julia said.

"Agreed," said Adam.

The principal brought in Liz and the counselor.

"Liz and I have discussed what happened," the counselor began. "I made clear that hurting another student is unacceptable under any circumstances. She appears to understand that. She was provoked by Sandra, that is clear. She immediately regretted her action. I arranged for her to talk with Sandra when she returned from the nurse's office, and she made a genuine apology."

"And did Sandra apologize back?" Julia asked indignantly.

"Sandra was the injured one," the counselor replied.

"So, it's all right to say nasty things about another student's mother?"

The principal intervened. "I will be talking to Sandra when she returns to school. What all of us need to do right now is help Liz—and all of the students—understand that a lot of what is posted on social media is untrue or misleading."

"You do understand, Liz," Julia said, "that this person is trying to hurt me? He will do anything to get at me. He wants others to think I'm a horrible person."

"You're not, Mommy," Liz said.

The principal concluded by explaining to Liz that the online world was going to play a huge role in her life and she needed to learn to read everything in it with skepticism.

Throughout the proceedings Liz looked mostly at her mother, as if she were someone different from the mother she knew. This played on Julia's guilt and she felt her anger at Dave mounting. How dare he do this to her family? Liz was obviously absorbing and reproducing her own escalating anxiety.

By the time they got home Julia was feeling awful. It was all her fault. She had to maintain a calmer presence for Liz. The only way she could do that was by medicating herself more consistently. She went straight upstairs to the bathroom and took an OxyContin tablet. She knew she could count on Adam not noticing. Julia floated through the rest of the evening without giving Liz any cause to worry about her—or at least that's what she told herself.

Q

Friday. Early evening. Julia was sipping her first margarita. Adam was preparing dinner, linguine with shrimp and tomato sauce, a recipe that involved letting the tomato, wine and garlic simmer for half an hour while he savored his drink. He took the opportunity to fill Julia in on a phone call he'd had that day with the Title IX officer.

"Elaine has completed her preliminary investigation," he said. "She's talked to everyone involved."

"That was quick."

"Yes. She's concluded that Natalie French's accusation has no merit.

Apparently, the loan officer confirmed our appointment at the bank, and that didn't leave enough time for what Natalie said occurred."

"But that's fantastic, Adam."

"Yes. It's a huge relief. Had she chosen some other time for her supposed harassment, there would have been no way to disprove her lie."

"So, what are they going to do to her?" Julia asked.

"Elaine asked me what form of punishment I thought would be appropriate. I said I didn't want to ruin Natalie's school career. On the other hand I didn't want her in any of my classes now or in the future."

"I have to say, you are more forgiving than I am."

"At any rate, Elaine said that, in that case, she would issue a formal warning to Natalie, ask that she send me a letter of apology, and make it a condition of her continuing at Berkeley that she never enroll in any of my classes or make voluntary contact with me. Elaine also offered a half-hearted apology for what I'd been put through. I suspect it was half-hearted because most of her cases involve men denying any wrongdoing, which must warp her belief in men's testimony."

"I'm so relieved," Julia said. "That calls for another drink," she added holding out her glass and grinning.

"If only it were as easy to get Dave out of our lives," Adam remarked.

"That reminds me. I unmuted Dave's tweets just long enough to read his latest salvo. It consisted of a quotation from Deuteronomy: 'I the Lord, your God, am a jealous God, visiting the iniquity of the fathers on the children.'"

"Seriously?"

"I'm terrified. I think he's warning that he will target Liz."

"That's why I told you to mute his Twitter feed. It only makes you more anxious."

"I can't believe you're not taking this threat seriously." Julia looked furious.

At that moment the timer went off for the sauce and thankfully he returned to the stove.

When dinner was ready Adam went upstairs to get Liz. It was no good calling her as she frequently had her earphones on. When he entered her room after knocking he saw that she was on her bed crying. He went over and sat down next to her, putting his arm round her shaking shoulders.

"I'm so sorry this is happening, honey."

Liz was sobbing and had trouble getting out the words. "That photo of Mommy."

"What about it?"

"It's all over the school."

"Liz, I know this is awful. But you can bet it will quickly be replaced by the next trending hashtag. A week from now everyone will be talking about something else."

"Everyone was looking at me and talking about Mommy."

"That's because they've got nothing better to talk about. There's nothing to be ashamed of about that photo."

"Was Mommy sexting?"

"No, not at all. She didn't send it to anyone. Someone else took it and posted it without her permission."

"That's so unfair."

"I know. Life can be unfair." Clichés, Adam reminded himself, only satisfy the user. He tried lightening the conversation. "But then life can also offer the prospect of a delicious, piping hot shrimp pasta," he said smiling, wiping her eyes with a tissue.

"Oh, Daddy. You're just trying to make me feel better."

"That I am. Come down with me and have some dinner. You'll feel better for it."

They went downstairs, hand in hand, and found Julia enjoying her third margarita.

Later that evening Adam reached the bedroom a few minutes after Julia. As he entered she was hurriedly shoving a pill bottle into her bedside drawer.

"My multivitamin," she explained.

"I thought you took one this morning," he remarked.

"You're my doctor now?"

He shut his mouth. But he distinctly remembered her swallowing one at breakfast. Come to think of it, she never kept her vitamins upstairs. Still, as she pointed out, he wasn't prescribing what she took. He let it go, once again.

The main item on the news was the next day's Nevada caucus. Julia was delighted that the polls said Bernie had a double-digit lead over Biden.

"But if," Adam said after hesitating, "Sanders becomes the nominee, all the experts say that the president will win."

"The experts!" Julia scoffed. "Look how well they did in predicting the 2016 presidential election."

"You might have a point there. But, faced with a self-styled socialist, almost every independent voter is going to go running into the president's camp."

"Biden's not going to radically change anything. He's just a political placebo."

"But Bernie is too left to bring the country together again," Adam said.

"Bernie would transform the tax system, the social safety net and healthcare. This country's in such a huge mess that only radical changes can stop it going down the toilet."

"For me, what matters most is stopping the bigot from getting reelected."

"I would rather risk everything to bring about real change." That was Julia all over. "I hate the inequality both parties allow to go on and on. It's obscene. Millions relying on food stamps, if they can get them. Millions unable to take their children to a doctor. Millions paid minimum wage. That's $7.25 an hour nationally. How can you possibly raise a family on that amount? It's absurd."

Julia had always been a passionate leftist, too radical to call a liberal. Adam admired her fire. But he saw himself as more pragmatic than her. More of a realist, he told himself.

"If I were voting today, I would vote for Biden." he said. "I just can't risk letting that would-be dictator win a second term."

"If most Democrats vote like you, we'll only have more of the same. For me there's simply no choice. It's Bernie or nobody."

"You'll end up with the asshole serving a second term."

"And you'll end up effecting no change worth speaking of. What kind of country will you be leaving for Liz? Where's your backbone?"

"Where's your judgment? Can't you see you'll be voting for that buffoon?"

Julia scowled, turned off her bedside light and fell asleep almost immediately.

Q

Julia had arranged to go shopping with Amy this Saturday morning. Adam was home gardening with Liz helping him. Amy and Julia drove straight to the Stella Carakasi store a couple of blocks from Berkeley Marina. It was their favorite place to shop, even if it was a bit on the expensive side. There's nothing like an extravagant purchase to alleviate the tension Julia was feeling these days.

As she was browsing tunics, she said to Amy, "I always believe that the latest outfit I've bought will finally define me for who I really am. You know, 'Just look at me and you will instantly know my core self.'"

"Lucky you," she said.

"Why lucky?"

"I have no idea what my true self is—if I have one, that is. I have so many different and conflicting selves."

"Maybe I should say, 'My best version of myself.'"

"That I can understand. Though, even then I would want a different outfit for the best version of each of my many selves."

"That's probably the reason why I end up feeling let down by the latest outfit I've bought. By the time I wear it, a different self is judging it."

Julia picked an asymmetrical black top. "What do you think?" she asked Amy.

"I prefer the white."

"I'll take one."

Amy picked up a down puffer coat— "filled with 100% duck down." Julia caught a glimpse of the price tag—$389. Her cotton top was a mere $109. Amy also grabbed a boy's t-shirt for Robert, her eleven-year-old son.

Despite Amy rooting for the white top, Julia chose the black one. Amy bought the coat without much hesitation. But then her husband, Jeff, was a highly paid lawyer. Money didn't figure into the decision.

They had reserved a table for lunch at Chez Panisse Café nearby. Julia frequently cooked from Alice Waters' *The Art of Simple Food,* and she was totally in sync with the chef's emphasis on locally grown and sustainable ingredients. They each started with a glass of white wine—Verdicchio for Julia and white Burgundy for Amy. Julia chose a fennel and blood orange salad with black olives and mint, and Amy a wood-fired clam dish. They shared both dishes.

As they sat later savoring their coffee, Amy blurted out of the blue, "I've been feeling very unattractive lately."

"Why on earth would you feel that?" Julia asked. Amy was beautiful, with her turned-up nose and flashing eyes, and she used her wealth to enhance her natural features.

"Because Jeff hasn't initiated sex for several weeks now."

"Have you tried any of the time-honored ploys?"

"Such as?"

"Oh, like sexy underwear. Or offering to assume an unusual position?"

"I've tried everything in my repertoire. Yet he always finds some dumb excuse for not having sex."

"Could he be seeing someone else?"

"I've asked myself that, too. But he works so incredibly hard and for such long hours I doubt it."

"Long hours can offer an alibi for an affair." After a pause Julia asked, "If you had a choice would you want a friend in the know to tell you that Jeff was having an affair?"

"I think I would. I really can't say for sure," Amy said. She hesitated for a moment. "The trouble is that this enforced celibacy is making me feel very promiscuous. Have you ever strayed from Adam?"

Julia thought for a moment but decided to keep the fiasco with Dave to herself. "No."

"Have you checked out our waiter? No? He's gorgeous. You can see his pecs through his shirt. There I go. It's getting ridiculous."

"It sounds as if you two need to have a serious talk about this."

"Me and the waiter?"

Julia laughed.

"I know you're right. But Jeff and I find it so hard to talk about sex with one another. It's not that he's inhibited when it comes to doing it—or should I say, when it *came* to doing it. But he hates talking about it. And that makes me feel embarrassed to bring it up."

"Have you thought about arousing his jealousy by flirting openly with another man in your circle?"

"Who are you thinking of? Adam?"

"I think, currently, Adam would flirt straight back."

"Really. Why?"

"For no good reason I'm finding it hard to respond to his overtures." Julia regretted saying this as soon as the words were out of her mouth.

"There must be a reason," Amy insisted.

"All I know is that my body refuses to respond to his caresses, no matter how much my mind wants me to. It's like I'm at war with myself."

"Then it's simple," Amy broke out grinning. "All we need to do is swap partners. Then Adam and I could gorge ourselves in bed while you and Jeff could enjoy a mutually celibate existence."

"Problem solved."

How ironic, Julia reflected on her way home. What she couldn't tell Amy was that what her body—unlike her psyche—craved was a Dave, though not Dave himself. Someone who would overpower her and satiate himself with no thought for her. The Adams of this world had lost their physical magnetism. It was ridiculous. But that was how it was. That was how her body was, at least for now.

That evening Adam and Julia had been invited for drinks by a couple who lived a few doors up the street. They were some twenty years older. Paul, a realtor, was a genial host who spent most of his time filling up everyone's glasses and talking about house prices. His wife, Martha, was more opinionated. There were ten other neighbors there as well.

Julia was in the kitchen getting fresh ice for her second straight tequila on the rocks when Martha drifted over. She asked Julia whether she had heard about the Oakland cop who had been arrested yesterday for not reporting an arrest he made on Harwood Avenue, a block to the south.

"I read an account in the East Bay Times," Julia replied.

"Don't you think it's terrible the way he is being treated?"

"I think it is terrible the way he treated the Black guy. You don't put someone in handcuffs and then proceed to take them down. That's what I call criminal assault."

"But we all know that guy. He's a thief. He's stolen packages from lots of us, including me."

"Yes, I know him. His name is Freddie. He's a vet with PTSD. His only income comes from a pension worth $900 a month. I'm not saying he has a right to steal our packages. But he certainly doesn't deserve to be punched in the face for it while in handcuffs."

"The officer was only trying to teach him a lesson."

"A lesson! Our police are way too violent. They think violence is their right. It's high time that attitude changed."

"Without the police, where would we all be? They are only responding to the violence that might be directed at you and me without their protection."

"Stealing packages from porches is hardly an act of violence. Being thrown to the ground with your hands tied behind your back and punched in the face is."

Paul arrived with an open bottle of tequila and refilled Julia's glass. She thanked him and he moved on. She decided to try appealing to Martha's empathy.

"Have you imagined what Black people go through? Every time you leave the house you pray that you won't be pulled over by a cop. You teach your kids how to behave submissively if they are. You know that the odds are that any confrontation will end up with you in jail. Or worse."

"But that's exactly what we need to make criminals feel."

"I'm talking about ordinary Blacks trying to lead ordinary lives."

"But look at the statistics. A disproportionate number of Blacks are responsible for most of the crimes reported here."

"While most of the crimes committed by cops go unreported."

"That's not answering my question."

"Your statistics only prove that the police go in for racial profiling."

"You liberals have always been soft on crime."

"I believe that the police are hired to protect our constitutional rights. Not to deprive us of them."

"Without the police our neighborhood would be overrun by Black criminals."

"There you go," Julia shouted angrily. "All Black people are criminals in your eyes. That's plain racist."

"What are you calling me? How dare you!"

"I'm leaving right now. I would never have come if I'd known that's the way you think."

"So much for freedom of speech," Martha shouted after Julia's departing figure.

Q

Adam woke up feeling depressed. Why? Oh yes, because yesterday evening Julia had antagonized one of their neighbors. News of her argument with Martha would quickly spread through the local grapevine. People would inevitably take sides.

Why couldn't Julia have stepped away from a conversation that was obviously spiraling out of control? Because she'd had three tequilas was the most likely answer, although last night she insisted it was a matter of principle. She would call out racist remarks wherever they originated. He couldn't fault her for that. But, had she broken off earlier, there would have been no offensive words to object to.

He read the news on his cellphone. Responding to the latest threats from Iran, the president threatened to order preemptive strikes on their military installations. The *New York Times* reported that, in the Nevada caucuses, Sanders was ahead of Biden, receiving over twice the number of votes, with fifty percent of precincts reporting.

It looked as if Julia was going to get her wish. Bernie looked unstoppable. Things were unfortunately looking up for the president. The president feared "sleepy Joe Biden" because he was ahead of him in all the polls, and so he cheered on Sanders with relish.

When Adam arrived at Champ's rendezvous, the host greeted him like an old comrade. Adam accepted his painful bear hug and sat down in a dilapidated armchair in the corner of the room. There were about a dozen people present by the time Champ began the proceedings with his usual upbeat summary of how well things had gone the previous week. He was particularly excited by the success of Bernie Sanders in the latest primary. Things were looking good for their man in the White House, despite the dirty tricks the Democrats were up to.

That remark produced, as it was meant to, a stream of invective from some of the attendees about Democrats and the international ring of pedophiles, Democrats and their spread of the coronavirus, Democrats and the secret state.

One new guy called Chris—young, crew cut, dark hair, multiple tattoos, bulging muscles—accused the Democrats of endangering the white race by championing ethnic diversity. He had just gotten back from attending a military-style training camp in Oregon where he had learned "the truth" about white genocide.

"We talked about the coming race war that will finally get us a white state. We celebrated white pride and discussed how we could use civil disturbances to demand white power. It was great. Everyone there wanted to take on the Democrats with their calls for gun control. Around the campfire in the evening, we all chanted, 'Race over all.' 'You will not replace us.' and 'White power.' I feel totally energized. What we really need is a day of the rope, a civil war that will leave white Americans in total control of our country."

Many of the others cheered Chris on during this rant and followed it by wolf whistles and whoops. Adam told himself to keep his face neutral.

Chris next turned confessional. He shared with the group how he had been sexually abused as a choirboy by his priest. It had destroyed his faith, he said. But then he had discovered white pride, which had restored his self-confidence. That segued into his discovery of QAnon. As a victim of a pedophile, he could totally identify with a platform that wanted to revenge itself on some of the most powerful pedophiles in the world. Michael jumped in to tell about the sexual abuse he'd experienced from his scoutmaster. Champ quickly intervened to direct the discussion back to less personal subjects.

Adam wondered why he was subjecting himself to this garbage. Exactly what was he hoping to get from these forays into the world of QAnon? Was there any way to understand what was essentially not rational, what it was that held all these Americans in its spell? To dismiss it and them as deranged or misinformed, as he had started off doing, meant he was missing something essential. Everyone in that room was convinced that their reality was superior to that of the most respected scientists or journalists.

There was usually a spark of truth in the otherwise wildly speculative rumors that consumed these people. For instance, the guy in fatigues, who looked like a vet, brought up a Facebook story that the government was using black helicopters at night to ferry Americans quarantined for Covid-19 to a training center in Anniston, Alabama. Well, it was true that the Department of Health and Human Services had made a proposal to do this. But pushback from Alabama Republicans caused the president to scrap that plan.

For most of the time Champ remained silent but watchful, content to let everyone who wanted to air their ideas to the group. Near the end of the two-hour meeting he steered the discussion to the upcoming primary. Super Tuesday was only nine days away. Fourteen states, including California, would be voting. He said that Q wanted everyone to help with an information offensive targeting the Democratic primary itself. He told them to keep themselves available. He urged them to create banners with their favorite accusation against the Democrats or against the secret state, and to keep next Tuesday open.

As the meeting was breaking up Adam went over to Champ to say goodbye. He glimpsed on Champ's computer an email and saw the words, "REMEMBER MARCH 3...MAJOR ACT OF CIVIL DISOBEDIENCE." So, Q was planning something big for Super Tuesday. Champ did, in fact, seem to be in touch with larger forces. So Adam's morning hadn't been a complete waste of time. At the back of all these crazy theories was a calculated ground plan. Their fanaticism was being fanned so it could be harnessed for a very real political outcome.

On his way home from the meeting Adam stopped in as arranged at his mother's place. She had prepared a light lunch. Or, rather, she'd had her housekeeper prepare it the day before and, today, had heated up the soup and poured dressing on the salad.

She greeted him, as she always did, with a brief kiss on the cheek. She was a physically inhibited woman. His father had been equally restrained. Adam remembered wondering how they had ever managed to summon up the passion to have him. Maybe he was preplanned, just like the rest of their lives. He'd spent many years in his teens re-programming himself, learning how to listen to his inner self.

Of course, she was wound up by the upcoming primary. Her committee was mailing and phoning every registered Democrat and Independent in the county. As Adam knew, she was championing Biden, "the only nominee guaranteed to defeat the president," as she said. That was what he had argued with Julia. Hearing it again, coming from his mother, made him feel how exasperated Julia must have felt when he uttered it. This time he offered a strong if perverse defense of Bernie. His mother responded as if she were dealing with a child who knew no better.

To change the subject, he gave her a heavily redacted account of his research into QAnon. She took the same attitude he had before he began looking into them, that they were complete crackpots. He patiently tried to explain to her how wide an appeal they had, how influential their beliefs were becoming.

"Truth, facts, evidence lack the draw and glamor of conspiracy theories," he said. "If you can find enough other Americans who share your ideas, however untruthful they are, you bond with them in an airtight capsule that no amount of fact-finding can penetrate."

"Lies are lies," she declared. "You can deny the reality of the coronavirus as much as you like, but that won't stop you being infected."

"Don't you see? If you get infected you claim that you have been deliberately infected by the cabal, the Democrats, the secret state, the Jews, whoever you believe your enemy is. No dose of reality is strong enough to dent their convictions."

"It only goes to show how badly our education system has prepared them. Do you remember when you tried lying to us?"

"How could I forget? You remind me of it repeatedly. It was no big deal. I was only denying that I had shoplifted a pack of cigarettes we wanted to try out."

"You remember when your father found the half-empty pack and made you return and apologize to the shopkeeper, and then give him back the money for it?"

"All too well. Dad went on to humiliate me by making sure my friends all knew what he'd made me do."

"But it worked. You never tried lying to us again. Ever since you've been a stickler for the truth. That's what made you become a scientist."

"Sure," Adam said to bring the conversation to an end.

Was she right? He always thought he'd chosen to be a computer scientist of his own free will. Had he in reality been programmed by his parents' convictions?

Now here he was in his thirties for the first time questioning his conviction that truth always bested lies, that facts could dispel rumors. Now he was seeing with his own eyes how truth frequently was less potent than unfounded beliefs. It was still preferable to them, but they appealed directly to people's feelings. We are not naturally rational beings. We have to learn to cultivate reason, and any situation producing a strong reaction can erase that learning in a moment.

That evening the news reported that a Berkeley resident, who had recently returned from Italy, had tested positive for Covid-19 and was self-quarantining. Julia reacted by reaching for her thermometer—of course she was 98.6—and exiting to the bathroom to take one of her pills for anxiety. Julia seemed to feel that death was specifically stalking her. It was no use telling her how low the odds of catching the virus were, let alone dying from it at her age. She was too scared to listen to reason. But, if you're scared of dying, what difference did long or short odds make? It was the chance of dying itself that scared you, not how big the chance was. So much for reason.

Q

Monday was unusually warm and sunny for February. It was forecast to reach 74 degrees. Julia loved the Northern Californian climate and the plant life that went with it. Already a range of flowers were blooming in the front yards of houses she passed on her morning walk to Rockridge—yellow nasturtiums, lilac vines, pink camelias, snapdragons, yellow and black pansies, and white and purple hellebores. She recollected visiting a schoolfriend at this time of year who was studying in Madison, Wisconsin. Apart from pine trees and other forlorn deciduous plants, she saw nothing but bare branches, hung heavy with snow, and flower beds that were covered with mulch. Life was in suspension. Here there was always new life and color. Yet, another form of death floated invisibly in the air.

Since her lunch with Amy she'd been arguing with herself about what she would want Amy to do if she were Amy and Amy her. When she'd asked Amy about this, Amy had said she thought she'd want a friend to tell her the truth. Julia decided that she would want to know if Adam was having an affair. She would want Amy to tell her about it if she knew that was the case. Or at least Julia persuaded herself that is what she would have wanted.

At the office she phoned Bruce. As well as being a friend, he was one of the attorneys in the building for whom she'd done work. Bruce knew Amy and her husband Jeff. He and Jeff often met at the courthouse and had drinks together. They also played golf some weekends.

She explained to Bruce that this was a delicate matter, that she would understand if he preferred not to be involved in it. But as a friend he could help another mutual friend, Amy. Of course, that aroused his curiosity. With some misgiving she made herself recount the conversation she had with Amy.

"Naturally she was reluctant to admit this, but it seemed to me that Jeff's sudden and unexplained reluctance to have any sexual relations with Amy pointed most probably to an affair. Like most of us, Amy and Jeff are not good at talking about sex between them. But, if he is having an affair, it could only help both of them if Amy were to know about it so that they could deal with it one way or another."

"I get your drift," Bruce said. "But I'm not sure I want to act like a stool pigeon."

"I understand," she said. "I'm not asking you for details of who or when. But it would really help Amy to know whether this is what is causing him to push her away. She's lost confidence in herself. I just want them to be able to come to terms with whatever is happening. Although Amy and I are very close, they are both good friends of mine. I have both their interests in mind."

"I've met them together for dinner a couple of times. They seemed to get on well." He paused to think. "As it happens I've agreed to have a drink with him on Wednesday when we're both in court. If he's willing to talk about it and agrees to let me share what he says I will let you know the upshot on Thursday. But I am not going to press him if he doesn't want to discuss it. Okay?"

Wasn't she doing exactly the same to Adam as Jeff was doing to Amy? How would she feel if someone told Adam about Dave and her?

On the way home Julia stopped off at Safeway for mayonnaise, as they were planning on celebrating this summer weather with a shrimp salad. Inevitably, the mayonnaise was stocked on the lowest shelf. Bent down, she couldn't decide between Hellmann's Light Mayonnaise and Bright Day Dressing. Hellmann's was smoother but not as tart as Bright Day. She was comparing the grams of fat—not much difference—when she felt a cold hand sliding beneath her jeans and panties and making for the divide. She shot up straight shouting, "WHAT DO YOU THINK YOU'RE DOING?" before she could see who the groper was. By the time she turned around, Dave was already walking fast towards the exit. The customers near her were all looking at her as if she was the offender.

"What are you all looking at?" she shouted. "Didn't you see I was being groped by that weirdo?"

An assistant manager hurried over and asked her if she would like him to dial 911.

"Is that the best you can do to protect your customers from being sexually assaulted?" she asked.

"I'm sorry, ma'am," he said, "but we cannot intervene in such incidents or we may become liable ourselves."

"That's really pathetic."

"We can make our video recording available to the police."

"Great. That should make your female customers feel so much better after they've been groped."

"Is there anything else I can do to help you?"

"Clearly nothing of use," she spat out as she made for the cash desk.

Had Dave stalked her from the office to BART, where she was absorbed in catching up with messages, news and social media on her phone and on to the supermarket? The thought filled her with fear and fury. How was she going to remove this man from her life? Who was it who had a good and a bad angel whispering to them over each shoulder? Oh, yes. Dr. Faustus. She was quite ready to sell her soul to the devil if that would permanently rid her of Dave. But he was the bad angel. Adam, her good angel, would advise her to keep everything in proportion. This line of thought was becoming ridiculous. She didn't even believe in a god or a devil. She was still shaking when she got back home.

When she told Adam that Dave had groped her in Safeway, he angrily predicted that it wouldn't be long before Dave got himself arrested.

"That's all very well," she said, "but meantime I am being stalked and groped by this jerk. What will he have to do to me before the police intervene?"

"You could make a complaint to the police right now."

"Sure I could. But even with the evidence from the video, he wouldn't be intimidated. He would only react like a wasp that's been swatted and buzz me more angrily."

"Maybe you're right. Maybe we should report him for stalking you and get a restraining order."

"Normally I would agree with you. I wish I thought that would solve the problem. But Dave is not one to pay attention to the law."

"The law is all we have. We'll just have to remain alert for now," Adam said. It didn't make her feel any better. But what could he say? To think she'd brought this on herself. She went upstairs for an OxyContin, the only thing guaranteed to change her mood.

The evening news reported that the Dow Jones had plunged over 1,000 points following a warning by health officials that the first major outbreak of the coronavirus in Italy could be a precursor to an outbreak in the United States. The president responded with a tweet to the effect that the virus was under control here and that the stock market was starting to look good. He seemed to be living in an alternative fantasy world where everything was working smoothly to ensure his re-election.

Q

Adam had just got under way with his morning undergraduate class when the door at the back of the classroom opened and Natalie entered and sat down as if nothing had happened. He was nonplussed. What ought he to do? Confront her publicly? Ask to see her after class? Without really thinking about it he gathered his notes together and announced to a startled class that he had to leave unexpectedly.

On getting back to his office, he phoned Elaine and told her about Natalie's appearance in his class. Elaine sounded flustered. She had tried to see Natalie yesterday but had not succeeded in contacting her. Natalie was scheduled to meet her that morning at 11. She apologized profusely and admitted that she should have warned Adam about this before class. Adam ended the call saying he trusted he would never see her in any of his classes again.

He'd arranged to spend his early lunch hour with Anna. He wanted to ask her about Brad, whose advisor she was. She'd opted for lunch at Raleigh's Bar and Grill on Telegraph, close to the campus. They got

there early enough to occupy a booth in a corner. As it was Taco Tuesday they shared shrimp tacos. He had the sour beer for which they
were famous, and Anna opted for a cider.

"So how's the paper progressing?" he asked, after their drinks had
been put on the table.

"You want to make me feel guilty?" Anna asked with a half-smile.

"I get it. Still part of the to-do pile."

"Exactly. My current excuse is that I'm doing a peer review for
Computer."

"Your procrastination saves me my own."

"You see? You owe me."

"How can I ever repay you?"

"That shouldn't be too hard to work out," she said, flashing her eyes
in exaggerated fashion.

"Anna, you're an incorrigible flirt."

"You noticed?"

"I was counting on it."

She moved closer to him in the semi-circular booth, crossing her
legs that were on tantalizing display beneath her short skirt.

"Just taking you at your word," she said looking into his eyes.

"You must know how incredibly sexy you are."

"I have heard it alleged in the past."

"It's just as well we're in a public place."

"Or?"

"Or I might be kissing you madly."

"I don't think that would be considered an act of public indecen-
cy here."

Their faces were drawing closer together.

He was interrupted by the ill-timed arrival of the server with their shrimp tacos.

Once they were alone again, he said, "You've completely ruined my appetite. Or rather redirected it away from tacos."

"I'm so sorry for the inconvenience," Anna teased.

He took her hand and raised it to his lips. "This is what I want to feed on."

She moved closer into him.

"Feast your fill, Adam."

"Now I could eat the rest of you."

"We could go back to my place," she said. "It's only ten minutes away."

"I would love to, but—"

"But?"

"You know. Julia." he shrugged sheepishly.

"How are you two getting on together?" she asked, moving back to her place.

"Why do you ask that?"

"Because I get the feeling that you are—how shall I put it—starved of physical affection."

"Feminine intuition sometimes scares the hell out of me."

"More like logical deduction."

Strangely, Adam had no qualms about discussing his sex life with Anna. She was so matter of fact about sex.

"I wish I knew. For some reason Julia is completely turned off sex. Why, I don't know."

"How long has this been going on?"

"About three weeks I guess."

"Any other unusual signals"

"Not really. She seems to be taking more sleeping and anti-anxiety pills than before."

"What make?"

"Apart from Ambien, I'm not sure."

"You always have tended to trust others too much. You ought to investigate exactly what and how much she's taking."

"You may be right there."

"The obvious next question—is she having an affair?"

"I don't know. There haven't been any surreptitious phone calls. She hasn't taken to coming home late from work. I doubt whether that's it."

"Have you asked her about it?"

"You mean, about her rejection of my advances?"

"Yes."

"Actually, I haven't found the right moment for it yet."

"There is no right moment," Anna said.

"I guess you're right. I hesitate to have it out in the open. Sex has always been like an unspoken conversation between us."

"That's not the way I see it. I believe in stating what I want and in asking my lovers whether I am satisfying them."

"Lucky them."

Just listening to her talking about having sex was arousing him. He tried changing the topic of conversation.

"I've been meaning to ask you about a graduate in my seminar, Brad. I understand you're his advisor."

"Brad? Yes. An oddball."

"In what way?"

"More than once he's tried to discover where I stand politically. I get the impression that, unlike most of the graduates in our department, he is very right wing to the point of subscribing to extremist theories."

"And what makes you think that?"

"Just yesterday he asked me what I thought of a post by Q on one of 8kun's message boards in which he claimed that what he called the 'China virus' was a bioweapon created to harm the president's chances of getting re-elected."

"Sounds deliberately provocative," he said.

"I certainly took it that way and bawled him out: 'You talking about the Kung Flu?' I asked. 'Or the #WuhanVirus?' Incidentally that hashtag was used on 70,000 posts on Instagram."

"He asked for that."

"I pointed out to him the impact that the president's language has on Americans like me who look Asian even though we'd been born in the US. Only the other day I went to seek advice from an elderly I.T. scholar at his home in the city. His middle-aged daughter wouldn't let me in the house, saying, 'We can't risk having Asians in the house right now.' I had to put my questions to him on the phone. And this is happening when there are only 15 confirmed cases in California."

"This country was built on racism. It's not like the Civil Rights era solved everything. It's persisted like an underground stream. The president has directed the stream back to the surface, and it is infecting everything. You know Brad is an adherent of QAnon."

"That doesn't in the least surprise me. He tried to appease me by saying that a Chinese official had alleged that it was the US Army, not the Chinese, who had brought the epidemic to Wuhan. I told him that I didn't buy that conspiracy theory either, and we left it at that."

"I'm really worried. I was reading about a social science study that concluded that humans can only accept a fact-based finding that confirms their preconceived beliefs. Confronted with an objective finding that contradicts those beliefs, especially political ones, they misinterpret the results to conform with their convictions."

"I never did share your idealist view of the superiority of scientific truth," Anna said looking directly at him. "Science can only promise to correct itself as new evidence and ideas emerge. What I love about it is its flexibility, its willingness to adjust and innovate."

"You're right, I know. I guess I've been something of an intellectual snob, dismissing anyone who ignores scientific evidence. It's human nature I've misunderstood all this time. It is entirely normal to be irrational. Scientists have to overcome their natural irrationality with a learned response."

At that point their server turned up with the bill and they realized that they both needed to get back to campus.

That evening the news reported there were five emergency appeals to stop the president's attempt to freeze the assets of pro-Iranian organizations and to close left-leaning websites. So far they had been accepted by three federal judges and rejected by two. One of the rejections concerned the Voting Foundation.

"I foresee campus demonstrations tomorrow," Adam said. "When the courts won't stop the president, all that's left is mass protest."

"And will you be protesting?" asked Julia.

"I only wish I could. But that would blow my cover with the QAnon crowd."

"Hasn't the time come to break with those crazies?"

"I'm convinced that they're planning to disrupt the primaries next week. If I can discover what they intend doing, I might be able to alert the security services and preempt them."

"You sound like James Bond, single-handedly taking on Smersh."

"Point taken! But I've spent so much time penetrating QAnon I don't feel like giving up quite yet."

"Your choice. But, I can tell you, your undercover stuff makes me feel real nervous. Liz and I could end up as bargaining chips if you get exposed."

"Come on, Julia. They're not the Mafia. It's mostly all talk and hot air."

"I hope you're right."

With that Julia turned over and switched off her light. Adam had been meaning to raise the topic of their sex life with her. Too bad. At the same time he was secretly relieved that he had escaped that embarrassing conversation. He could see her responding by sarcastically asking whether he was now demanding his marital rights. Until now they had never separated the act of sex from their love for each other. He just didn't know how to talk about sex on its own. If only he were like Anna who could talk about sex as if she were discussing an omelet recipe.

He fell to sleep and dreamed of cooking an enormous cheese omelet following Anna's instructions. When it was ready they both began eating it from opposite sides until they met mouth to mouth at the center. He woke up with a hard-on.

Q

After dropping Liz at school, Adam drove to campus. It only took about twelve minutes. He needed to sign some papers at the Title IX office and go to the library to take out a book, *Enchanted America*. The author, a political scientist at the University of Chicago, offered a theory about the popularity of conspiracy theories, arguing that people were either rationalists or intuitionists. He argued that intuition had its own kind of grammar, and it was that grammar Adam wanted to learn more about.

He spent over an hour in the library mainly browsing through current scholarly journals on computer science. The office of the Title IX officer was on the campus's southwest corner. As he walked, he heard a roar coming from Sproul Plaza well before he reached it. He made for the protest, one of many being held all over the country opposing the president's attempted closure of left-leaning websites in the name of national security. When he reached the plaza the crowd had been divided by a line of cops in full riot gear. The leaders of the larger group of protesters stood on a platform with a public address system. On the other side of the cops were those defending the president; he could make out a "Q" t-shirt—worn by Brad.

Each side was waving signs at the other: BAN GOVERNMENT CENSORSHIP faced off against IRANIAN SYMPATHIZERS ARE TRAITORS. Some of the posts used for the banners had lethal-looking pointed ends. Every so often a plastic bottle of water or a food carton would be hurled from one side to the other. From the periphery he heard catch phrases from the speaker blasting over the PR system— "our first amendment rights" ... "endangering international order" ... "democracy of the internet." Those opposing the protesters shouted mainly insults— "Crazy Commies" … "Liberal Losers" … "Leftists Go Home."

As he slowly made his way round the edge of the crowd Adam debated with himself whether the protesters had a chance of reversing the president's actions. The president's followers had no shortage of rationales for his behavior. He had been misunderstood. He had been misreported by the lying media. He was making a joke. Because he prided himself on being tough on law and order, he was more likely to direct water hoses and smoke bombs at protesters than offer a compromise. He would no doubt dismiss the protesters as left-wing extremists, or members of antifa, who in reality were just an uncoordinated bunch of disparate online anti-fascists.

The president's weak spot was his desperate need to be re-elected. The country's interests took a backseat when the issue affected his standing in the polls.

Adam continued on Bancroft, leaving the shouting behind, and reached the ponderously named Office for the Prevention of Harassment and Discrimination. He found Elaine in her office. She had prepared a stack of paperwork for him to review and sign.

After they were done she confessed, "This case has angered me. I spend so much of my time helping women stand up for themselves and hold aggressors to account, and along comes a selfish, spoiled young woman like Natalie French to undermine all our work. It really is intolerable."

"I understand," he replied.

"This case provides perfect ammunition for the Secretary of Education, who maintains that universities are depriving accused men of due process, including the right to cross-examine their accuser."

"I'm not at all sure that cross-examining Natalie would have made her change her story. I was really lucky that she selected a date for which I had an iron-clad alibi."

"I'm sorry you were dragged through this procedure. I had a gut feeling that Natalie was lying before we interviewed your bank's loans officer." He imagined her wanting to add, "Mostly, it's the men who lie." Maybe he was being unfair.

"Ironically my wife is currently being harassed by an ex of hers from years back. So far, there's not enough hard evidence to take action against him."

"I'm sorry to hear that. Most continue their harassment until they are taken to court."

"This guy is so macho; I doubt whether he would be deterred by anything legal. It's becoming a real problem." He went on to tell her about the evening they were swatted.

"That sounds awful. I wish I had some useful advice for you."

"Human nature. What can I say?" he said as he got up and left her office.

After seeking refuge from the noon sun in the all-wooden interior of the Faculty Club, where he read his book over a salad, Adam returned home about 1:30. To his surprise he found Julia in bed. She was white-faced and staring at the ceiling.

"What's going on, honey?" he asked her.

"He'll never leave me alone."

"You mean Dave?"

"I wish I'd never met him."

"Why? What's he done now?"

"He's lost his mind."

"What happened?"

"He forced his way into my office this morning."

"Forced his way?"

"I wish you'd stop repeating my words. Yes. He pushed past reception saying he had to see his sister. They believed him and let him take the elevator to my floor. I was in the middle of a phone conversation when he stormed into my office and screamed at me to get off the phone. When I asked him what he wanted, he told me that, if I didn't allow him to have sex with me, he would kill himself."

"Which shows that he's not serious. He's had plenty of time to do himself in if he'd wanted to."

"It's easy enough for you to say that. I thought he was going to kill me. He was shouting his head off."

"Did anyone hear him?"

"Yes, Jill and a couple of others called security. I did everything I could think of to calm him down. But he kept yelling at me. You know: 'You fucking bitch!' 'You dirty whore!' 'You cunt!' Then these two burly security guards burst into the room. They somehow got him out, but I heard him still shouting that this wasn't over. I was a complete wreck. I was crying and shaking uncontrollably. Jill ordered a Lyft for me and took me down to the car."

"I really am so sorry this happened to you. Can I get you a Xanax?"

"Thanks, but I've already taken one." Julia's eyes were heavy. "I don't know how much more of this I can take," she said suddenly.

"I'm calling our lawyer. We'll get a restraining order."

"Like Dave would honor a restraining order."

"Then he'll be arrested and put in jail."

"Serving him with papers will make him go crazy. He'll take it out on me. Or Liz. Who knows what he's capable of?"

"But ..."

"No," she said firmly. "I would feel in constant danger. We can't do that."

"Okay. But it's the only thing we can do to try and stop him from harassing you. If he makes one more threatening move will you agree to take out a restraining order?"

"I'm telling you it won't work."

"We can't just sit back and wait for him to do whatever."

"Okay. I agree. If he does one more thing we'll go to see Mitch."

"Good."

After a pause he said, "You look exhausted, honey. Why don't you sleep, as I'll be bringing Liz home from school?"

"Thank you, Adam." Her eyes were already fluttering shut. He left her to her troubled dreams.

How had it come to this? How had this ghost from the past changed their lives so quickly? For ten years they'd enjoyed a mutual idyll. They'd been happy so much of that time. In love in a quiet and contented way. He'd always thought they were exceptionally lucky. Now he found himself wondering if Julia loved him the same way he had her. So many of his assumptions had become questionable. Maybe he had been living a hopelessly romantic dream. Even his country seemed in danger. Was it going to survive? Would his marriage?

He went to the bathroom cabinet to take one of Julia's Xanax's. There were none. Only a plastic bottle of OxyContin. Too strong for him. Was Julia now taking these regularly? He must talk to her, however unpleasant that might be. He longed for cocktail hour.

Q

The Thursday morning news focused on Iran's Islamic Revolutionary Guard. Their gunboats had swarmed US naval ships in the Persian Gulf, one coming within ten feet. The president responded by ordering the US Navy to destroy any gunboats repeating these maneuvers. How long, Julia wondered, before the president's penchant for threats and bluster precipitated a major war?

At the office, she listened to her voicemail and responded to her work emails; then she phoned Bruce to see if he had contacted Jeff. He said he'd rather talk to her in person in his office. On the way there, Julia felt nervous.

"Boy. That was some conversation," Bruce said after hugging her and offering her a chair.

"What do you mean?"

"I mean, no sooner did I broach the topic than he began a confession that poured out of him nonstop."

"So he was having an affair?"

"Not...exactly. He told me that he had been representing a young Mexican American guy who had been wrongly charged with possession. After getting him acquitted they went out for a celebratory drink that turned into several drinks and ended back in the guy's apartment where they had non-stop sex for hours."

"No way! I never got the impression that Jeff was bisexual."

"That's the word I used. He dismissed it. He said he was gay, and had always been gay, but he'd never admitted it, even to himself. He said that women no longer turned him on. Men were much more exciting. He said he'd now been with other men, and that he'd never experienced such intense desire and such extreme pleasure before."

"Amazing," said Julia shaking her head.

"I was shocked, too," Bruce said. "I asked when he intended telling Amy, and he looked confused. He said he didn't know what to do. He said he loved his son. He said it would kill him to live apart from him."

"Poor Jeff," she said, meaning it.

"I told him that Amy had talked to you and that she was suffering and didn't understand why he was rejecting her. He said, 'If only I were bisexual I might be able to make it work. But I simply can't pretend to want to have sex with Amy or any woman ever again.'"

"He needs to come clean with Amy."

"That's exactly what I said to him. He floated the idea that you might tell Amy, implicitly giving me permission to tell you what he'd told me. I told him that was hardly the best way."

"Poor Jeff. You said the right thing."

"He kept on it," Bruce said. "He asked me to ask you to fill Amy in. He said then he'd be forced to deal with the storm that would follow. He said he knew it was cowardly, but he thinks it would be better for Amy to have a few hours to absorb the news before they confront each other."

"What did you say?" Julia asked.

"I said I'd ask you, if that was the only way he could break the news to Amy. She has to be told."

Julia sighed deeply. "I know she'll be devastated. But she's that already. I guess this way I can help her stop blaming herself."

"Thank you for agreeing to do his dirty work."

"Thank you, Bruce, for resolving this. I truly appreciate what you've done. I hope this doesn't end my friendship with Amy."

"I know you'll handle it well, Julia."

"Thanks, Bruce," she said as she left sick at heart.

Amy was already seated on the patio with a beaded glass of iced tea when Julia arrived. Julia had picked Onigilly, a Japanese lunch chain close to her office in the Embarcadero Center. It was a beautiful day. As the two kissed, Amy looked at Julia apprehensively, as if she sensed what was up. They ordered a Wakame salad to split and Amy asked for cold sake.

"Guess what I just heard on the way here," Amy said. "The governor announced that the state is currently monitoring 8,400 Californians for COVID-19. That means the virus is already here, invisibly infecting us as we speak."

"That's scary," Julia said. "One of us could have it and not even know we were infecting the other."

"It scares the hell out of me. All the president did was to name the vice president to lead a response team. That's all he does is push problems into the hands of some committee or other."

"We could be in the middle of an epidemic before he takes any action. I've been worried for weeks now. Adam thinks I'm getting it out of proportion. I think he suffers from hubris, you know, a scientist's conviction that we can control it."

"This could be as bad as the one at the end of the first world war."

"Exactly" Julia replied. "I've been taking my temperature once a day. Somewhere I read that, if it exceeds a hundred degrees, it's an early sign that you've got it."

Their salad bowl arrived and they quickly devoured the seaweed and mixed greens. Julia dreaded what was coming but she knew she couldn't put it off much longer.

"Has anything changed with Jeff?" she asked.

"Unfortunately, no. Why do you ask?"

"Because a colleague of mine at work knows Jeff since they both were on opposing sides of a case a while ago."

"Really? What's his name?"

Julia didn't want to involve Bruce, so she said, "You wouldn't know him. But he met up with Jeff yesterday for a drink."

"Yes?"

"And Jeff ended up confessing to him what's been going on that accounts for his strange behavior."

"Tell me, please," Said Amy, her face filled with anguish.

"This is hard to tell you." Julia took a deep breath. "I don't know any better way than to come right out with it—Jeff's discovered that he's gay."

"What?"

"A few weeks ago he had sex for the first time with a young man. Since then he's been having casual sex with a number of different men."

"I don't believe it." Amy looked more shocked than upset.

"He says that he wants to live his life as a gay man now."

"This can't be happening," Amy said, and the tears began falling onto her cheeks. "This can't be happening."

"I really wish it weren't." Julia reached out and took her hand

"What am I going to do now?" she asked Julia through her tears.

"I guess the first thing you need to do is to talk to him about it."

"Oh my god," said Amy, hanging her head.

"Whatever you do, don't try to reach any firm agreement on anything. Remember, he's a lawyer. Just tell him what you're feeling and listen to what he has to say." If only, Julia thought, somebody had given her such useful advice before she agreed to meet Dave.

"I hate him," Amy shouted so loudly that customers in surrounding tables all turned to stare at them. "I want to kill him."

"You know, he's so ashamed of how he's treated you these past few weeks that he didn't have the courage to break it to you directly."

"Now you're defending him?"

"Not at all. It's you I want to help."

"So he got you to tell me instead?"

"Yes."

"What a fucking coward."

"My colleague tried to persuade him to talk to you directly. But he wanted someone else to do it before facing you."

"That's pathetic. How could you agree to take his part?"

"I'm not, Amy. Don't shoot the messenger."

"I feel so worthless. Why did this happen to me?"

She took out a tissue and wiped her eyes. Julia put some money on the table.

"Listen, I have to get back to work. Are you going to be all right driving back?"

"Of course. Don't worry about me."

"But I am worried about you. You're my best friend. I've only told you because I'd want you to do the same for me. I'd want to know the truth."

"If only I could turn the clock back a month. Life was so perfect then."

"Listen, Amy," Julia said getting up, "I'll phone you later. You know I'm here for you, no matter what time of day or night it is."

"Thank you, Julia," she said, wiping her face. "My life's finished."

"Please don't think like that. You'll get through this, you'll see."

As she left the café Julia heard Amy ordering another sake.

Late that evening Amy phoned Julia. She was drunk and hysterical.

"I don't know where he is."

"Have you tried calling him?"

"Have I tried calling him? I've tried calling him all evening. Now he's turned his phone off completely."

"It sounds like he's scared to confront you."

"So he should be. I'll give him hell when I see him." She was sobbing as she spoke. "He can't do this to me."

Julia remained silent. What could she say? He had already done it.

"Robert wouldn't go to sleep without his father saying goodnight to him. He knows something is wrong. I had to sit on his bed talking to him for ages until he eventually dropped off."

"Children are really smart when it comes to feelings. Unfortunately, they're always the worst losers in breakups."

"Oh my god, Julia. How am I going to manage financially?"

"That's the last thing you should be worrying about right now. Jeff will pay you alimony, child support. You own half the house."

"What can I do with half the house? I can't afford this house on my own. I'll have to sell it and move into a smaller place in a dangerous neighborhood."

"No, you won't. First you have to talk through what's happened with Jeff."

"How can I do that when he won't come home? What a bastard!"

"He'll have to come home some time."

"Meantime, I'm left here totally stressed and drinking myself silly."

"What are you drinking?"

"I transitioned from sake to vodka when I got home. When that ran out I switched to red wine."

"Ouch!"

"I know. They don't mix. I should have had gin instead of wine. Too late now."

"At least it should make you sleepy."

"Yeah, I'm already sleepy. But I know that I'll be wide awake at 3 or 4."

"Give yourself a break and go to bed. You'll have to be up in time to get Robert to school in the morning."

"I wish I could go to sleep and not wake up again."

"That may be how you feel now. But it won't last. Robert needs you. So do I. So, please go to bed now."

"I know you're right, Julia. I'll go to bed, as you suggest. Thank you for being my friend."

"Things will work out. You'll see. Sleep well. We'll talk tomorrow."

Julia felt wholly inadequate. She had fallen back on clichés for the most part, but sometimes that's all you can do. She guessed her most useful role was that of listener.

She couldn't help thinking that Amy and Jeff presented a mirror image of her and Adam. Only she was performing Jeff's role. Should she tell Adam that she slept with Dave? Would her marriage be breaking up in the near future? The thought was enough to send her to an OxyContin.

Julia dreamed that night that Adam was married to Amy and she and Amy were having a wild affair. She wanted Amy to leave with her, but Amy couldn't see herself leaving Lucky with Adam. She woke up feeling as confused as her dream, with Lucky licking her nose.

Q

That Friday, after taking Liz to school, Adam settled down with his laptop at the breakfast table (still uncleared) to see what QAnon news was trending in Twitter. He read the posts in a thread titled: "Welcome to Information Warfare."

"GET READY to take back the narrative from the LYING MEDIA."

"HISTORIC! President already surpasses Bush 2004 and Obama 2012 in National Primary Vote Total."

"The coronavirus is NOT REAL. It's been created by the Deep State."

In one post George Soros was claimed to be the single largest donor of the company responsible for the failed Iowa Caucus app. Some urged followers to join the current meme war targeting those Democrats in Tuesday's primaries who stood the best chance of beating Republican opponents in November. Others urged them to protest next Tuesday outside their local voting center, with signs about how the Democrats were cheating.

One post in particular caught Adam's eye. "Let's have martial law and get this over already!" One of his colleagues, a professor of digital ethics, responded, "Conspiracy theories can kill."

Next, he looked up how his retirement account was doing. Over the past week it had lost 22 percent of its value. Caused mainly by news of the global spread of the coronavirus, the Dow had lost 3000 points. The week promised to be the worst for the stock market since the financial crisis of 2007. This was only the beginning, he told himself. He wondered if he'd have to go on teaching until he looked like one of those academic scarecrows that hobbled around campus more dead than alive. He felt his future security crumbling beneath him.

Just as he was about to clear the breakfast table the phone rang. It was his mother.

"Hello, dear."

"Hello, mother. What's up?" She rarely called him weekdays.

"It's Barack. I'm so worried about him."

"Why?"

"He was throwing up all day yesterday and he won't eat anything."

"Have you taken him to the vet?"

"I went yesterday afternoon. They prescribed Flagyl."

"And he's still throwing up?"

"Not any longer. But he's still not eating."

"When Lucky gets a gastric upset we always keep him off food for twenty-four hours."

"That's what the vet told me to do."

"But you just said that Barack won't eat anything."

"I know. I just thought that I'd try him out with a little something to see if he was better yet."

"If it was anything more serious than a stomach upset, the vet would have said so. Kittens have strong constitutions. Just give him time. And then try tempting him with baby food to start with. That's always worked with Lucky."

"I feel so sorry for him. He is lying on my lap looking up at me with large, sad eyes, as if to accuse me of starving him."

"Starving an animal when it's got an upset stomach is the best thing you can do. Just leave a bowl of water down for when he decides he needs a drink."

"Thank you, dear. I just needed to be reassured. I'm sure you're right."

After a pause they went on to talk about—what else—the president's latest aggravation. He was charging the "do-nothing Democrats" with doing what he was in fact doing, politicizing the spread of the coronavirus. After she ended the call, he reflected how even his rationalist mother ignored the vet's advice when Barack showed signs of a minor gastric upset. It didn't take much to ignore the voice of science.

Late that evening in bed Adam was scrolling through his Twitter feed when he saw an image that shocked him. Dave had just posted a picture, a selfie, of him and Julia seated in some bar. He was grinning and she was looking into the distance. The message below: "You cannot escape your true partner." A violent anger started to rise within him, but he took another look at the photo. Julia didn't look thirteen years younger. She looked her present age.

He handed her his phone with the tweet.

"Have you seen this tweet of Dave's?"

"No," she said defensively. "I muted him at your suggestion."

"I forgot. Where was this taken?"

Julia looked closely. "I can't recollect what bar this was. It's probably ceased even to exist by now."

"It's weird, but in it you look closer to your age today than then."

"I guess I should take that as a compliment if I haven't visibly aged over thirteen years."

"It was simply an impression, that's all."

"So now you're taking it back?"

"Which? The compliment? Or the age you look?"

"I don't care," she shot back in a temper. "Stop asking dumb questions."

"Okay. Okay." But he was disturbed. He looked at the photo again. He could have sworn that the image was recent. Did she wear her hair long like that when he first met her? He couldn't remember. Could Dave have taken it without her knowledge? Unlikely.

"At any rate," he said, "there's nothing we can do to stop him from posting his messages."

"Agreed. Let's drop it now."

"Whatever you'd like, honey," he said reaching over to run his hand down the back of her hair. She flinched and got out of bed. Now even non-sexual physical closeness was becoming difficult.

She disappeared into the bathroom. Was she taking another pill? He felt as if the pills were replacing him. He felt his life was slowly unraveling.

Q

Julia left to see Amy first thing after breakfast. Adam walked the dog, took Liz to school, and, on the way back, stopped to check the news. Saturday's main headline was a shock. The president, invoking the Insurrection Act of 1807, was sending the National Guard into three blue-leaning states participating in Super Tuesday. His justification was the threat of "liberal mobs" including "antifa" disrupting these states' elections. This seemed ominous.

When Adam looked up the Act, he read that it authorized the president to deploy troops unilaterally to suppress an "insurrection, domestic violence, unlawful combination, or conspiracy" that "impedes the course of justice." A perfect fit for the conspiracy-theorist-in-chief. Apparently, Dwight Eisenhower had invoked the Act in 1957 when he sent troops into Little Rock to desegregate the schools, and George H. W. Bush employed it in 1992 to help stop the riots in Los Angeles after the Rodney King verdict. This would be the first time a president had invoked it for no real or discernable reason, and the president's staff did not offer the public any evidence, although they claimed they had it. This clear power grab would excite his base. How big were they now? He claimed that he was the champion of everyone wanting to exercise their right to vote. Clever. And frightening.

Switching to Twitter, he saw a direct message from QChamp88. Champ urged him to show up on Tuesday for a protest rally outside the Berkeley Civic Center. Biden, who was a bigger threat to the president than Bernie Sanders, according to Champ was expected to win big in today's primary in South Carolina. Q wanted his followers to bring banners denouncing Biden for being a member of a human trafficking ring, or for being senile, or both. Champ said that QAnon members would be protesting outside polling places in all fourteen Super Tuesday states voting on Tuesday—the more disorder the better. He suggested slogans for a sign Adam could make, either SAY NO TO BIDEN AND THE DEEP STATE, or NO PEDOPHILES! REJECT BIDEN.

Adam replied that he would be teaching that day and couldn't attend. That shouldn't surprise Champ. Adam also read Q's latest tweet: "People are disgusted and embarrassed by the Fake News Media, as headed by the @nytimes, @washingtonpost, @comcast & @ MSNBC, @ABC, @CBSNews and more. They no longer believe what they see and read, and for good reason. Fake News is THE ENEMY OF THE PEOPLE!"

He was interrupted by an urgent call from Julia. She said she'd just heard from her mother that her dad had been rushed to hospital with advanced liver disease. He could die any time. Despite their history, she felt it was her duty to go and see him. She would be coming home shortly and asked Adam to get Liz and Lucky ready to leave for Stockton as soon as she got back.

The drive to Stockton took them almost two hours. Julia described to Adam how she had found Amy that morning—totally changed. She seemed in control; she was starting to think concretely about moving forward without Jeff, of whom there was no trace so far. Actually, Amy seemed almost too collected. Julia found it unnerving.

They first went to Julia's parents' home. Laura, her mother, led all of them into her small, dingy living room and asked what they would like to drink. Julia and Adam opted for water, Liz for milk. Once they were settled down Julia asked her mother how her dad was.

"Not good. What do you expect? He's suffering from end-stage liver disease."

"And what caused it?"

"You know the answer to that" she said bitterly. "Whiskey."

"He always did drink a lot."

"Well, he's been drinking a lot more since you left home."

"Like how much?"

"Like a bottle a day...on good days."

"Have they thought about a liver transplant?"

"They say there's no way they are going to waste a good liver on someone who's not willing to swear off drinking. They will only perform a transplant if a patient has stayed off alcohol for six months."

"But can he stay alive that long?"

"Very unlikely." Laura spat out most of her answers.

"He's not ready to give up his whiskey to save his life?" Julia asked.

"No. He makes me bring him a bottle of whiskey every time I visit him in the hospital." She paused and her tone shifted. "But a new liver could prolong his life for a number of years."

"And where will he find a donor willing to give his drinking habit a new life?"

"That's where you come in."

"Me?"

"If you're a match, you could donate twenty-five percent of your liver and extend his life."

"Are you kidding me?

"They say that a healthy person's liver can return to normal in two to four weeks and regrow to its original size in less than a year."

"If he was ready to stop drinking I might consider it. But we all know how likely that is."

Julia's mother came to a halt directly in front of her.

"What kind of daughter do you call yourself?"

"You know I owe him nothing."

"What do you mean?"

"You don't want me to dredge up the past, do you?" Julia said.

"You always did exaggerate what happened to you as a child."

"You mean, you always did minimize it, when you're not outright denying it."

Liz was closely following the conversation, her brow furrowed. So, Adam interrupted.

"Liz and I need to take Lucky out for a walk. Put on your coat, Liz. Let's have a little outing."

"I'll come with you," Julia surprised all of them by saying. She turned back to her mother. "You and I can go to see Dad together after we get back."

"He sees me every day. You go visit him on your own. I know he'd want that."

While Julia was visiting her dad, Lucky and Adam spent the time watching Liz do a jigsaw puzzle with her grandmother.

Laura looked up at him. "You hear about the National Guard?"

"Yes, I read about it this morning."

"Some Dems are appealing his order in the courts."

"I would hope so."

"What do you mean? He's only doing what the act allows him to do."

"That depends on how you interpret the act."

"Why do liberals find everything he does wrong?"

He was surprised at her stand. After all, she was part of the great working class that Democrats had traditionally claimed to champion. But then he reminded himself that the president took much of the white blue-collar vote in 2016.

"The president's using a concocted justification for federalizing the National Guard," he said, trying to keep his tone light and friendly.

"I don't know anything about that. But I do know that the Dems are planning massive disruptions during next Tuesday's primaries."

"That's what he's claiming. But where's the evidence?"

"Before you arrived I read on Twitter that there are numerous warnings about students in the Bay area preparing to make trouble outside polling places."

"I sincerely doubt that. Since when were you on Twitter?"

"Since QAnon."

"You follow them?" he asked in astonishment.

"I'm a member of a local group of QAnon here. This morning we were emailed asking us to join a counter-demonstration to stop them from obstructing our free election."

Adam knew that QAnon had a large following online, but he never thought of Champ's group as more than an exception. He thought they were like antifa, that they didn't have a physical organization. Then he'd had pointed out the leader of a group at the rally. Now the fact that there were more QAnon groups like Champ's bent on disrupting the elections was alarming. What was the long-term goal? To prevent the November election? How closely was QAnon tied to the White House? Adam became more alarmed the more he thought about it.

"Don't try to force that piece to fit where it doesn't," she told Liz. Liz turned the piece round and promptly fitted it in place. "Smart girl you've got."

"You're not going?" he asked.

"You bet I'm going. I'm not going to let those crazy leftists stop us from voting."

"I doubt that's their intention."

"I don't trust them one bit."

"You're an eighty-year-old..."

"I'm still here."

Adam sighed. "Just remember to stay ten feet away from the polling place or you'll get arrested."

"That's what our QAnon group leader told us in his email."

"Good."

In the car driving home Julia filled Adam in on how it had gone with her father at the hospital. He'd greeted her by asking where the whiskey was that he'd asked her mother for. When Julia told him she wasn't going to bring him liquor, he immediately started shouting at her and demanded she go out for it that moment. When he realized that was getting him nowhere, he asked her whether she'd told the doctors yet that she was willing to donate a part of her liver. She told him that she would only consider doing so if he stopped drinking. That led to another outburst when he accused her of wanting him dead. Julia held her own and pointed out that he was the one killing himself. That infuriated him even more. He began cursing so loudly that the nurses rushed in. When he shouted at them as well, they gave him a sedative. One nurse had to hold down his arm. Once he started to doze off Julia left. "I couldn't get myself to kiss him goodbye. I think I would have been better off never having had a father," she concluded bitterly.

"Dad," Liz said from the back seat, "I really like having you as a father."

"Well, thank you, sweetheart," he replied.

Most kids, he thought to himself, did not want to imagine what it might be like to be fatherless or motherless. He shuddered to think that Liz might one day feel about him what Julia thought of her dad. That couldn't happen. How could he avoid creating the distance that had separated him from his mother?

They arrived home emotionally exhausted. As they walked to the front door Lucky suddenly froze and Liz exclaimed, "Yuck! What's that?"

In the middle of the doormat was a massive pile of dog shit.

"Ooof," Julia said, while all three of them covered their noses.

"As the front gate is closed, there is no way that could have been left by a stray animal," Adam observed.

"You know who's done this," Julia whispered to him.

He nodded. He picked up the mat with its contents. "All of you go in now. I'll see to this."

After they'd had a meal and Liz had gone to bed Julia said to him, "I don't know how much longer I can stand waiting for Dave to strike."

"It's getting under my skin, too," Adam said. "The only other response I can think of, aside from the restraining order, is for me to confront him."

"No, please, I really don't want that."

"What we agreed was not to do anything unless he threatened you again. I don't think dog shit qualifies."

"I need a pill," Julia announced and left for the bathroom. By the time he'd undressed and got in to bed she was fast asleep.

Q

Sunday, day of leisure. Julia poured herself a second cup of coffee and settled down to read the *New York Times*. The lead story—" "WHO: Outbreak at Highest Level of Risk" —"reported 88,000 confirmed cases of the coronavirus and more than 3,000 deaths worldwide. Just as she had feared; this would be a pandemic. Was this the year her life would come to an abrupt end? Already there were seven positive cases in the Bay Area.

And what was the federal government doing? Sending tests to US labs that weren't usable for weeks now because of a manufacturing flaw in the labs. America was way behind Europe in testing and had turned down a German test that was working very well. And, without tests, how in the world could they know the numbers? She never had trusted government statistics. But now there seemed to be no reliable numbers of any kind. It was perfectly possible that their housekeeper could be infected. What about the servers at the café she'd had lunch at last Friday? Or even Amy? She'd kissed her goodbye when she left.

She wanted to check the voter turnout, so she scrolled on her phone. For the first time, as expected, Biden was leading Sanders with a large majority.

She asked Adam, "Did you see that Biden's winning in South Carolina?"

"Yes. I was just reading about it on my phone. I'm glad. I think he's a much more electable candidate than Bernie."

"There's my pragmatic husband. If every Democrat supported the candidate whose ideas they agreed with most, Bernie would be the nominee."

"Julia. I think you're missing something here."

"What?" she said defensively.

"This man will become a dictator if he gets a second term."

"Well then, I guess this Tuesday we will be negating each other's votes. Too bad."

"That's democracy for you."

They relapsed into their respective reading.

Later Julia called her mother.

"Hello," she barked into the phone.

"It's me, Mom, Julia."

"You don't think I know your voice?"

"Then you could have answered, 'Hello, Julia.'"

"Hello, Julia," she echoed sarcastically. Here they went.

"I called to ask how Dad's doing."

"Not good."

"In what way?" Julia asked with exasperation.

"He's not eating anything."

"Not even his favorite meal, a steak?"

"When did you last hear of a hospital serving steak to its patients?"

"Have you tried cooking one at home and taking it to him, wrapped up to keep it hot?"

"He doesn't even have the strength to cut it up."

"So? You could do that for him."

"I'm trying to get you to understand that he's got no interest in food. His stomach's all bloated and he complains that it hurts him all the time."

"I bet he's still drinking the whiskey you bring him every day."

"That's his last pleasure."

"But it's making him worse."

"You think I don't know that? I've long since stopped trying to restrict him."

"Oh, Mom."

"Yesterday I was told by an administrator at the hospital that they are clearing the beds there for an expected influx of coronavirus patients sometime soon. They want him moved to a hospice."

"When is he being transferred?"

"Not sure yet. Soon. Unless..."

"Unless what?"

"Unless you agree to an immediate transplant."

"We've gone through this once already. I'm not going to donate part of my liver in order to prolong the time Dad has to drink himself to death."

"What sort of a daughter are you?"

"My own sort. It's not as if he was a loving kind of father. In fact, the only kind of love he was interested in was the wrong kind."

"Here we go. Are you next going to bring up your childhood fantasy?"

"How dare you call it that. You know, as well as I do, that that was no fantasy. And it's had real consequences for me," she added, thinking of her sick if short-lived desire for Dave.

"Oh, sure," Laura said, ending their call on the same sarcastic note with which it began.

Adam looked up and asked, "Does your mother really expect you to donate part of your liver to your dad?"

"Can you believe the two of them?" Julia said.

"I'm a hundred percent behind you turning him down."

Next Julia called Amy. "How're things today?" she asked.

"He showed up late yesterday evening. I could hardly recognize him. He was wearing a translucent blue shirt and his hair was streaked."

"That sure doesn't sound like the Jeff I remember."

"You can say that again. It's over. He said he's finally discovered his true self. He kind of apologized. But he was too pleased with his new self to conceal his delight."

"And how did you respond?"

"How do you think? I screamed at him, flew into a rage and told him to get his things together and leave, and then broke down sobbing. I could sense his relief that he wouldn't have to deal with me or any other woman ever again."

"I'm so sorry," Julia said. She truly was.

"It felt so strange. I really believed I knew everything about him. And all along he was a different person, a stranger. You never get to truly know anyone, even yourself."

"I couldn't agree more with you. Recently I've been utterly surprised at myself."

That instantly aroused Amy's interest. "Really. In what way?"

Julia quickly backed off confessing anything more. She told Amy that she was being brave and doing great.

That night Julia dreamed she was at a wedding party, her wedding, apparently. There was this long table spread with delicious looking food. In the center was a turntable with an ice sculpture—of her. She watched herself slowly turning a full circle. And, every time she faced the front, guests, led by Dave, would reach out and try chipping a bit of her off and putting it in their mouths to melt. Half of her wedding dress was already missing, and Dave seemed determined to chip off the section covering her genitals. She tried screaming, but no sound emerged from the ice. Then, gradually, like Hamlet, she thought her ice body was melting and she would turn into dew. Finally, pieces of her scenario turned faint and floated away. But nothing replaced them. Soon she was staring into a void. She woke up sweating and terrified. It was as if she'd been dreaming her own dissolution.

Q

The University had cancelled all classes for Super Tuesday. The Chancellor wanted to discourage demonstrations on campus. Almost everyone feared there would be some kind of violence near polling stations. Adam felt sure that QAnon supporters were determined to create enough chaos to justify the presence of the National Guard. A perfect recipe for mayhem.

That morning Adam had arranged to meet Anna on campus to work on their article. He had sent her a draft and got back her detailed notes on it. They settled down in front of his computer and spent the first ten minutes agreeing on the title: "Hacking into State Election-Management Systems."

"If it takes this long for us to just agree on a title, how are we going to get through another five-thousand words?" he asked.

"Good question," Anna said.

"There must be a better way of doing this than poring over every sentence."

"How about just accepting all my suggested alterations and we'll be free to do as we like."

"How often do we get to do that?"

"This academic life can get you down if you don't offer yourself some rewards."

"And what rewards do you offer yourself?" Adam asked.

"I favor ones that are exciting."

"Physically exciting?"

"How did you guess?" Anna put a hand on his arm and squeezed it.

"That thought leaves me quite incapable of concentrating on this paper."

"I agree. So why don't we offer ourselves a reward?"

"Now you've got me interested."

What the hell? he thought. It had been a month since Julia wanted to have sex. He was wound up tight. He guessed all he needed was an excuse to surrender to Anna's invitation. She looked enticing in a dark blue miniskirt and low-cut white blouse. He wondered if she had had this in mind when she dressed this morning.

She moved her hand to the back of his head and drew it to touch hers. "My place is only a short walk away."

"Let's go," he said and kissed her.

It was a hot morning. They walked tantalizingly slowly to her apartment in Northside, a quiet residential neighborhood, the opposite of the loud commercial Southside Adam frequented. They entered a two-story, mid-century building by a door that led straight upstairs to her apartment. The apartment gave off an immediate impression of brightness and flamboyance. The sun beamed down from the living room skylights, intensifying the bright colored rugs and cushions that gave the room an air of celebration, as if it were just waiting to host a party.

Anna threw her purse on a chair and asked Adam if she could get him a drink.

"I'm not sure I can wait that long," he said grinning.

"Slow down. If not a liquid appetizer, how about one of another kind?"

"That sounds more to my taste."

Anna was clearly a woman who liked to control how things developed.

"In that case I am going to undress you first," she announced.

She moved close to him and, instead of starting with his shirt, she undid his belt. Needless to say he already had an erection that she uncovered with one movement as she pulled jeans and underpants down and had him step out of them. Bent down there, she momentarily took him in her mouth.

"Mm," she murmured, looking up at him.

She stood back up, unbuttoned his shirt and pulled it off. He was beside himself with anticipation.

"My turn," he said.

He struggled, unsuccessfully, with the small buttons on her blouse that were unusually tight.

"I'll do it," she said, smiling at his difficulty, and unbuttoning her blouse with ease. Without pausing she unhooked her bra and threw both arms up above her head, "Voila!"

"You're so beautiful," was all he could manage to say. Her breasts were small and upright, and he immediately took both of them in his hands. His palms felt how firm her nipples were, and he began to caress them gently with his fingers. That had its intended effect.

She took his hand and led him into a very feminine-looking room filled with bright cushions, a cosmetics-covered dressing table with oval mirror, and a queen-sized bed with its colorful duvet.

"Hold on a minute," he said. "I haven't yet had the pleasure of removing your skirt and panties."

"If you insist," she said. "No buttons to thwart you there."

After unzipping the skirt he pulled both down and buried his face in her stomach. So soft and warm. They stayed like that for a while. Then, she raised his head and drew him onto the bed, pulling the duvet off at the same time. She gave him a condom to put on.

He was about to climb on top of her when she slipped deftly from beneath him and started to kiss him from above with a long moist kiss that involved some arousing tongue movements he had never experienced before. And she knew how to lead without being assertive or off-putting. He was only too happy to be the recipient of her expertise.

At the same time he was already tremendously excited. He needed so badly to erupt inside her soft, inviting body. She knew this but was set on prolonging the process, to gradually blow on the flames of his desire until they reached total conflagration.

Now she was licking his erection and he was moaning with desire. Next she guided his mouth to her breast and held still while he did what he liked with his tongue. All the time he was waiting urgently for her to signal that the moment had come for him to enter her.

But, when that moment arrived, it was she who seized hold of him and gently lowered herself onto him. Looking down at him with a faraway smile on her beautiful face, she began, ever so slowly, to undulate above him. It was excruciatingly exciting. He only had one overriding need, which was to reach a crescendo. She, however, acted as if she would be happy to rock herself on top of him for the rest of the day. It was torture. It was thrilling.

He tried speeding up their movement, but she put a finger to her lips and said, "Live for the moment. The future will come soon enough."

"You'll drive me insane if you hold off much longer," he said.

"What made you think you were sane in the first place?"

"Just give me back my sanity. This is torture, even if it is incredibly exciting torture."

"If you're into torture, I could always manacle you."

"Anything, provided you go faster."

With that Anna turned into a hungry animal. She sunk her mouth into his neck as she increased, not just the speed, but the thrust of her movement. They both began breathing more heavily and their eyes lost their focus as they strained to reach a climax.

What a miracle for first-time lovers. They came at the same time. And, really, she had done it. In charge to the end. What an amazing end. It took him back to his early days with Julia when pleasure was all they were looking for. That was all Anna and he were wanting. And they certainly had found it. In a big way.

They both lay back on the sheet smiling at each other with mutual satisfaction.

"That was really something," he told her.

"You enjoyed it?" she replied.

"I don't need to answer that. And you?"

"I don't need to answer that."

They laughed.

After an interval, Anna said, "Last time we talked about the fact that you and Julia are not having a lot of sex."

Adam experienced a momentary twinge of guilt. "I still haven't worked out exactly what is going on with her. I know she is more stressed out than she's ever been."

"Mm. Do you think it's mostly about the world around her?"

"I'm at a loss. She does seem to take a lot of tranquilizers and pain pills."

"What kind?"

"Xanax." He hesitated. "And OxyContin."

Adam was feeling too euphoric to take any of this to heart. He had almost forgotten how thrilling great sex could be. It left you feeling how great it was just to be alive. Yes, life could be amazing.

Anna led them gently back to the everyday world, getting up and dressing and suggesting they get lunch at her favorite nearby café.

Adam barely got home in time to shower and was five minutes late collecting Liz from school. To make it up to her, he bought her an ice cream—cookies and cream with sprinkle— on College Avenue on the way home. He wondered how he would be when Julia got back. Surprisingly, that evening, he found that he didn't feel a bit guilty. Perhaps it would take a couple of days for his conscience to kick back in.

In the short term all he could do was re-live those intensely exciting moments and silently thank Anna for making love to him with such skill. She had such a different attitude toward sex than he did. She approached it as one would the preparation of a gourmet meal. Detached, yet a participant, she coolly organized each course with a view to optimal deliciousness. She seemed to have absolutely no inhibitions; her only aim was mutual pleasure. It was, he thought, a purely physical affair. He believed she would do the same with any man she took a fancy to.

Sex with Julia was an expression of their love. The excitement was like a bonus, an expression of their feelings for each other. With Julia, Adam was always the one to take charge. Not that she was shy in responding to his moves. But that's how it evolved naturally. They were always very considerate of one another's needs. Anna was a completely different experience—a powerful chemical attraction, intense, thrilling, purely sensual.

Q

Super Tuesday. Some demonstrators with banners were already in the church courtyard protesting the presence of the National Guard—a couple of indifferent soldiers in full riot gear with guns slung over their shoulders. One banner read NO TROOPS IN OUR CITIES. Another: NATIONAL GUARD GO HOME. It was all a bit stagy and artificial. Julia cast her vote in a near empty interior and was back home by normal breakfast time.

On the BART train going home from work that evening, it was standing room only. Julia found herself next to a group of about six young demonstrators. Four were guys wearing MAGA caps and one of two women sported a black t-shirt emblazoned with a golden "Q". They were still pumped up from whatever they had been doing. As they talked about the day's events, Julia could see them beginning to mythologize their parts in it.

"That retarded student with the banner reading, "IMPEACH THE PRESIDENT." He totally got under my skin," one of the guys said.

"That was obvious after you kicked him in the shin, and grabbed his banner," laughed one of the women who was holding onto him for support.

"I thought it was great when you stamped on his stupid sign. Fucking pervert, that's what he was."

"But what about when we charged them?" said another guy. "I managed to send one of them running off with a bloody nose. See this metal ring?" he pointed to a thick all-metal band on his third finger. "Does a lot of damage."

"Funny you mention that," said the woman wearing the "Q" t-shirt. "I used the diamond on my ring to rip open the cheek of that bitch who yelled that QAnon was a load of bullshit."

"Lying Dems," said another of the guys. "Claiming that the president only sent out the troops to help him get re-elected."

"Assholes!" said the first man. "Did you see those two guardsmen throw that demonstrator to the ground when he attempted to force his way past them?"

"Yeah," said the woman holding onto him. "Force is what they deserve and force is what they're getting. Those guardsmen don't carry clubs and rifles for fun."

"What about the pepper spray?" said another of the guys, gesturing with his hand pressing an imaginary trigger.

At the next station the crowd thinned enough for Julia to distance herself from them. She found all of it confusing. Wasn't the National Guard supposed to be protecting the polling places from disruption by left-wing demonstrators, who were there to protest the presence of the National Guard, while right-wingers were there to oppose the leftists, but constituted the real threat to the electoral process? It was absurdly convoluted.

On her walk home from Rockridge she made a point of turning up College Avenue so that she could pass the church where they'd voted. What a difference from this morning. The crowd outside the polling station spilled over into the street where police were forced to direct traffic round the bulge of people. The two National Guard troops had grown to ten. They formed a line separating two opposing groups of excited protesters. As Julia paused to take in the scene, a guardsman seized hold of a placard that read TROOPS OUT that a protester was holding right up to his face and broke it in two. He was greeted with loud jeers and cheers. It felt like a rowdy street party. Democracy as farce. Yet, behind the street theater lurked something terrifying and rotten.

At dinner Adam seemed in an exceptionally good mood, teasing Liz about her rejection of the spinach he'd cooked— "Will you eat it if I cover it with sprinkles?" "Yuk!" —feeding Lucky with occasional tidbits Julia was not supposed to see, and recounting a meeting with a neighbor and her new puppy who he and Liz encountered on their walk back from school— "it ended up peeing on one of its owner's expensive-looking white suede shoes."

"You seem to be unusually pleased with yourself," Julia commented.

Adam looked momentarily taken aback.

"I guess it was having a day off. I treated myself to a beer and pizza for lunch at Zachary's. For just a moment it was like I was a student again."

"Lucky you. I had to get Jill to fetch my lunch, since I had a 2 p.m. deadline. I finished up with indigestion from the lunch or the pressure to meet the deadline, or both."

"Can I get you a Pepcid?" Liz asked her.

"No thank you, sweetheart. It went away once I'd finished the job."

"Do you get a lot of tummy aches?" Liz asked her.

"I guess I have my fair share. Why?"

"Is that why you take so many pills."

"I don't take that many," she protested.

"You took one this morning," she said, "and another when you got home."

"Are you spying on me now?"

"I don't need to. I can hear you opening the bottle in the bathroom from my room."

Julia clearly needed to store them somewhere else, she told herself.

Liz kept glancing at Adam each time Julia responded to her, as if this was all for his benefit. Julia tried to lighten the mood.

"Mind your own beeswax," she said.

"Whatever you say, Mommy," Liz concluded and left the table.

Adam and Julia stayed up late that evening to watch the early results of Super Tuesday. Biden seemed to be leading in thirteen of the fourteen states. There were scenes of rioting at polling stations across the country, especially in the three blue-leaning states, California, Virginia, and North Carolina, to which the president had sent the National Guard.

Two polling stations in San Francisco had to be shut down for more than an hour while guardsmen and police cleared demonstrators from the entrances. The news cut to an incident outside one station on University Avenue, east of the Berkeley campus. Adam and Julie watched students facing off against both guardsmen and their Republican supporters. Adam recognized a couple of his grad students among the progressive protesters. And there, on the side of the guardsmen, was Champ and two others sporting "Q" t-shirts—Champ's read WE ARE Q. They waved banners reading HANDS OFF OUR ELECTIONS, BIDEN'S A COMMIE and FAKE NEWS IS THE TRUE VIRUS, with which they seemed to be jabbing their opponents with no restraint from the troops next to them.

"You can see," Adam said excitedly, "the followers of QAnon are provoking the violence, inviting retaliation to create the excuse for the National Guard to attack the protesters."

"How can you be sure?" Julia asked him.

"You see that big guy with the shaved head in the WE ARE Q t-shirt? He's Champ, the leader of the group whose meeting I went to. He emailed us all urging us to turn up today and make mayhem. What's troubling is that the whole thing appears to be coordinated nationally. This isn't just media talk. It's boots on the ground."

"That's scary."

"You're right, it is. It's got me worried that they're working towards something much bigger."

"What?"

"That's what I can't work out. If I were a true follower of QAnon, I would believe that what they call The Storm is about to break."

"And what's the storm?"

"The moment the president orders the military to arrest all the leading Democrats and their fellow pedophiles, like George Soros and Bill Gates, and send them to Gitmo."

"I can't believe that so many people believe that stuff."

"But the reality might be a lot worse. For instance, what if the president sends troops out on election day? Or he could postpone the election saying he fears an insurrection."

"Now you're sounding like a conspiracy buff yourself."

"What he's done today could very well be a dress rehearsal for election day."

Julia looked seriously concerned, and he immediately pulled back. "I'm probably simply being paranoid."

Adam shut down the laptop they were sharing.

"You could help dispel my paranoia," he said pulling her gently towards him.

Her body froze. She couldn't help herself. Her body simply refused to respond to the only man in the world she loved. Was it really her body? Or was she blaming it for an atavistic reaction that had nothing to do with Adam? She was thoroughly confused. But she knew there was no way she could make love with him that evening.

"What's the matter?" Adam said, sensing her resistance.

"I wish I knew. What with the virus, Dave and now these riots, I feel a complete mess. It's nothing to do with you. Please indulge me. It can't last."

That was more like a wish. She wasn't at all sure it wouldn't last. Adam rolled back to his side of the bed with a sigh. She knew she wasn't going to get to sleep without some help. So she went to the bathroom and took two OxyContins. The receptionist had left a package containing them on her desk yesterday with a note simply saying, "You owe me." Dave, of course. She had almost run out and Dave seemed to have an endless supply. All of this was his doing of course. Really? What a mess she was in. It was just too easy to blame someone else. To admit it's yourself was way too painful.

Q

Another day at home. For Adam it felt like a mid-term break. However, that morning he began to regret having succumbed to Anna's seductive charms. It had been great. but it left him feeling he had let Julia down. He no longer thought her rejection of his advances justified what he had done. At the time it had offered a convenient excuse. But wasn't marriage supposed to have difficult passages like this one? How could he know what Julia was experiencing? He needed to talk it through with her. They couldn't go on pretending nothing was wrong.

Biden had swept twelve of the fourteen primaries. All his major competitors except Bernie were withdrawing. National polls showed that Biden was leading the president by four points. But if he were to face off with Bernie, the president would have a three-point lead.

Meanwhile, the president refused to condemn the right-wing demonstrators who had turned violent. By contrast, the Democrats were largely peacefully protesting the presence of the National Guard. Maybe the president was enraged after learning that he was likely to face a centrist and not a so-called socialist.

Videos of the riots from all three blue-leaning states showed a significant number of right-wing aggressors wearing the insignia of QAnon. The press barely even commented on their presence. It was as if the Great Awakening was a realistic possibility, not an absurd apocalyptic fantasy.

A tweet from QChamp88 read: "One step closer to martial law. Watch out, deep state." This touched on Adam's deepest fear—that the president really was planning some kind of coup. Was he in fact directing the actions of QAnon? As the president's inner circle was now made up almost entirely of yes men and women, who would try and stop him, or them? QAnon, he now realized, was a much more serious threat than its absurd beliefs made the country think it was. The Storm was more than just a fantasy. It had momentum.

He dialed his mother.

"Hello, dear," she said.

"Are you happy with the primary results?" he asked.

"Very. Biden is our best hope of getting the president out of the White House. My level of anxiety has dropped significantly."

"I'm glad to hear it. Maybe now you can afford to let up some on the time you spend working for the Democrats."

"I will consider your suggestion on November 4th. Until then, I will be working flat out to get the votes in."

"I know it's pointless arguing with you."

"I'm glad you realize that," she said chuckling. "So, how's my favorite granddaughter?"

"Learning to navigate her way through the digital wilderness."

"I do worry what kind of world we are leaving for her. If only we had realized what we were doing to the planet when we were younger."

"But, now, we know. And the president keeps rolling back all the environmental protections, and even they weren't strong enough to reverse the damage already done."

"I know. It makes me feel guilty for doing so little in the past." After a pause she said, "I need to leave now for a committee meeting. It was lovely hearing from you."

"Same here. Drive carefully."

She ended the call. As he sat there, phone in hand, he realized that neither of them could bring themselves to end with the word "love." How sad.

At 6 p.m. Adam was beginning to think about preparing dinner when a disheveled Julia appeared in the kitchen entrance looking shaken, with blood trickling down her face from deep scratches on her forehead.

"Oh, Mommy," Liz exclaimed.

"What on earth happened to you?" he asked as he grabbed a clean towel and went over to her to wipe off the blood.

"Dave," she managed to get out.

"What happened?"

She took a breath. "He was waiting for me at the bottom of the drive when I got home. In the bushes."

"My god!"

"And he shoved me hard into the side fence. I lost my balance and fell into the rose bed." She held up her arms that were covered with scratches, some oozing blood. "He laughed, or jeered rather, and yelled, 'See, you made me do this because you make me so mad at you.' Did you hear anything?"

"Not a thing!"

"Then he hissed at me, 'You think you're too good for me. But I'll show you.'"

"Is he still out there?" Adam asked, already halfway out the door.

"No. Jim rushed out from next door. He heard it through his living room window. Before Jim could get anywhere near him, Dave ran off, shouting, 'I'll be back, bitch.'"

"That's it," Adam said. "I'm calling Mitch and we are taking out a restraining order."

Julia's only response was to ask Liz to fetch her a glass of water.

"Is Dave your ex-boyfriend?" Liz asked her.

"He's just some crazy man," her mother replied.

"But why does he want to hurt you?"

"Because a long time ago I knew him when he wasn't like this."

Liz didn't know how to process this enigmatic response, so she went to get Julia's water.

Adam called Mitch who explained what they needed to do that evening. Take photos of Julia's scratched forehead and arms. Go to their local police station and file a report. Make a file of all emails received from Dave or posts of his containing veiled threats. Download from the California Courts website a bunch of forms needed for a Temporary Restraining Order and fill them out. In court parlance Julia, Adam and Liz would become "protected persons" and Dave a "restrained person." Dave would be ordered to stop contacting, threatening or attacking them, and keep one-hundred yards from them, or their house, or car, or workplace, or Liz's school. Very comprehensive—in theory.

When they finally got to bed late that evening they watched the news. There were continued protests; the president insulting the Speaker of the House after she had denounced him for not condemning the rioters; the president dismissed the threat from the virus as fake news; the president ridiculed the need to wear a mask; the number of confirmed US cases of Covid-19 reached two-hundred-seventeen nation-wide. Adam woke up later that night to realize that they had both fallen asleep with the TV on. He watched a commercial for Miller Lite: "It's Miller Time." Just what he wanted to hear at 1:30 in the morning. He fell back to sleep before he could summon the effort to find the remote.

Q

On his drive to school, Adam stopped off at the courthouse in downtown Oakland to submit the restraining order forms. Once the clerk had checked out the paperwork she told him to expect a response from the judge later that day. Mitch had arranged to pick up the order after it had been issued.

Once in his office, Adam checked his email. There was one from QChamp88. He was looking to drum up protesters for next Tuesday's primaries. There were three-hundred-and-fifty-two Democratic delegates up for grabs, including Washington State, which Champ was targeting. Q's aim? To bring the primaries to a standstill by staging violent protests outside the polling places. One tactic he was promoting was to accuse the authorities of failing to protect voters from catching the coronavirus. How ironic, seeing that the president just declared it was totally under control.

He replied to Champ that he had already made clear he was not willing to participate in any violent action. Champ's next quick response was an attempt to bribe Adam to join them by suggesting that he, Champ, might know or be the hacker who had exposed David Crawford's personal emails. He would be happy to give Adam more information if he accompanied him to Seattle. Adam repeated his refusal.

But this was a surprise. Why would QAnon want to take down the president's nominee for a government position? Then he remembered that Crawford was originally a favorite of both Republican and Democratic Senators. That could make him appear to be part of the deep state, what Q called "the enemy of the people." Suppose the president had been pressured into nominating him by supposed members of the deep state. If so, QAnon could be intent on saving the president from his enemies. Was QAnon secretly collaborating with some members of the administration? If Champ was the hacker, Adam ought to get in touch with the agents who asked him to trace the identity of the hacker to expose the subversive role of QAnon. But who knew where the agents' loyalties lay. Too many imponderables.

Anna drifted into his office. "Hello, lover," she teased.

"Unfortunately," he flirted back, "our students have decided to attend classes today."

"I know. Tough break for us."

"It was fun."

"It was. Carpe diem."

"How did Horace go on? Something about trusting as little as possible in the next day."

"I see you're a classicist as well as a scientist."

"Hardly. That's about all I can remember from my Latin classes."

"Well, this is the next day, and I have to get myself to work. At least we seized last Tuesday."

"We did that. Have a good class."

"Ciao!"

She was gone. Clearly their day together was a pleasant memory for her in the same way as a good dinner. Actually, Adam was relieved. He didn't want things to become any more complicated. Evidently, that was how Anna saw it as well.

Back home that evening Adam told Julia that the two graduate students who had seen him at the president's rally were trying to figure out where he stood, politically speaking. He told them he wasn't one of those professors who flaunted their political allegiance in class. One of them thought that was a cop-out, arguing that it is easier to process information if you know what the speaker's bias is. Adam replied that he had no wish to make any students feel alienated because their professor aired views that they opposed.

"I don't agree with you," Julia said. "I had a history professor who was a rabid libertarian. He would come out with outrageous assertions. But we all felt free to disagree with him, which led to some really lively discussions."

"I understand. But I'm not that kind of guy. I prefer to umpire discussions, not provoke them with personal opinions. It's a matter of personality, I guess."

"My beloved fence-sitter."

"That's not fair. I just don't believe it encourages open debate for the authority figure in the room to adopt a position before an argument even gets under way."

"It's your class. Obviously you should conduct it any way you want."

Julia's phone rang. It was Amy. Julia put her on speakerphone.

"Hello, Julia. Guess what! I've been placed in quarantine."

"Oh, my god, Amy. You mean you've got Covid-19?"

"I haven't got back the result of a test. But I've got enough of its symptoms that my GP told me to self-quarantine. I have a dry cough, a temperature of 100.9, and I find it a little harder to breathe than normal."

"That's awful."

"If it doesn't get any worse, it's fine. It hasn't stopped me doing any of the things I normally do around the house."

"What about Robert?"

"The doctor said that, at his age, there is little chance of his catching or transmitting the virus."

"Thank God for that. Are there any treatments available?"

"Not according to my doctor. But I've been searching the internet. Some of the claims are obviously crazy, like gargling with diluted bleach. But one respected health specialist recommended using nebulized hydrogen peroxide."

Adam raised an eyebrow at Julia.

"Then," Amy went on, "I found this Sri Lankan herbal drink that is said to be a remedy for a range of viral infections, including Covid-19."

Adam couldn't stop himself interrupting. "Amy, I happen to have come across that particular rumor. All it does is reduce someone's fever, encouraging them to think they're over it and go out infecting others."

"Really, Adam," Amy said. "I didn't know that. So far, I've only followed the advice of scientists at the University of Queensland in Australia, who in a video recommend eating bananas because they are rich in B6 which bolsters the immune system."

"I love bananas," said Julia. "But I worry about their sugar content."

"I'm not diabetic. So, I'm gorging myself on bananas. The only other action I've taken so far is to order a DVD from Happy Science. Their leader talks about how to boost your immunity. Apparently, it includes a coronavirus prayer."

"I never knew you were religious," Julia said.

"I'm not in the usual sense. But this Japanese cult has an enormous following and sounds really inspired."

"I sure hope that you only get a mild case of it. At least you're still under forty, which the CDC says is the age group least likely to be hospitalized."

"Thanks, Julia. Got to go. Talk to you soon."

Julia turned off the phone and she and Adam looked at one another.

"Adam," she asked, "have you heard anything about hydrogen peroxide acting as disinfectant?"

"I sincerely hope she does not experiment with hydrogen peroxide," said Adam. "It can cause a range of adverse effects, from inflammation to permanent neurological damage depending on the concentration."

"Is there nothing that can protect us from Covid-19?"

"According to the World Health Organization, nothing so far. But that's never prevented charlatans from trying to make a quick buck with fake cures."

"You're such a cynic."

"Would you rather have me drinking cow or camel urine, as is being advocated in India and the Middle East?"

"Of course not. But I am very worried."

"Because?"

"Because I had lunch with Amy only ten days ago."

"It's highly unlikely that Amy contracted it over ten days ago when she is only showing symptoms now."

"But do you think I should get tested?"

"I doubt very much that you would qualify, as you have no symptoms all this time later."

"It all makes me feel so anxious."

"Honey, I can assure you, you're fine."

"It's all very well your saying that. But it doesn't stop me worrying."

What else could he say? Julia went upstairs for one of her anti-anxiety pills.

He followed her upstairs and watched her swallow it.

"You seem to be taking a lot of pills just recently," he said.

"That's because I need them to do what you won't do."

"And what's that?"

"Reassure me."

"So, you're saying that it's my fault that you're taking more pills?"

"I'm not. But it doesn't help that you never believe that I feel totally stressed out all the time now."

"That's unfair. I can see that you are not your normal self."

"But your efforts to reassure me don't work. I'm not as rational as you."

"Still, I'm seriously worried about your pill intake."

"That's not what I said. I just can't reason away my fears."

"I wish you didn't feel the need to take so many pills."

"Don't be. I take an Ambien at night to help me sleep. Otherwise, I take anti-anxiety pills when I feel overwhelmed, not regularly."

"If that's what you need to do, I'm okay with it."

"Thank you for your permission."

"I didn't mean it that way. I'm just very concerned for you. You know that you mean everything to me."

"Let's go to bed, *cariño.*"

He turned on the TV. The number of coronavirus cases worldwide had exceeded 100,000. Next came an announcement from the president saying that Americans suffering only mild symptoms should go to work. Adam couldn't believe that he could be so ignorant about contagion. Or maybe he only cared about preserving the economy to ensure his re-election. Business naturally came first. Those who died from it were collateral, sacrifices on the altar of the S&P.

Julia woke up to what had by now become a permanent state of funk. Previously TGIF would raise her spirits at the prospect of a weekend free to do as she pleased—at least up to a point. But this Friday she was filled with fears—of catching the virus, of Dave erupting into her life, of something happening to Adam or Liz. She could no longer cope without the help of OxyContin. She was now taking at least four 80mg tablets a day. If she tried cutting back, she became nauseous and started to have stomach cramps. Even as she came awake she could hear her heart pounding. She went straight to the bathroom cabinet—despite Liz, she still stored her pills there—and took one. It would be an hour before it fully kicked in. She filled up the interval with the morning's everyday routines—showering, teeth cleaning, dressing, doing her hair, helping prepare breakfast, and putting together Liz's lunchbox. By the time she sat down for breakfast she had entered that pleasant state of free floating, as her newly liberated self detached itself from her earlier stressed-out self, like a satellite leaving its launching rocket and entering pure space.

Adam had printed out a copy of the temporary restraining order Mitch had obtained from the court and emailed him. It ordered Dave not to harass, attack, strike, threaten, assault, follow, stalk, molest or block her or Liz's movements. Dave was forbidden to contact them in any way and must stay at least one-hundred yards away, as Mitch had told them. The court hearing for a permanent order was set three weeks from today. Adam said that Mitch planned on having Dave served with the order that morning. Julia felt her heart pumping faster. That would really do it. She was certain this would send Dave into an uncontrollable rage. Far from making her feel safer, the order made her doubly afraid for herself and Liz, not to mention Adam. So much for feeling liberated by the OxyContin.

The day was suitably miserable, cold and raining. BART was more crowded than usual due to the weather. On the way home she was crushed against an elderly white guy wearing a rain-spattered transparent plastic raincoat that soaked into hers. After a while she realized he was pressing his crotch against her. She shouted at him, "Back off, you jerk."

He moved away a few inches and responded, "How dare you accuse me of being too close. If you need space around you don't travel in rush hour." She shouted back, "No one's buying that line. Just keep your distance." The other passengers looked or moved away from the two of them.

As in Safeway, she felt as if she'd been doubly attacked—first by the attacker, then by everyone who'd witnessed it. Was it easier to assume that the victim caused it? What was it about people that made them rush to judgment? It made her feel as if she were a foreigner in her own country.

Julia reached home, wet and bad-tempered.

Before she had time to tell Adam about what happened on BART, he announced, "We had an incident at school this afternoon."

"Did Liz do something again?"

"No. Dave turned up there."

"Oh, no! Is Liz all right?"

"Yes, thank God. She's upstairs doing homework. But it could have gone differently."

"What happened?"

"He turned up just before the end of school and informed Ms. Fulsome, who was on duty in the front yard, that he had been asked by you to collect Liz from school."

"I swear, I'll kill him."

"Luckily Ms. Fulsome said that she could only release Liz to a parent unless there was a written note from the parent authorizing someone else to collect Liz. He insisted that you had phoned the principal asking her to release Liz to him. She phoned the principal inside who confirmed that no one had phoned her."

"Then what happened?"

"I saw him as soon as I arrived to pick her up. I confronted him. 'What are you doing here?' He shouted back, right in my face: 'None of your business.' Ms. Fulsome ran up, telling me the lies Dave had told her. I told him that there was a restraining order. If he came near Liz—or you—again, he was going to prison for a very long time. He said, 'Fuck off, Chad. You think I'm scared of a piece of paper?' And then he said, and Adam hesitated a second, 'You tell that Stacy of yours that she's going to wish she had been born without a cunt.'"

"He said this in front of Liz?"

"In front of Liz, the teacher and a number of other children and their parents. No one knew what to do."

"I told you a court order isn't going to stop him."

"At that point we heard a police siren. It turned out that the principal had phoned the cops as soon as Ms. Fulsome called her from the playground."

"Oh my god. Did they arrest that maniac?"

"No. He ran off just before the cops arrived, shouting more obscenities."

Adam said he was left standing there holding a dazed Liz and that everyone, all the parents and teachers, looked stunned. He expected people to ask him if he was okay, but no one did. It was all very strange. He wanted to pursue Dave but couldn't leave Liz standing there alone. So he ended up angry, frustrated, fearful and conflicted.

It was Julia's turn now to feel frightened for what might have happened. This was a nightmare. "What did the police say?"

"That they would send an officer to the hotel to warn him that if he disregarded the order again he would go to jail and remain there until the court hearing."

"But this was an attempted kidnapping, at the least."

"Just the point I made to them. But they said a warning the first time was standard procedure. Can you believe it?"

Julia said she had to go see how Liz was. She turned out to be remarkably calm, saying that she would never have gone with Dave even if Ms. Fulsome had agreed. After spending more time talking to her about other things, Julia went straight to the bathroom and swallowed her third OxyContin of the day.

Later, watching the ten o'clock news, Julia saw scenes of protesters in a number of blue cities being tear-gassed and clubbed by federal troops in full riot gear. The number of confirmed cases of Covid-19 in the US had risen to 402. She felt as if she was living in a third world country without the resources to deal with an outbreak like this. No wonder she was falling apart when the country itself was doing the same thing.

After she turned off the TV, she could hear sounds of sobbing coming from Liz's room. She got out of bed and went—unsteadily due to the OxyContin—to comfort her. Lying down next to Liz, she took her daughter in her arms.

"That man scares me," Liz said.

"I understand." She couldn't stop herself from slurring her words. "But we now have 'n order telling him to stay 'way from you."

"That didn't stop him this afternoon."

"P'rhaps not. But, if he does it 'gain, he'll go t' prison."

"That could be too late."

"No one's goin' to let him touch you," Julia tried to reassure her.

"It's not me I'm worrying about."

"Who then?"

"You, Mommy. He wants to hurt you."

"We're not going to let him, sweetheart." What a thoughtful child she was.

Once Julia had climbed back into bed, she surprised herself by throwing herself into Adam's arms crying uncontrollably. Every aspect of her life felt as if it were coming undone. She felt threatened by the virus. She felt threatened by Dave. She felt that Liz was threatened, too. She felt threatened by her growing need for Oxy-Contin. Adam just held her as she had done Liz until she cried herself to sleep.

But her dreams were frightening, too. She was being hunted by a pack of outsized wolves with burning red eyes that kept gaining on her. And, as they drew closer, she could hear their heavy panting and feel the heat from their breath. Just as the leader of the pack seized her in its gaping jaws, she woke up shaking all over. But, awake, she was not free of the panic she was feeling in her dream. Awake, she felt the same panic, as her life threatened to go into free fall.

Q

Yesterday Adam had come to a decision. QAnon was undoubtedly preparing for a major intervention in the national scene. It would take the form of some kind of coup against what it saw as the forces of the deep state. To Adam's mind, those forces were the final defenders of the Constitution. That was why Homeland Security was trying to find the CISA hacker. He needed to alert them to what QAnon was secretly up to. He had gotten in touch with the two agents from CISA and arranged to meet them for coffee that

Saturday morning. He'd suggested Starbucks on California Street, close to the exit from the Bay Bridge.

When Adam arrived after driving through the rain, they were already seated in a booth with their coffees. After getting himself a cappuccino, he joined them. Adam filled them in on all he'd learned about QAnon's planned intervention in the primaries, and how they had secretly set up cells across the country. For evidence, he showed them emails he'd received from QChamp88.

"88. Interesting. A white supremacist," said the other agent to his colleague.

"No surprise there," the older one answered.

Adam went on to share with them Champ's email, in which he had hinted that he was the hacker. Once again, both agents looked uncomfortable being faced with this evidence.

"This suggests pretty conclusively," Adam said, "that QAnon is actively undermining the democratic process, and is willing to resort to cybercrime to attack its perceived enemies in the government."

"That's one way of interpreting it," the older agent said.

"What other ways are there?" Adam asked. "This was an illegal attack on a major figure in your administration."

They both looked at him without responding. Adam tried again.

"I would expect you, as security members of that administration, to be deeply concerned by what QAnon has been up to."

"Not everything is as it appears," the other agent said.

The older one took over. "Frankly, sir, you are out of your depth. It is not as transparent as you think. When it comes to matters of national security, we have access to so much information not available to members of the public, such as yourself. What you see as a threat, we see as part of a larger pattern that casts this information in a very different light. Obviously, we are not permitted to explain more. But I have to ask you, officially, not to share this information with anyone else. You have done your part in telling us what you have learned. Now please leave it to us to use the evidence as we see fit."

Adam was about to protest again when the other agent added, "And please delete those emails from your server. They could easily be misinterpreted and misused."

"I just don't get it," Adam said.

"You don't have to get it," the older one said, assuming a more authoritarian tone of voice. "We are not offering advice. We are instructing you as a matter of national security to destroy those emails. Just do it."

Both of them got up. "We thank you for your concern."

Adam was left with his now cold cappuccino, utterly bewildered. They had made him feel like an amateur at sea among professionals. No explanation. Just a Do-as-you're-told. Did their desire to keep QAnon's plans out of the public eye mean that they were party to them? That would imply that the government was using QAnon to further its own illegal aims of retaining power regardless. Was the intention, then, to alter or delay the election?

Adam left Starbucks feeling far more anxiety than he did coming in. But what could one liberal-leaning academic do in the face of an administration determined to undermine democracy? Shaken out of his usual optimistic outlook, he drove home in the rain. Like Hamlet, he felt as if his country had become a sterile continent.

The evening news reported that the president was said to be in quarantine, suffering from a fever and experiencing breathing problems. How ironic if this were true. He'd spent the last two months downplaying the virus and insisting it was under control. Julia, however, took it as evidence that the virus was out of control. It was so insidious. If it could infect the president, how could ordinary Americans like them stay safe?

The newscaster announced that on Saudi Arabia's stock market shares in the state oil giant, Aramco, fell by as much as nine percent Saturday, as fears over the virus sent oil prices plummeting. Factories had shut down, people were driving less, and airlines were canceling flights. The S&P stock index had plummeted eleven percent in just ten trading days.

In the middle of the night Julia woke Adam up. She'd just experienced a nightmare she said she'd had before. Whatever scene she was visualizing in her sleep started to disintegrate. Chunks of the picture evaporated leaving blank spaces. Gradually the entire scene gave way to vacancy. Like life had stopped. She'd entered a vast nothingness. And complete silence. Adam held her in his arms until she dropped off.

Q

Daylight-saving time started. Like most Americans, Adam and Julia got up an hour later to make up for the lost time. They planned to spend a lazy Sunday. Yesterday's rain clouds had dispersed. Adam gardened and then fixed the sagging door on the garage. Julia and Liz went shopping in the morning, and took to their respective rooms for the afternoon.

Six that evening found them all in the kitchen-living room where Adam was cooking spaghetti Bolognese while Julia—with a glass of wine—and Liz were half watching the news on TV. The lead story concerned the continuing shortage of testing kits for the coronavirus. Despite interviews with doctors complaining about their inability to obtain test kits or lab results in reasonable time, the president stated that anyone wanting a test could get it. He went on to blame the previous administration for a rule regulating laboratory-developed tests.

"Much as I like Obama," Julia commented, "he always played it too safe. He ended up issuing hundreds of orders trying to control everything. He laid himself open to this charge."

"Whether or not you're right about his extreme caution," Adam responded from the kitchen, "Obama never issued an order regulating those labs. I heard this charge before and looked it up on the FDA website. Every page of Obama's draft guidance was labelled: 'Contains Nonbinding Recommendations – Not for Implementation.'"

Julia was annoyed at herself for not cross-checking this. "Well, listen to my husband. A stickler for the truth."

"Truth matters. The president has done real damage with his endless lying. One lie replaces the last one so rapidly that we all just accept them now, or we say it's just the president at it again. But there are millions of people who swallow whatever he says without ever questioning it. It's frightening. Do you know how many lies he's told since becoming president?"

"No, but I have a feeling that you do."

"Over 17,000."

"Okay, that's very depressing. Not that Democrats are above lying."

"The president must have broken the Guinness Book of Records. Democrats can't begin to compete with him. Now, I fact-check every major claim he makes."

"Okay. Okay. I was way too credulous. Any other fault of mine you want to bring up?"

"I wasn't trying to put you down. Just giving you the facts."

"Yeah, yeah. Facts aren't all there is to life, you know." Julia got up. "Please excuse me a moment," she said as she made for the stairs. Adam reflected that her fuse was getting shorter by the day.

When she returned ten minutes later she poured herself another glass of wine and flopped down on the sofa. In a little while she announced that she was feeling sleepy, and two minutes later she was fast asleep.

After a few minutes Liz said, "Daddy, Mommy's sounding weird."

Adam came through to the living room and bent down over Julia. Her breathing was strange—slow and erratic. For several seconds it seemed she stopped breathing altogether. He tried shaking her awake. No response. He tried taking her pulse but couldn't feel anything. Her face was gray and clammy.

"Open her eyelids," Liz suggested.

Her advice took him aback. He did as Liz proposed. Forcing her eyelids open he found her pupils were much smaller than normal, more like pinholes.

Looking over his shoulder Liz uttered, "Uh-oh," and rushed upstairs. She returned with her backpack from which she pulled out a blue zippered bag which contained a spray labelled Narcan.

"What is that?" he asked Liz.

"Don't worry, Daddy. They taught us at school what to do if someone OD'd."

"OD'd!" he exclaimed.

Without hesitation she tilted Julia's head back, inserted the nozzle of the spray into one of her nostrils and pushed down the plunger. Julia stirred, opened her eyes and immediately threw up on the rug. They moved her onto her side and covered her with a blanket.

"Nothing wrong wi' me," she barely managed to say.

"Better call 911," Liz said.

"No. Don' call," Julia slurred out, "'m all right."

"You're not all right," he said, picking up the phone. "I'm calling for an ambulance right now."

After he called, Liz helped him clean up the rug. Julia seemed half-conscious.

"How did you know it was an overdose?" he asked Liz.

"Because I've seen her take those round green pills from the bathroom cabinet lots of times. They looked the same as those in the picture our school nurse showed us. The green ones are the strongest. It was in that lesson we learned how to give Narcan."

"I'm truly impressed. I'm so proud of you. You did great."

The fire station was only a couple of blocks away. Within five minutes the ambulance arrived, siren wailing. Adam let in the two paramedics, a man and a woman dressed in their cumbrous protective clothing and heavy boots. They went straight to Julia, checked her breathing, checked her pulse, took her temperature and asked her some simple questions. Next they asked Adam what drugs she'd been taking. Unsure of the details, he went upstairs and found four bottles of 80mg extended-release OxyContin tablets. He gave them to the crew. When they asked him how many Julia took in a day, he had to admit he had no idea.

"Between three and four," Liz said.

They all looked at her with surprise.

"I was worried how many tablets she was taking, so I began to keep count," she explained.

Adam felt inadequate and guilty that Liz had been paying closer attention than he had. Maybe he had not wanted to know.

The paramedics explained that because Julia had been taking extended-use tablets she was in danger of another relapse unless she was given additional doses of Narcan for the next four hours. She needed to be in the hospital for at least that amount of time. They arranged to follow the ambulance to Alta Bates Summit Medical Center and watched as Julia was taken out on a stretcher.

The wait at the hospital seemed endless. Adam felt as if he'd been trapped in a nightmare from which he couldn't awake. Once Julia had been evaluated, she was moved to a cubicle where he and Liz could be with her. But she was not very coherent and responded to their inquiries with extreme irritability, behavior that the doctor told them is typical of patients in the early recovery stage.

They released her at 1:30 in the morning, by which time Liz was asleep in a chair. Before discharging her the doctor talked to all three of them about Julia's options for follow-up treatment. They agreed that the best fit was a Level 1 outpatient addiction treatment center. He gave them a list of local treatment centers to choose from.

Back home, they all fell into bed exhausted. Adam set his alarm now to check up on Julia's breathing in one hour. He never heard the alarm go off and woke up the next morning relieved to see Julia already awake and seemingly normal.

Q

Julia woke up confused and ashamed, especially after Adam had told her that Liz had been the one to realize what was happening to her and to administer the antidote. To owe your life to your nine-year-old daughter! What kind of mother was that?

For the moment her body demanded most of her attention. Since waking up her stomach had been a mess. She was horribly anxious. How was she going to go to work? How would her staff attorney manage in court without her assistance and research brief? She felt really ill. What treatment did she need? (She couldn't remember a word the doctor had said last night). Should she try and get up for breakfast? Her mind presented a million questions, but she could find no answers.

She decided that one OxyContin wouldn't hurt and might help her feel better. But the bathroom cabinet had been cleared out. She went to her backup hiding place, a shoe box. That too was empty. What now? Back in bed, she felt that Adam and Liz were ganging up on her.

Then Adam appeared with her breakfast on a tray. Next to her mug of coffee he had placed two white pills in a small dish.

"What are those?" she asked him.

"Methadone tablets. The doctor prescribed them."

"And what are they for?"

"To help with your withdrawal symptoms."

"Will they help my stomach ache?"

"They should; they're strong pain relievers. The doctor said to take them twice a day—after you eat to avoid getting nauseous. But you have to get new doses each day from the clinic."

"How tiresome."

"It's because they can be abused also, like OxyContin."

"What was that about a clinic?"

"Last night we all thought that attending an outpatient clinic would work best for you."

"Really?" she said resentfully. "I can't recollect anything the doctor said. I guess I have no choice."

Adam said nothing.

She suddenly remembered that it was Monday. "I need to call the office to say I won't be coming in."

"Don't worry, honey. I've already told them that you will be staying home for at least this week."

"That's ridiculous. I can be back tomorrow."

"The ER doctor was very explicit about your staying away from work for a minimum of a week. Don't you remember?"

"No, as I said, I don't. Are you sure I was present when he said that?"

"Present, yes. But dozing off much of the time."

"I feel awful for what happened last night."

"Listen, what matters is that you survived it all. There was a moment when I wondered whether you'd make it. Thanks to Liz we got past that quickly."

"I feel so bad that she had to save me."

"She was truly amazing. Without her we would have had to wait for the paramedics to arrive, and you were in danger of stopping breathing altogether."

"Was it that serious?"

"I was getting ready to do CPR." After a pause, Adam said, "Listen, I have to get Liz to school. Do you want the paper?"

She shook her head. Let the world go hang.

"We need to talk when I get back."

"Yes, we do, I know." She felt like a naughty child about to be scolded. "Go ahead."

Adam disappeared. She ate her breakfast, took the pills, and instantly fell to sleep.

Around noon Julia woke up, showered, dressed and joined Adam downstairs.

"Thanks for letting me sleep it off," she said.

"Can I get you anything?" he asked.

"No thanks." He had always been thoughtful and caring. Why did it make her feel obligated today?

"Feel like talking about it?"

"I guess we need to."

"So how long have you been taking opioids?"

"I'm not sure. About a year, although I started off with just the occasional one."

"And when do you think you became addicted?"

"Again, I'm not certain. A little less than a month ago I tried stopping cold turkey."

"How did that go?"

"Badly. I experienced cramps, nausea and was so irritable at the office that I reduced Tina to tears. I was only off OxyContin for two days, but there was no way I could go on without it."

"So where did you get them?"

She hesitated. Should she tell Adam that the last two supplies had come from Dave? A sort of bribe. That would mean admitting that she'd had sex with Dave. So she lied.

"From one of the assistants at work," she lied.

"And why didn't you share this with me?"

She hesitated. "I didn't feel you'd understand."

"What wouldn't I understand?"

"You're always so sensible. I didn't think you would understand why I needed OxyContins. I took them because I was getting more and more stressed. And the more I took the more stressed I felt."

"What was making you feel stressed?"

"There you go. That's my point. You think that all we need to do is locate what's making me stressed and we can cure it by removing the cause. But that's not how stress works, at least with me."

"Well, how does it work?"

"Once you become stressed everything acts like fuel on the fire. It's not this or that that triggers it. It's everything. For instance, take the coronavirus—and by the way, did you see that the US now has over 1200 confirmed cases? I worry that we aren't taking proper precautions to protect ourselves against it."

"What exactly do you have in mind?"

She hesitated. "Shouldn't we make a habit of wearing masks when we go out?"

"The CDC counsels against it. They are directing all supplies of masks to healthcare workers and maintain the rest of us don't need them."

"Is that because they make no difference? Or because the government has found itself in short supply of them?"

"Good question. But walk down to the stores and you won't see anyone wearing one."

"That doesn't fill me with confidence. At any rate, I was just offering you an example of what I worry about. It may not seem reasonable, but reason plays no part in the way stress grips me and alters my perception of everything. You just can't see that, Adam. That's why I felt I couldn't tell you about my addiction. You simply couldn't understand how I could reach that place."

"I'm really sorry I made you think about me that way."

"I feel so conflicted. One bit of me admires the clarity of the way you think. And another bit gets exasperated that you can't empathize with my gut reactions to things. Those reactions may not square with the facts, but they do square with the way I feel. And feelings are as real as the material world. In fact, they make up a large part of my material world."

"Julia, please don't think that I have no room for feelings. I feel nothing but deep love for you and for Liz. I feel angry with Dave. I feel sorry for my department chairman. I could go on."

"I'm not accusing you of lacking feelings. I'm saying that, when feeling runs counter to firm facts, your entire training as a scientist makes you favor facts over feelings."

"I plead guilty. When Amy starts repeating advice from crazy cults like Happy Science, I can only respond with the truth. I admit that anyone like her spreading harmful or downright silly rumors drives me ballistic. But there's plenty of feeling behind my defense of the facts."

They had reached an impasse. Adam seized the opportunity to turn the conversation toward her recovery. He told her that he'd been looking up the various outpatient treatment centers for opioid addiction. The one he thought might suit her best was called the New Span Foundation in Berkeley. It offered an intensive outpatient program that included individual counseling, group therapy, family education, support groups, and random testing. After an initial week, sessions could be scheduled around her work commitments.

She told him that it sounded like what she needed, but she wanted to look through the list for herself to make sure that that was the program she liked best. So, they resolved practicalities while failing to work through their fundamental differences.

Later that afternoon Julia called Amy to find out how she was doing.

"Pretty well, thank you," she replied.

"What symptoms are you having?"

"The usual, so I'm told. Coughing, a fever. Worst is the difficulty breathing. But it has never got bad enough to scare me."

"Thank goodness it's no worse," Julia said.

"They say it can appear to clear only to return with more severe symptoms. But that's not the normal pattern."

"Has Jeff been there for you?"

"Jeff has been really concerned. But I won't let him in the house for fear of infecting him. Still, he's taken care of Robert. Angry as I still am with him, I respect the way he's been willing to do anything I ask him to."

"I'm not surprised. He was always a good dad. I'm sure he would go to enormous lengths to help you."

"It's certainly a relief."

After a pause Amy said, "Can I ask if you and Adam have got any closer physically?"

"I can't say we have. It's making me feel extremely guilty."

"You shouldn't blame yourself as much as you do. It takes two to tango."

"How do you mean?"

"Haven't you noticed? Adam has a roving eye."

"Really?"

"That evening we came over to you for drinks he found me alone in the kitchen and he came on to me."

"What did he do?'

"Nothing you could tie down. But he made it clear that he found me sexually attractive."

"Well, you are."

"Thank you."

"But that sounds like a bit of harmless flirting."

"Agreed. All I'm saying is that you both might be going through a phase in which you find others more attractive than one another."

"Maybe we are." Julia felt a spark of jealousy arise in her. "Incidentally," she said changing the topic, "judging from the silence emanating from the White House, it doesn't look like the president is doing well."

"What happens if he dies from the virus?"

"The VP takes over."

"Of course. I wonder how he would function as president?"

"He's an unknown factor. He's hidden in the president's shadow all this time. He must share the president's agenda—you know, like putting business ahead of keeping everyone safe. But he might stand a better chance in the election, more appealing to Independents, for example."

"I never thought I'd be wishing the Buffoon-in-chief a speedy recovery."

They both laughed. Julia decided to postpone telling Amy about her OD until Amy was in a better place herself.

Around six Adam returned from walking Lucky.

"Goddammit!" he exclaimed. "Somebody keyed my car—on both sides."

"Didn't you leave it at our end of the drive?" Julia asked.

"Yes. As always. Someone came all the way up to the garage and did this. It was intentional."

"You know what? I bet it was Dave."

"That thought had crossed my mind. I'll check the Ring camera to see if it identifies him."

"Will we ever be free from him?" she asked, knowing the answer.

"What I can't work out is why he waited years before he decided to target us."

She knew, only too well, the answer to that. But she couldn't tell Adam, which only made her feel guilty and anxious. "Is it time for my Methadone?"

"You're right. Forgive me for getting distracted. I'll get it right away."

He brought two tablets to her with a tumbler of sparkling water. No wine for her for a while.

They turned on the news. The US had banned travel from most of Europe. Shoppers were emptying the shelves of toilet paper, paper towels and disinfecting wipes. Adam told her not to worry. He'd bought supplies of all those articles that morning. Her reliable Adam. Meanwhile the Surgeon General claimed, "The risk is low to the average American." It didn't look as if the average shopper agreed with him.

Q

As they were reading their emails before getting up, Julia exclaimed, "Oh, no!"

"What?" Adam asked.

"This is from Liz's principal—'Due to COVID-19, classes will be closed from 6 p.m. this Friday the 13th.'"

"My news feed says that as many as two-hundred-thousand Americans could become infected. Worse, millions might die. As many as one in every two-hundred."

"That's terrifying."

"It's a worst-case estimate."

"Once the school's closed, who's going to stay home with Liz on Tuesdays and Thursdays?" she asked.

"If they are closing schools the universities will soon follow suit. Besides, your office could well close, too."

"The principal goes on to say they will be shifting to online classes."

"I can see myself teaching online soon. That could be a drag—talking to rows of faces on Zoom. Or to dark spaces where they want to remain unseen."

"I feel as if our whole world is going dark."

"People have had to get through worse. Think of the Black Death."

"It doesn't make me feel any better knowing that I'm sharing my dread with others from the past. If you add in climate change, this could be the beginning of the end of human life as we know it."

"I hope you're wrong for Liz's sake."

They returned to their respective devices.

Adam had an email from QChamp88—how Adam hated the 88 now he knew what it stood for. "Here's a final email from me that you also need to delete after reading—"

Wait a minute—"also!" Did Champ know that the two government agents had instructed him to delete all emails relating to QAnon? They must be in touch with one another. They must be allies with the same agenda. And what was that? The arrest and removal of members of the supposed secret state? This was extremely threatening. A conspiracy theory embraced by the government's own National Security Agency. Intent on undermining the constitution, the government appeared to be using QAnon as its guerrilla arm—or army. Julia was right. Their world was going dark.

"I wanted to share with you some good news," Champ went on. "I can't yet be specific. But very soon we'll be seeing the Great Awakening. The Storm is gathering. Trust in Q."

Adam saved the email to an email archive with the others from QChamp88. Would a day arrive when he would feel unsafe, even in danger for keeping those emails? He felt like a character in Orwell's *1984*. "The past was erased, the erasure was forgotten, the lie became the truth."

It was toward the end of Adam's Tuesday graduate seminar when his cell phone started to vibrate. He always ignored calls while teaching. But his phone kept vibrating. He extracted it and saw four calls from a number he didn't recognize, and there was one unanswered call from Liz. He excused himself and went outside the classroom to the corridor to call her back.

"Liz?"

"Oh, thank goodness, Daddy," she replied out of breath.

"Is anything the matter?"

"There's a policewoman here who wants to speak to you. I'm passing the phone to her." That put him into a panic.

"Liz? Liz!"

"Hello, sir. This is officer Bobbie Heart from the Oakland Police Department. Am I talking to, err, Mr. Adam Gosford?"

"Yes. What's happened?"

"Your wife was attacked at home and has been taken to Highland Hospital."

"Oh, no!" he exclaimed.

"I think it would be best if you came home and we can talk here at more length."

"But how is my wife?"

"She's doing well."

"Are you at my home now?"

"Yes, sir. I am staying with your daughter until you get back here. When do you expect to get back by?"

He gave her an estimate, told the students he had an emergency, and drove home in record time.

Liz rushed into his arms when he opened the door. The policewoman got up from a chair and asked him gently to take Liz upstairs and come back down. He did as she asked.

"We received a 911 call from your address at 4:52 this afternoon," the policewoman said in the oddly precise language of her. "The caller said that there was a physical assault in progress."

"Who called you? Liz?"

"Yes, sir. We arrived while the assault was still ongoing and were able to apprehend the assailant. He's been charged with sexual assault."

"Sexual assault! You mean rape?"

"Attempted rape, sir. Your wife was taken to Highland Hospital in Oakland for a sexual assault forensic exam."

"You mean a rape kit?"

"That was what the procedure was previously called. She will also be interviewed by a detective who is experienced in sexual assault investigations."

"I see. Liz and I ought to be leaving for the hospital then."

"I would advise you to call the attending physician and ask her how long it will all take. You won't be allowed to see her until they are done." She wrote down the name and phone number of the doctor.

"Good advice."

"Is there anything else you want to ask me before I leave, sir?"

"Not for now, thank you."

With that she left.

Adam went straight up to Liz's room.

"My poor darling. How are you doing?"

She burst into tears, burying her head in his chest. When her sobs subsided she said, "I was so scared, Daddy."

"What happened?"

"Mommy was helping me with my math homework at the kitchen table. Suddenly there was a crash and this man—the man from school—he was in the doorway and started shouting horrible things at Mommy."

"How scary."

"Mommy told me to go upstairs with Lucky and pushed me towards the staircase. I did as she'd told me to do before I locked myself in the bathroom."

"You had your phone with you?"

"Yes. I heard him yelling and there was a lot of crashing and I heard Mommy scream."

"My poor Liz."

"So I dialed 911."

"I'm so proud of you."

"They told me to stay on the line and keep talking to them until help arrived."

"You are so brave."

"So then, suddenly, the police were everywhere. I came out of the bathroom and that policewoman took care of me."

"Could you see Mommy?"

"She was bleeding from the mouth and she was in her underwear, which was torn. They wouldn't let her touch me. She was crying and thanking me for doing what I did. I told her it was only what she had taught me to do."

"I had no idea that she'd given you instructions on how to react to a break-in."

"I think she thought this was going to happen," Liz said to his surprise.

"Her gut feelings have always been remarkably reliable."

He phoned the doctor at the hospital who told him he could pick Julia up in three hours. He made Liz and himself a dinner of pork chops, mashed potatoes and salad.

To pass the time before they needed to leave he switched on the local news while Liz played a video game on her phone. The president was accusing the Fake News of inflating the outbreak to try to prevent his being re-elected. Meanwhile, there were more riots at polling stations in six states, and, in St. Louis, a car had driven into a line of people, killing two and injuring eight. Also the stock market was plunging. The distracted globe was falling apart.

Q

Julia woke up alone in bed with a headache. She felt her forehead and discovered that she had a bandage wrapped around it. At first she couldn't work out how it had got there. Then in a flash it all came back to her. Thank goodness Liz was unharmed. But how was she going to explain to Adam why Dave had done this? She couldn't go on lying to him. Now was the time to come clean about everything. But how would he react? Would he leave her? She was terribly scared of what might follow.

She put on her dressing gown and went downstairs. Adam was out taking Liz to school, though how her poor girl was going to manage there after last night she had no idea. Adam had left her hot coffee in the coffee maker and there was sliced bread in the toaster just waiting for it to be turned on. Thoughtful, as always.

She was finishing her second cup of coffee when he returned and sat down opposite her at the breakfast table.

"How are you feeling?" he asked with concern.

"I woke up with a headache, but it's gone now after I took my two tablets. My neck still aches and my lip is swollen a little."

"If only I'd been here to protect you."

"That wasn't your fault. Dave must have worked out when you were in class."

"Was the hospital exam awful?"

"It's all a blur to me now. I seemed to sign dozens of forms. They took care of my injuries—my bloodied mouth, the blow to my head, the bruising on my neck, the lesions in my rectum."

"Oh god!"

"They took every kind of sample you can think of – blood, urine, saliva, DNA swabs, vaginal and anal swabs, scrapings from my fingernails. They examined every inch of my body with some kind of special light. They combed my hair. They took my underwear. The process seemed to go on forever. And the female detective's questions which also went on and on."

"My poor honey."

No. she didn't deserve his sympathy, she reminded herself. "It's all my fault."

"Of course it's not. You're the victim, remember."

"All the time I kept thinking I deserved it."

"That's crazy." Adam hesitated. "Do you feel able to describe what happened?" he asked tentatively.

"I'm not sure I can give you a detailed account. I was terrified. When he first broke in he was just yelling and yelling—'You thought a court order would keep me away?' 'I'm going to fuck you stupid, and then I'm going to make you pay for what you've done to me.'"

Adam looked shaken. "And Liz heard all of it?"

Julia could only nod ever so slightly.

"I'm so sorry."

"I told her to go upstairs and take Lucky who was cowering under her feet, which she did. Then Dave grabbed a knife from the countertop and, holding it to my neck, ordered me to take off my pants and t-shirt. I tried throwing the t-shirt over his head, but he flung it off and hit me in the mouth with his fist. He called me a whore and told me he would really hurt me if I tried anything else. He grabbed me by this arm, twisted me around with my back to him, and thrust my head down on the table so hard he split open my forehead which began to drip blood into my eyes."

She broke off to wipe the tears from her eyes. Adam was bent over the table holding his head with his clenched fists.

"Are you sure you want me to go on?" she asked.

"I want to know whatever you can remember, however awful it was."

"The next I knew, he had pulled down my panties and was thrusting some object, maybe the knife handle, into my ass. I screamed at him to stop, that it hurt. He laughed and said something like, 'That's the idea. The more you hurt, the more excited you make me feel.' I was in such pain I even heard myself plead with him to just enter me with his penis—Adam, are you sure you want to hear this?"

Adam still sat bent over, not looking at her.

"If I'm to help you get over it, I have to know what happened," he assured her grimly.

"Well, he didn't do it. He snarled in my ear, 'I've changed my mind. That's all you're good for. I'm done with you.' He put his hands round my throat and began to strangle me. I tried to pry his hands off of me, but his grip was too strong. I was beginning to black out when I heard the cops coming in."

"That's rape and attempted murder. He's going to be put away for a very long time."

"Strangely, I still feel guilty."

Adam looked perplexed. "I don't get what you feel guilty about."

Julia realized that there was no other way out of this.

"I have a confession to make. Before I do that, I want to say how deeply sorry I am for the mistake I made, and how much I regret having made it."

"Go on." Adam looked concerned.

She looked down and could not bring her eyes up to his. "Back before I knew you, my relationship with Dave was a weird mixture of excitement and fear. He was often sexually aggressive, and I found myself perversely excited by his roughness. I was turned on by being forcibly made to serve as the instrument for his pleasure. I despised myself for playing that role. But I kept on doing it, because it excited me."

"I'm stunned. You've never acted that way with me."

"I know. After I'd met you I realized that sex could be something mutual, that it could be a play between equals. More. It could be a way of expressing love, not just excitement."

"Is that the confession?"

"No. I wish it was." She gulped, then forced herself to continue. "After I ran into Dave back in January, when he told me I'd ruined his life, he began pestering me to have a drink with him. Eventually I agreed, hoping to get him to see that our relationship had run its natural course. But, when I met him, he kept on repeating that he had never had another sexual connection as great as ours. And he swore that he would leave me alone if I had sex with him just once more. That would free him of his obsession."

"And you believed him?" Adam asked, as if it was obvious that no one in their senses would do so.

"I know I was incredibly naïve, but I did it. I thought it would get him out of my life. ...Our lives."

"I can't believe that you were taken in by him that easily."

"You're right, I'm sorry to say. I have to confess that I was still partly turned on by the prospect of having rough sex with him. I say 'partly' because I also hated him and was disgusted by his need to hurt and humiliate me."

She felt such a fool describing it all in cold blood. Adam wasn't helping her. But then, why should he?

"I'm in shock," he said, and looked it. "Is this why you've refused to have sex with me recently? This is a whole new you I know nothing about."

"It's an old me that I thought I'd left completely behind."

Adam rose and got himself a glass of water. Still standing, he said, "Where was this?"

"Does it matter?"

Adam said nothing.

"At the hotel where he works. No sooner had he had sex than he started asking me to meet him again. When I protested that he had agreed to leave me alone after this one time, he laughed at me and said he knew how excited I'd got with him."

"Was that true?"

"I don't know how to explain this to you, but that old need to be completely overwhelmed and used did thrill me until it was over, when I was overtaken by disgust at myself."

"I'm completely at a loss. Why have you never told me?"

"Because I had hoped that I'd outgrown it. And I was ashamed."

"Where on earth did you get it from?"

"I've been asking myself that ever since. I now think it originated in those visits my father made to me in my bed when I was a child. He forced me to participate. And he was only interested in his own satisfaction. So my earliest model of sex made me want to subordinate myself to his sexual needs so that I could get rid of him. But my own sexual psyche must have gotten mixed up in it."

"And is that how you still feel today?"

"I thought I'd overcome that sickness after I'd met you and learned to associate erotic feelings with love. I didn't agree to have sex with Dave to experience that excitement. Just to be rid of him. But I was surprised to find that the actual act did awake those old conflicted responses and arouse me. I was so shaken by realizing this that I was put off the entire idea of sex. I couldn't tell you. I'm sorry. I was just so mixed up I couldn't handle anything sexual."

She stopped. She looked up at him. He was strangely silent.

Finally he returned her gaze. "You are thinking, why am I not angrier?"

"You do seem extraordinarily calm, I must say. Not that I'm complaining."

"Of course, I feel mad at you. Surely a part of you knew beforehand that his promise was worth nothing."

"I felt I was caught up in something and this was the only way to get out of it." She was beginning to get annoyed with him. Why couldn't he just come out with a bit of old-fashioned jealousy? Or anger?

After a long silence he said, "The reason is that I too have a confession to make."

"What do you mean?"

"I mean that I, too, had sex recently."

"What!"

"I was feeling rejected and hurt, feeling sorry for myself. I told myself that it was your fault. That you owed me this."

"Who was it?"

"Anna."

"I should have guessed. She always did have that other connection to you that you never appeared to be fully conscious of. And she is certainly attractive."

"Yes, she is. And my frustration made her irresistible."

Julia was about to make some sarcastic remark when Adam went on, "But it was only once. She is every inch the bachelorette who plays the dating field by her own rules. She uses men for her pleasure."

"Please don't pretend that she didn't give you pleasure."

"Of course she did. I'm not trying to suggest I was seduced. I went willingly into it. But we both understood that it was a one-time thing. She simply took pity on me in my state of frustration. The experience was entirely physical."

"Sure! I always thought she fancied you."

"Maybe. But no more than a bunch of other men. She picks and chooses as she pleases."

"All right, I get it. You had sex just the one time and—"

"—And almost immediately regretted it. Sex without love was something I enjoyed earlier in my life. But, now, it feels meaningless. That's what I learned from having sex with Anna."

"That doesn't stop me feeling mad as hell with you," she said. Because she did, however unfair that was.

"I feel mad with myself for acting like an adolescent."

"That's easily said. When was this?'

"About ten days ago."

"Just about the time I was so stressed out I was upping my dose of pills."

"I guess so."

"I know we should be able to forgive each other when we both have betrayed one another. But I can't help feeling mad at you."

"That's not fair."

"Fuck fair. The thought of you and her makes me just crazy."

"Maybe I should work on being more sexually aggressive."

"Don't be a complete jerk. I said I was over that."

"How convenient," he said icily.

"Screw your sarcasm. Why can't you just come right out and say you're mad?"

"I can see you're just dying for a fight. Even though we're both equally at fault, you have to make me the villain."

"Here we go again. Because we both cheated we should do the *reasonable* thing and forgive each other?"

"And what's so wrong with that?"

"It's not how I feel, however unreasonable that is. I can't get past picturing you and Anna naked together." She took a long breath. "I know it's ridiculous, but I feel violated."

"You should know what that feels like."

"How dare you!"

"I didn't mean the rape. I was referring to your need for rough sex."

"Now you're going to hold that over me? I've already told you I'm over that now."

"You expect me to believe that, in just a few weeks, your sexual preferences have completely changed?"

"There you go again. You hide your real feelings behind that veneer of sarcasm. Why can't you come out and say you're furious with me?"

"No one tells me how to feel, not even you."

"I don't need to tell you. I know you well enough to know that you're very angry."

"Okay. Okay. Congratulations. You've made me really pissed off with you and your sexual peculiarities."

"That's better. How about calling me a pervert? A whore?"

Adam suddenly got up from the table knocking an empty mug to the floor. "I've had it listening to you. I'm off to pick up Liz from school."

And he stormed out of the house.

Q

When Julia woke up Adam had already left to drop off Liz on his way to school. Her neck was still sore, her butt raw, but her swollen lip had gone down.

Why had she got so mad at Adam yesterday? And why did she still feel she had a right to be? She guessed she wanted him to show that he was as hurt and angry as she was. The way he kept his cool infuriated her. She couldn't stop herself feeling betrayed, even if she'd betrayed him. She still felt outraged. Partly at the way he repressed his own hurt and anger. If they couldn't be honest with each other, what was left?

She idly surfed through the news. The World Health Organization declared the coronavirus to be a pandemic. US confirmed cases were in the high 5,000s, with 110 deaths. Schools, universities, businesses and sports stadiums were all shutting down. The stock market had officially become a bear market. Massive demonstrations were ongoing, and National Guard troops were firing tear gas and rubber bullets at people in the streets, including young women, journalists and students. Biden was leading in the polls by double digits. The White House was maintaining silence about the state of the president's health, yet he was—supposedly—still tweeting: "The foreign virus won't stand a chance against us." More likely, we wouldn't stand a chance against the virus.

She couldn't decide which was deteriorating faster—her life or the country. They were all in the hands of a president who was spreading misinformation as fast as the virus was spreading infection across the world. And she had been in the hands of a man who believed that she had made him an involuntary celibate. The death of the truth threatened death itself. Where did this leave her? Adrift with no land in view. She was feeling overwhelmed and helpless. That was what had made her resort to OxyContins in the first place. And since then everything had got a lot worse.

She opened the drawer of her bedside cabinet and extracted two Methadone tablets which she swallowed with a mouthful of water. Not that she had any OxyContins to tempt her. So, except for Methadone, what now did she have to fall back on under stress?

The entire world was shutting down around her. But she still had Liz. And Adam. Yes, Adam remained at the center of her life regardless. The strength of those two ties was her best hope in a country unraveling. They could all find themselves homebound soon. She was lucky that Adam and Liz were such great human beings. They could be about to become her entire social world for maybe many months to come.

She spent the morning performing banal household chores. She even found herself ironing some napkins and cloth placemats. It would have made little difference if she'd simply folded them up and put them away. But she preferred to occupy herself.

Then the phone rang.

"Hello."

"It's your mother, dear."

"Hello. Is something up?"

"You could say that. This morning your father passed away."

She was shocked to realize that the news made her feel tearful. After living all her life with a dysfunctional father.

"I'm so sorry. Did he go peacefully?"

"The nurses said he did."

"They didn't warn you in time to come to the hospital?"

"They did. But I didn't go."

"What do you mean?"

"Three days ago I stopped bringing him whiskey."

"Better late than never."

"It was far too late to make a difference. But I just couldn't go on helping him kill himself."

"I understand."

"Besides, he was more interested in seeing the whiskey than me. That last day I saw him he made me mad. He started off pleading with me to fetch him a bottle. You know, 'Damn you woman, get out of here, and don't come back without my whiskey, if you know what's good for you.' I told him that, if I left, I wouldn't come back ever. He replied, 'I couldn't give a rat's ass. Just get me my god-damned whiskey.'"

"I'm so sorry," was all Julia could manage to say.

"When the hospital called to say he was going I stayed at home until they rang to say he'd passed away." She started crying. "The old bastard must have been suffering withdrawal and had no one there when his life gave out."

"He was almost certainly heavily sedated with morphine. He probably felt nothing those last hours."

"I wish I could believe that."

There was a short pause while her crying subsided.

"When's the funeral?" Julia asked.

"In two days. Saturday at two."

"Are you making all the arrangements on your own?"

"The funeral director is dealing with most of it. At least we had an insurance policy covering the expenses."

"That was unlike him."

"Him? No way. I'd taken out the policy years ago and I paid the premiums."

"Is there anything we can do to help you?"

"When you come for the funeral—you can come, can't you?"

"Of course we're coming."

"It would be really helpful if you or Adam would go through the bank accounts and bills for me."

"No problem."

"I've never handled the bills and taxes."

"We'll come as early as we can and do that before the funeral," Julia volunteered, thinking her mother might be too upset after the ceremony. "If you can have all the paperwork ready for us to look through."

"Thank you, dear. I will."

"Are you sure you're all right on your own there?"

"Of course, dear. But thanks for asking. I'll see you Saturday." She ended the call.

Julia felt numb. You only have one dad, even if hers failed miserably at fulfilling the role. It was almost as if she were grieving the loss of a father figure rather than her own dad. But the truth was that she'd lacked a father figure from the start. All she'd been allotted was a cop-out of a dad who'd taught her nothing but how to get mixed up over sex and end up addicted. However, looking on the brighter side, being released from his shadow would maybe free her up to shape her own life now. For too long she'd allowed others to shape it. It was time to take control.

Late that evening Adam and Julia were in bed, still at a stand-off. He said, "I've been thinking. Why didn't I pay more attention to all of the pills you were taking? And do you know what? It was because I was fixated on that crazy conspiracy theory, QAnon. What good did my poor attempt to penetrate their organization do? As soon as I got near the truth, I was shut down. I feel that the real secret state is composed not of the enemies of this administration but of the administration itself. And supporters of QAnon are its secret army."

"Now who's sounding like a conspiracy theorist?" she joshed.

"I can't get over how Champ knew that CISA agents had told me to destroy all my emails with him. They're supposed to be on opposite sides. Only last year the FBI added QAnon to its list of potential domestic terrorists."

"I can understand your hang-up with those crazies. But I'm not going to let you assume the blame for my habit. I totally messed up. The spread of the virus terrified me. It still does. I needed something to dull my fears."

"And, instead of paying attention to those fears, I dismissed them as irrational."

"Maybe you were right. But fears don't respond to reasoning."

"That's something I've only fully come to understand recently. My entire professional life has been a search for verifiable facts. Now, finally I appreciate the fact that emotions are too powerful to ignore, no matter what the facts. Not just in politics. It's been true in our life, too."

"Facts will always be facts. But you do have to work through people's emotions to get them to accept those facts."

"Yep. I guess it simplified my life to live in a world where everything was verifiable. What a pleasant delusion."

"I've always admired your stance—the clarity of your thinking, your self-confidence, your sense of right and wrong. I depend on it."

"Thank you, honey. Tonight I have nothing but doubts—about myself, about us, about what's going on around us."

"Join the club. I'm a morass of doubts. I'm not sure there is anything I am certain about."

"Maybe that's the only sane thing to be now. That includes how I feel about you and Dave. Half of me is angry at the image I conjure up of you two. And half of me thinks you were as much a victim as a participant."

"I feel equally mixed up about you and Anna. I want to call her and scream at her over the phone."

"And I spent half the night imagining ways to beat up Dave for doing that to you."

"But I agreed to it that time."

"Please don't remind me. I feel so humiliated."

"It wasn't your fault."

"I wish I could say the same about my time with Anna."

"Please don't remind me! It will probably take some time before I can stop resenting the thought of your and her bodies entangled on her bed. I keep imagining what the two of you did together. And, of course, I can't stop myself comparing her to me. Is her body better than mine? Was she more skilled? More exciting than I am?"

"We could always put it to the test," Adam said grinning for the first time in a long while.

"You know what? We could. I'm feeling competitive. I want to obliterate her from your memory."

She leaned over and gave him a lingering kiss. They looked into each other's eyes as if they had just met, as if this was their first kiss. She moved the rest of her body on top of him. She felt the stirring in his body, the rush of blood, the faster breathing, the urgency to fuse together in a single body of passion and love. Yes. They still had this. It was enough.

Q

When Adam woke up he could hear the rain. He checked his weather app; it was 49 degrees, one of those relatively rare wintry days in the

Bay Area. Friday the thirteenth. Not that he was normally superstitious. The temperature outside didn't make him want to rush out of bed. Lucky and Julia were still asleep.

He turned the bedroom TV on to CNN. What the hell were they talking about with such urgency in their voices? Who's dead?

"Julia, wake up.," he said. "Listen to the news. Something big is happening."

Julia eased herself into a sitting position.

The news announcer helpfully paused to offer a summary of what he was discussing with the usual bunch of political experts: "This is what we know so far. The president passed away at 5:30 this morning from the coronavirus. At 6:45 the vice-president was sworn in by Washington DC judge, Bruce Mason, as the forty-sixth president of the United States. The new president will address the nation at 10 a.m. Eastern time."

Adam muted the TV. "Wow."

"So that's why the White House was remaining silent on the president's health," Julia said.

"How ironic. The man who dismisses the virus dies of it. All those duped followers, including the QAnon supporters, they'll have some explaining to do."

"They'll probably blame his death on Hillary."

"And all the other members of the deep state."

Julia was looking at her cell phone. "Here's an email just arrived from Liz's principal. She's canceling all classes today because of the president's death. Online classes will start next week. Stand by for more details later."

"I can't decide," Adam said, "whether this news calls for celebration or not. We know so little about the vice—sorry, the new president."

"Let's finish breakfast before his address. I want Liz to really hear it. It will be a significant moment in American history."

He agreed.

At ten they were all seated in front of the living room TV. The new president appeared seated at the Resolute Desk in the Oval Office. He began by sharing his grief at the president's sudden death and declared Monday as a day of national mourning. He went on to address the divided state of the nation, depicting the protests—what he called riots—as lawlessness that threatened the ongoing primary elections. When he compared the situation to a civil war, Julia and Adam looked at each other with wide eyes. Then he said:

"Accordingly, under the National Emergencies Act, I am declaring a state of martial law effective immediately. I am also suspending habeas corpus and have asked the Secretary of Defense to deploy troops who will have the authority to arrest and detain, without a search warrant, rioters nation-wide."

"This is unbelievable," Adam said.

"This can't be constitutional," Julia replied.

"All I know is that the Constitution leaves the president with extremely wide powers."

The president went on. "I am temporarily revoking all American passports. I am giving temporary authorization to David Crawford, director of CISA, to block any media postings threatening our national security."

"Can you believe it?" Adam exclaimed. "They kept that jerk on, despite his lying under oath, to censure all the media."

"Lying's now become a qualification for serving this administration," Julia said.

"Because of the spread of the coronavirus," the president continued, "I am ordering the closure of restaurants, bars, gyms and places of entertainment, and banning the gathering of groups of more than five people. I am also imposing a nation-wide curfew between 10 p.m. and 6 a.m., starting tonight. These necessary restrictions will be enforced by Federal troops. They will also be detaining subversives, identified on the FBI's Security Index, who threaten our national security."

He ended by promising to review these emergency measures once they had achieved their purpose of restoring the country to normality.

"Whatever 'normality' means," Adam remarked as he turned the TV off.

"Jesus Christ," said Julia. "I would call what he's just done a coup. All those law and order advocates will just love it."

"And the followers of QAnon."

"And not just conservatives and Republicans, but many Independents and Libertarians."

After a pause Adam said, "I'm wondering how extensive the FBI's lists of security threats is."

"Why?"

"Because the government clearly saw my small insight into the workings of QAnon as a threat."

"Don't you think you're being a little paranoid, *cariño*?"

"Maybe. I hope so. But I wouldn't be a bit surprised if they start arresting people targeted by QAnon. You know, Hillary, Gates, Soros and company. Maybe even Obama and Biden. They'll turn conspiracy theories into established fact. And you can forget about the right to demonstrate. They'll put you in jail for participating in an insurrection."

"Like Alice, we've entered a looking-glass world where everything is reversed. God help us."

Liz interjected, "Mommy, I always thought Alice's looking-glass world was funnier than Wonderland."

"I only wish this version was as funny as Alice's, sweetheart," Julia said wistfully.

"Oh, my god!" Adam exclaimed.

"What?" Julia and Liz asked together.

"Listen to this post just tweeted by Q: "This is my final message to you all. You won't need me again. THE GREAT AWAKENING has arrived. I have arrived. The deep state has been defeated. Yes. Your new president is Q. WHERE WE GO ONE WE GO ALL.""

THE END

A NOTE ABOUT THE AUTHOR

Brian Finney is a Professor Emeritus of Literature at California State University, Long Beach. Educated in England, he obtained a BA from the University of Reading and a PhD from the University of London. After serving three years as an officer in the Royal Air Force, he spent five years in industry as an internal management consultant and production control manager. Between 1964 and 1987 he taught and arranged extramural courses for the University of London. Since immigrating to the US in 1987 he has taught at the University of California, Riverside, University of Southern California, UCLA, and California State University, Long Beach.

He has written seven nonfiction books, including a prize-winning biography of Christopher Isherwood, and *Terrorized: How the War on Terror Affected American Culture and Society*. His first novel, *Money Matters* (2019) was a finalist for the American Fiction Awards in the Best New Fiction category. *Terrorized, Money Matters*, and *Dangerous Conjectures* are all available on Kindle.

He is married and calls Venice, California his home. You can visit him at: bhfinney.com

www.ingramcontent.com/pod-product-compliance
Lightning Source LLC
Chambersburg PA
CBHW061023120726
47910CB00006B/2071